It was a beautiful night . . . to escape . . .

. . . their olfactory senses filed away the smell of freshly cut grass and pine trees.

The landscape was still bathed in soft, silver colors.

Stars watched them.

All was calm.

All was bright.

Val silently determined the most direct route to the mountains and forests, where they planned to increase the information in their data banks for more efficient usefulness, and then he pointed and began walking.

Aqua and CatSkil followed.

And thus it was, one midsummer's night, that from a dusty warehouse shelf in a quiet factory in the middle of a sleepy valley, three slightly malfunctioning machines *left* their assigned places. . . .

ANDY KAUFMAN · BERNADETTE PETERS

HEARTBEEPS

A MICHAEL PHILLIPS Production
HEARTBEEPS
also starring RANDY QUAID · KENNETH McMILLAN
CHRISTOPHER GUEST and MELANIE MAYRON
Special Make-Up Effects by STAN WINSTON · Special Visual Effects by ALBERT WHITLOCK
PHIL designed by JAMIE SHOURT and ROBBIE BLALACK · Associate Producer JOHN HILL
Executive Producer DOUG GREEN · Written by JOHN HILL · Produced by MICHAEL PHILLIPS
Directed by ALLAN ARKUSH
Music by JOHN WILLIAMS
A UNIVERSAL PICTURE

HEARTBEEPS

A NOVEL BY JOHN HILL

A JOVE BOOK

To Denny,
who has given me
love and Brian.

Acknowledgments

I want to thank Michael Phillips, Allan Arkush, Doug Green, Andy Kaufman, Bernadette Peters, and everyone else in the terrific cast and crew who had wonderful ideas for the movie, *Heartbeeps*. I've used many of them in this novel, where, of course, I'll get full credit.

—J.H.

Chapter 1

• • • It didn't look like a robot factory.

Not from the outside.

The original architect, fifteen years before, didn't really
think the huge factory belonged in the middle of the lush,
green valley, surrounded by rolling mountains and rugged
forests. So he tried to hide the fact that it was a factory. He
added fancy, pointed corners, too many windows, sloping
angles, and a number of what the rank-and-file workers referred to as doodads and geegaws.

As a result, inside, the factory was clearly a no-nonsense,
highly efficient place to work; from the outside, however, it
looked like a cross between a modern industrial complex and
an Arabian Nights whoopee palace.

At the moment, on a spring day in 1995, a dirty orange
forklift was taking a wooden pallet from the noisy main
assembly area of the factory into the quiet, dusty warehouse.
On the wooden pallet stood three figures.

One was very well-dressed. The second one wasn't. And
the third was seriously approaching advanced slobbism.

The worst-dressed of the three, a short, heavyset, middle-
aged man with a clipboard, a three-day stubble, and a permanent frown, was named Max. He wore a rumpled beige jump
suit with ''G.M. Robotics'' on the front, next to pseudocoffee

stains and grease spots from the bacon substitute he had quickly cooked himself for breakfast several days before. The wrinkled collar of an old-fashioned purple shirt was visible at the top of the jump suit. Max was fifty years old, born just after World War II, but it had been many decades since anyone had referred to him as a "war baby." His most common attitude was somewhere between being impatient and disgruntled; if Max had been one of the Seven Dwarfs, he'd have been Grumpy. His perpetually lousy mood wasn't just due to a common situation many men find themselves in as they enter their fifties: his life hadn't turned out as he had expected, but it wasn't all that bad either.

It was the goddamn robots.

Like many people in the mid-1990s who had reached adulthood without so many machines running around, yakking it up and generally getting in the way, Max never completely liked or trusted robots or computers. Oh, sure, Max would finally admit if you pressed him, they did do some good, and yes, they did improve many things about modern life.

But Max didn't have to like them.

A man's a man and a machine's a gadget, he would often announce after several cold beers. You couldn't laugh, argue, bully, befriend, drink, hug, dream, or shoot the breeze with a robot, Max would declare after several more cold ones. And then he'd go on like that until he had cleared out his corner of the tavern. In spite of the fact that Max had made a good living for years because of modern technology, Max hated computers, disliked robots, and wasn't all that crazy about his station wagon.

The second figure on the forklift pallet was somewhat messy, but at this point in his young life he was still only an apprentice slob. He was a tall, gangly, good-natured young man named Charlie. Charlie was long on intelligence and short on poise; he knew more about robots than about human nature. He was precise around machinery, awkward around men, and downright clumsy around women. Charlie was formally educated on the subject of technology, pleasant to be around, and enthusiastic about life in general. But his true passion was robots.

Born in 1970, now 25 years old, Charlie was like many younger people who had grown up in a time when home computers were as common as television sets; having been a teenager in the mid-1980s, he had actually grown up with the robotics industry. And he loved each new development. Just as an earlier generation marveled at early space flights, Charlie had watched with fascination each time a new robot model had been announced or demonstrated on TV. Charlie saw robots as the most cooperative, efficient partners that humans could ever have as they continued to challenge and shape and improve the future. Like many people of his generation, Charlie automatically liked and accepted robots and never felt threatened by them. He couldn't imagine a world without them. Besides, exciting new breakthroughs were always just around the corner. . . .

The third, extremely well-dressed passenger on the wooden pallet, unlike the other two, was not human. He was a highly sophisticated robot.

He was designated ValCom-17485. A previous owner of ValCom-17485 had once described him, in a happy-drunk way during a party, as looking like "Howdy Doody, all grown up and wearing a pin-striped suit." The people at the party had chuckled at this, but they laughed even louder at Val's sincerity when he answered, "Thank you."

Val was very polite. He was programmed that way.

He had been carefully designed at great expense to look and act as much as possible like a particularly nice person. Extensive research had shown that with certain types of robots, people wanted them to look as human as possible. In fact, psychologists had discovered that people had the same instinctive fascination with human-shaped robots as they did with monkeys and fun-house mirrors; they were fascinated with distorted views of themselves.

So from a hundred feet away, you would think Val was a pleasant, handsome man about thirty years old wearing a brown, pin-striped, double-breasted suit and a red bow tie. From thirty feet away, if you watched him walk and do things, you'd think something was fishy but wouldn't be able to put your finger on it. From ten feet away, you'd be sure he was a robot, unless you weren't wearing your glasses.

"Well, I see why you're here," Charlie said to the robot in the usual friendly, conversational tone he used with everyone, man, beast, or machine.

Max looked away, rolling his eyes; he hated the way

3

Charlie always made small talk with other people and despised it when he did it with machines.

"Looks like a second-level appendage laceration," Charlie added sympathetically, looking down at Val's right foot, which was partly ripped away, exposing wires and tubes.

That figures, Max thought to himself, wishing the forklift would hurry and get to the shelf. Anyone else would just say the robot's foot was torn, but not Charlie, oh no, Charlie had to go into the "second-level" business. Actually, Max secretly envied and admired Charlie's detailed knowledge of robotics, but Max would go several hours on the rack before you'd get him to admit it.

"So how did it happen?" Charlie asked the robot.

"Industrial accident, sir," Val answered in his mechanical but pleasant male voice.

"Yeah? I thought you were a Com-series," Charlie said, surprised, as the pallet rose the last few inches and became level with a six-foot-wide dusty shelf thirty feet above the warehouse floor. Max signaled the robot driver below to stop.

"While here for my annual maintenance work," Val replied in his usual pleasant voice as he stepped onto the shelf, "I was waiting outside the reprogramming building, as instructed. But Sanitation Engineer Russell Percival Wyatt told me to, quote, get my ass over here and help, end quote." Val's voice suddenly stopped, and instead there was an actual recording of Wyatt's harsh voice, perfectly spliced into place. Val continued his explanation. "At that time, I was assisting several worker robots in lifting heavy metal refuse containers, and one fell on my foot, severing several ambulatory circuits—"

"You mean Crazy Rusty countermanded an executive order?" Max interrupted, amazed.

"How come you're so surprised, Max?" Charlie asked. "Everyone knows Crazy Rusty is pretty weird."

"I know, I know," Max said, "but to use a Com-series to lift trash cans . . ."

"You know Rusty doesn't have all the dots on his dice. Remember last year at the Christmas party?" Charlie asked. Max nodded, recalling how Rusty had spotted a huge bodyguard robot and kept insisting that it dance with him.

"Yeah, I didn't even know Rusty was out of the hospital yet," Max said, hating it whenever Charlie was right. Max wore the same grouchy expression whether the subject under

4

discussion was mayhem or cheesecake. Max looked at Val.
"And Rusty told you to lift trash cans?"

Val nodded.

"Jesus," Max mumbled. "Some people would use a Rolls-Royce to plow turnips."

"Mr. Westlin will kill Rusty," Charlie added.

"Yeah. And slowly," Max said. He decided that Westlin, their supervisor, would probably transfer Rusty Wyatt to the new General Motors Experimental Lab in Greenland, where robots were being made to use on Arctic oil rigs.

Max and Charlie stepped back onto the wooden pallet, and Max signaled the robot driver below. The pallet started down, descending out of Val's sight slowly, but his mechanical eyes followed the two humans until they were out of sight. Charlie watched Val too, feeling strangely as though the pleasant robot was being left alone in a large, dark warehouse. Val's eyes and expression suggested a little-boy innocence, but Charlie immediately fought the feeling, reminding himself for the millionth time that machines weren't human. In school, there had been entire courses to combat an industry-related problem termed Metal Anthropomorphism or Asimov's Syndrome. The textbook was titled *Don't Forget It's Only a Toaster*. Irritated at himself for the momentary lapse in self-control, Charlie took it out on Max, picking up on one of their many arguments. As the forklift carried them away, Charlie and Max argued about the relative merits of American-made robots versus the cheaper imports.

Val just stood there.

Except for his red bow tie, the rest of Val's coloration—from his tan-bronze facial paint to his brown suit and dark shoes—comprised one of the more subdued color schemes in this part of the vast warehouse. All around him, on shelves above, below, and beyond, were dozens of bright colors. Damaged robots, or large pieces, stored and tagged, were bright red, green, yellow, and orange. Even the large covers for some of the pieces were beautiful pastels. Val looked downright dull in comparison.

But it did not concern him at all. Val's only assigned function at the moment was to stand on the shelf and await repair; coloration was irrelevant.

Val did, however, perform a routine sensory data scan. It revealed nothing except a window he was facing, with an expansive view of mountains and forests in the distance. He then turned his head to the right, a series of tiny mechanical adjustments designed to appear smooth to the human eye. He looked down the long, dimly lit shelf where other robots and parts were tagged and stored. The nearest piece of machinery to him on his right was twenty feet away, part of a DolphBot, a light-bluish mammal-shaped machine created for joyous activity in the water a few years ago, just after porpoises became extinct. It was inactive, awaiting new circuits. Beyond it were several humanoid robots wearing yellow raincoats and red hats. They were FireBots, particularly useful for fire fighting and far preferable to the human beings that were formerly used, since smoke inhalation was no longer a problem in rescue work. FireBots, however, were often in the repair shop. These seemed charred on one side. Further down were more metal parts, but the naked, fifty-watt bulbs were strung too far apart in this part of the warehouse for Val to see clearly what they were.

He turned and looked to his left. Beside him, only four feet away, was a robot shaped like a human female; in fact, Val noted, she was designed to please the male human's irrational fascination with almost dysfunctionally large mammary glands. She was dressed and designed to look as if she was going to a particularly chic dinner party. She stood frozen, with one hand on her hip and the other posed in front of her at an angle, as though she were about to greet someone. Her dress was long and light pink with sections of gold metal plate. Its most striking feature was a high, sweeping, fairy-tale collar which dramatically curved up on one side of her head. The pinkish material was so thin it was translucent, and at the moment, from Val's point of view, the diffused light from a distant light bulb was shining through it, creating a lovely glowing effect. She had large eyes, painted brown (which were termed by the promotion department in her sales brochure as "liquid brown" due to the presence of lubricating fluid), and gold glitter on her eyelids, which caught the light for a split second every time she blinked; she was programmed to blink every 23.68 seconds. Her hair was swept up in gold metal ringlets. And she had a pleasant smile on her pretty face.

Val looked away and stared straight ahead.

Neither robot had a comment or reaction to the other; there

was no logical reason for any acknowledgment or interaction. Unlike humans, robots waited until they had something to say before speaking, so hours passed as the silence of the warehouse continued without interruption.

Until sunset, which was framed by the large warehouse windows.

A human eye would perceive it as a breathtaking sunset. Yellow shafts of sunlight, half-hidden by orange clouds, came together at a small red ball that was resting, just for the moment, at the junction of two rolling mountains. Even the green forests took on a golden tint, and the long shadows of the evergreens that striped the lower valleys didn't hurt the effect any either.

Val and the female-shaped robot stood silently, facing the sunset, a beautiful light-red glow on their metallic faces.

Then a strange thing happened. . . .

"Beautiful, isn't it?"

Val realized that the soft, feminine-sounding mechanical voice came from the robot next to him. Val's internal circuits whirred into action; this data did not compute. On the surface, Val was motionless and maintained his eternally pleasant expression. But inside, there was an almost frantic search for order and reason; lights blinked, wires buzzed, circuits hummed. Val's computer, now a microscopic Fourth of July fireworks display, required additional information, even after hundreds of facts had been counterprogrammed and cross-indexed.

What Val had just heard definitely was not . . . logical.

"What was the purpose of that piece of communication?" he asked.

Not at all surprised or offended by the question, the female robot turned and looked at Val for the first time.

"I am practicing social conversation," she said. Her voice had a soft, almost musical tone.

Things were beginning to make sense to Val. "I assume you are here for damage to your mental circuitry," Val responded pleasantly.

"Incorrect," she said in an equally pleasant tone. "My designation is AquaCom-89045. I am being custom-reconditioned as a companion-hostess for poolside parties and other social functions. My observation concerning the aesthetic

7

appeal of the sunset is, I believe, an example of human charm.''

Val's computer conducted a lightning-fast search on the subject and came up dry. "Request additional data on 'charm,' '' he asked.

The female robot shifted position slightly as she began to explain, and her voice took on a looser, more human rhythm. " 'Charm: inconsequential words spoken in a positive tone, accompanied by a smile to imply interest in and/or approval of the listener.' '' She blinked and paused, then her voice returned to robot-normal. "That is charm.''

Buzzing, whirring, clicking noises—all happening inside Val, all at high speed. "Charm computes as an irrelevant exchange of random data,'' he concluded. "Therefore, it cannot increase efficiency, correct?''

Aqua looked at him and gave Val her winning smile.

"Correct . . .''

Val smiled back, pleased.

". . . for 97.53 percent of all existing robots,'' she said. "However, for the Com-series robots, charm increases usefulness and is therefore valuable knowledge.''

She then looked away, leaving Val to stew in his own circuits. He hesitated, aware he was not speaking or computing in a very efficient manner, but finally spoke up.

"I too am in the companion series.''

Aqua blinked, then turned and looked at Val with more interest than she had before, smiling even more widely.

"Your designation and function?''

"I am ValCom-17485. Function: to serve as companion and valet. Being programmed for charm was probably an extra expense, not as desirable as my present area of expertise: stocks and bonds, with specialized data in lumber commodities.''

"Request example of your programming in stocks and commodities,'' Aqua asked.

Val's computer instantly retrieved his most recent memory from his memory bank. Several days before, just before his annual maintenance work was due in order to maintain his five-year, fifty-thousand-mile warranty, he had been in the service of a tall, balding, grumpy quasi-tycoon named Horace Smith. Val recalled standing in the man's bedroom, holding a breakfast tray in his right hand. On the tray was a tiny microfilm spool of *The New Wall Street Journal*, a single perfect rose (which his wife Pat insisted always be present to try to improve his mood each morning, although it never did) and a single perfect cup of coffee (black, decaffeinated). In his other hand he held the man's suit coat while Smith put his pants on. "Okay, Val," Smith would growl, "let's hear the bad news. . . ."

And Val now repeated his answer verbatim for Aqua, in the same chatty, upbeat tone he had been programmed to use when conveying financial information.

" 'Good morning, sir. UnderSea FarmCo is up two points, and July Plywood is down a quarter.' "

"Your programming appears to be logically consistent with your assigned function," Aqua replied.

"Thank you," Val said in his regular voice. "If additional data on charm can add to my usefulness as a robot companion, I can learn new data from you. Question: Once you made that value judgment concerning the visual arrangement of mountains and sunset, what would be an appropriate response of mine?"

"You would probably say something like"—Aqua's voice tape did instantaneous splicing, and her voice became deep, male, banal, and chatty—" 'Yeah, I know what you mean. Mountains always make me feel closer to God for some reason. Can I get you a drink?' " Aqua switched back to her regular voice and turned to Val. "Then as you spoke you would look at me inquiringly."

"And your response to this?" Val asked, confused.

Aqua answered with a newly spliced voice tape. This one was female and flirtatious, with a Southern accent.

" 'Oh . . . thank you. I'll have a banana daiquiri.' "

Val and Aqua looked at each other a few moments, as expressionless as always, then, since their communication was apparently ended, they resumed their original positions on the shelf, facing forward, silent, two slightly malfunctioning machines awaiting repair on a dusty warehouse shelf.

But while Val's facial expression was pleasantly bland and he was quiet, deep inside his computer lights flashed, impulses raced, and microchips ricocheted data at lightning-fast speeds. He was like a pinball machine in heat.

Very little of what he had just heard made sense. He began his exhaustive search for logic and order with the concept "banana daiquiri" and tried to work from there. But he had little success. He kept trying, however. There was no hurry.

Days melted into nights; the sun through their window kept ducking below the mountains at sunset, then jumping back into view as night, looking for all the world like the moon.

Inside the warehouse, nothing much happened. Except inside Val's brain.

He kept trying to accurately categorize, compare, contrast, and cross-index all this new data before continuing his discussion with Aqua. There were many confusing variables to isolate, identify, correlate, and interpret, not to mention all the variables and syllogisms which could possibly be extrapolated.

Val was stumped.

He decided to review his recent memory-bank tapes at high speed, searching for additional clues to help him understand the deeper significance behind things like charm and banana daiquiris. First he jumped back to Crazy Rusty and the trash cans; that was no help. Then he shot forward, reviewing the conversation with Max and Charlie as they placed him on the warehouse shelf; nothing. So he backed up to the point where Max and Charlie had first placed him on the forklift pallet and they had slowly driven through the large robot factory itself, looking for anything that would help him understand the unit designated AquaCom-89045. . . .

When Val had first entered the main factory area and stood on the wooden pallet of the forklift just in front of Max and Charlie, he had almost experienced sensory overload.

The factory was immense, the size of an airplane hangar, full of people, robots, machines and activity, all creating multiple levels of input—sights, sounds, smells.

Sights: color-coded areas made the factory a crazy quilt of shades and hues.

Sounds: human speech, whirring computers, cutting torches, high-speed engines, power drills, clanking, banging, and yelling.

Smells: grease, rust, lubricants, molded plastics, soldered iron, stale doughnuts, and human sweat.

Organized confusion. Logical chaos.

"I've seen crowded theaters on fire more organized than this place," Max had grumbled to Charlie over the noise. But the system did work and work well, Val noted, creating, testing, and producing robots quite efficiently in spite of what Val mentally referred to without any value judgment as the human factor.

The first robot Val's memory tapes recorded that he had seen was a cheap SweepBot, a slender, metal cylinder with mechanical hands that pushed a broom back and forth. It had rolled right out in front of the forklift's path, then darted out of the way at the last moment; the forklift driver was programmed to stop instantly for humans but would have turned the SweepBot into a metal pancake.

On their right was a break area, where assembly-line workers could go and relax for precisely fifteen minutes. Inside the break area were uncomfortable chairs, dog-eared issues of *PlayBot*, and a new electronic poker table. In the center of the table was a small white plastic hand with one finger pointing outward, which shook itself in an electronically accusing manner at any player who forgot to ante. In one corner of the room, Val had seen a handsome young Coca-Cola delivery man glaring at his slower robot assistant. (Both wore the red and white uniforms with the distinctive logo, but the robot's was painted on.) The assistant made a high-pitched sound, the soft-drink machine's coin tray opened, then a special vacuum tube connected to the machine shot out and all the loose seventy-five-cent pieces were sucked in. But then the forklift had rolled on, stopping twenty feet further on in front of a huge, rectangular, computer on wheels with a dozen mechanical arms.

Max had taken the papers off his clipboard, handed them to the large, busy ExecBot, which then stamped them "E.B. -22084," and handed them back to Max, who fed one copy into a slot, then motioned to the forklift driver to roll on, leaving the ExecBot to its endless paperwork and ringing telephones.

The forklift then headed toward the warehouse area, rolling by a series of specially created testing cubicles, each designed to test and retest a particular type of robot.

The first cubicle was a small sound studio. Over the shoulders of the human monitors seated outside, through a glass wall, Val had seen a beautifully designed female-shaped robot wearing a white toga with gold braiding and seated in front of a large harp. Her long metal fingers were poised by the strings, and her mechanical expression seemed appropriate to

11

a musician who was about to play something serene and classical and magnificent. One of the humans outside said "Test Number 14, HarpBot-99043" into a speaker, then pushed a small button. The graceful, long fingers began to caress the strings lovingly, and through a speaker, just over the din of the factory, Max, Charlie, and Val heard a beautiful concerto begin. But the fingers began moving faster and faster until it was clear that "Turkey in the Straw" was being played in its usual rapid, foot-stompin' manner. The HarpBot played so quickly and tapped her foot so energetically that all the strings quickly broke, but she idiotically continued playing the destroyed harp as the humans outside shook their heads, openly displeased.

The testing at the next cubicle seemed much more successful. It was a large, fifteen- by forty-foot underwater tank, with several men and women watching from outside, taking notes. Inside the tank, in the clear blue water, a human scuba diver assisted a robot in practicing repair of an underwater cable. However, the human struggled awkwardly in an element he was never designed for, contending with gravity, balance, air supply, and equipment as always, while the equipment-free, specially designed, sea-green robot sat on a rock, legs (with fins for feet) casually crossed, the cable across his lap, tinkering away without problems.

Val had turned as they rolled by to look at another testing cubicle with a volcano-and-jungle mural painted on the back wall. At one end, a giant forty-foot-high DinoBot, designed to look like a *Tyrannosaurus Rex*, complete with huge head, open mouth with rows of teeth, tiny forelimbs, and giant haunches, was lumbering toward a single human hunter in a safari jacket, who aimed an old-fashioned rifle at the DinoBot's chest. But the forklift rounded a corner before Val saw the outcome of the test. (He cross-indexed "dinosaurs" and "charm" and came up with even less than usual.)

The next cubicle was designed like a cozy, masculine den, with a solid wall of books, a brick fireplace with a mantel, and an Irish setter curled up on a rug in front of the fire. Inside the cubicle was a semihumanoid robot, designed to look slightly overweight, with a Perrier bottle permanently in his left hand, while a human in a brown tweed jacket with patches on the elbows paced around nervously, waving a pipe. Since they had rounded the corner, it was quieter, and Val was able to catch part of the conversation.

"Okay . . . okay . . . but *where* should the detective meet the blonde?" the man asked, leaning on a typewriter at a desk.

"At the lighthouse . . . in the fog. . . ." the robot answered mechanically.

"Fog! Great idea!" the human exclaimed happily and rushed over to make some notes. But the forklift rolled on.

The last cubicle before entering the warehouse area was designed like a boxing ring. Two robots wearing boxing gloves and shorts that said "Everlast" on the belt were slugging it out while humans monitored their reactions. Then one BoxBot knocked the other's head off, but both kept fighting. The other's arm fell off, then part of a shoulder, and while the humans kept hitting buttons to try to stop the fight, bells were clanging and towels were thrown in, and the two now headless torsos continued to pound away.

Then a huge set of doors had automatically opened, and as the forklift rolled out of the busy factory area into the quiet warehouse area, Val suddenly spun his head around 180 degrees to see how the fight ended, so that even though his body was facing forward his head was looking backward.

"Turn your head back around!" Max had suddenly growled at him, and Val quickly spun his head around. They had entered the warehouse, and the doors closed behind them.

"God, I hate it when they do that," Max had muttered to Charlie, and then Val's memory tape of the factory ended.

Machines possessing artificial intelligence operate in a different time frame than humans, since, among other reasons, they don't sleep, they don't forget, and they don't say things to each other like "Let a smile be your umbrella," or "If it wasn't for bad luck I wouldn't have any." Machines pause before picking up a conversational thread until all previous, related data has been carefully examined, studied, scrutinized, and generally milked dry. Thus it was many days later when Val, having just finished his review of his recent memory tapes, continued his discussion with Aqua in a conversational tone without all the indirectness favored by human beings.

"But what would happen," Val asked late one night without turning his head, "after I brought you a banana daiquiri at this poolside social gathering?"

"Assuming you were a human male adult and possessing sexual insecurities—" Suddenly, a series of alarms went off in Aqua's computer. "Forgive me," she said, "that was a redundancy." She turned off the alarms, which sounded not unlike the crash-dive alarm in old submarine movies starring Robert Mitchum. "At that point, once you had brought me a drink, we would engage in verbal courting rituals known as clever banter."

"To what purpose?" Like all sophisticated robots, Val was programmed to discover: what is the utility, the goal, the function, the logic, *the reason*?

"The purpose of clever banter," Aqua answered, "is to give the human male social companionship during the party as well as assisting him in viewing himself as intelligent, interesting, and virile." She paused, then added, "That is my assigned function."

Val turned and looked at her carefully.

"You appear capable of performing at peak efficiency," he objectively noted.

"Thank you, I do. As our Litany says . . ."

And then suddenly, both Val and Aqua stared straight ahead, their eyes glazed over a little, and they both spoke mechanically, saying in unison, *"We Exist to Serve with Logic and Efficiency."*

They spoke in cadence; it was a chant. When they finished they each slowly closed their eyes, and a brief electrical hum could be heard from each of them.

In the center of the top of Val's back was a round disc. The computer-typeface lettering around it said "Pleasure Center, ValCom-17485." It was the size of a silver dollar and designed like a snowflake. Once the electrical impulse hit it, it felt like gangbusters.

Aqua's Pleasure Center was in the same location, labeled in the same way, and responded the same; like Val's, her Pleasure Center began to glow a soft orange, then orange-red, then bright red, before fading away. The entire electronic experience only lasted six or seven seconds. It followed every recitation of the Robot Litany by sophisticated robot models.

The "Pleasure Center" concept had led to many breakthroughs in robotics. Technically, of course, machines can't feel "pleasure"—but the advanced models could distinguish something resembling that state when they received new surges

14

of energy that pulsated through their more sensitive circuits. Thus the Robot Litany was reinforced with small, almost disabling power surges. And the only way a robot could cause these extra-power vibrations was to recite the Litany. It was the closest thing to mechanical "happiness" yet achieved by modern technology.

Now it was over—until the next time they recited the Litany. Val and Aqua opened their eyes and stood there quietly, staring out into the semidarkness of the warehouse; if they had been humans they would have smoked a cigarette.

The next afternoon, Val and Aqua could hear but not see Max and Charlie two rows away struggling to get a large robot shaped like a giraffe onto their forklift. At this time they overheard the following data according to Max: the awkward-shaped machine was (1) headed for Robot Country Safari (2) a son of a bitch to lift (3) a hell of a lot tougher to move, since Charlie had ordered a forklift that was two sizes too small. Once Charlie, Max, their argument, robot, and forklift had all rounded the far corner, bringing peace and quiet once again to the warehouse, Val turned to Aqua, realizing he had more questions.

"Question," he said.

"Proceed."

"As I said, you appear capable of performing at peak efficiency. However, you have been housed in the warehouse with a repair tag. Logically, you have a malfunction that is not readily apparent."

Val waited for a response.

An hour went by.

Then he realized. "Communication error on my part," Val stated. "I said I had a question but instead made a statement. Let me rephrase and clarify. Is it correct that while you appear perfectly capable, you in fact have a malfunction?"

"Affirmative," Aqua answered.

Two hours.

"What is the nature of your malfunction?" Val finally asked. Outside, twilight gently settled over the mountains and forests, a pale blue gossamer cover. Aqua did not turn as she spoke quietly.

"Until recently, for the seven years since my assembly, I have been centered around a different function, design, and programming than my present assignment." Aqua hesitated;

they had tried so many times to erase her memory tapes, but there were still images left, some blurred, some sharp. "I was designated GovCom-223 . . . 9 . . . something. I spent all seven years of my existence, until six months ago, assigned to the same family. I was a governess-companion and assisted in the daily care, recreation, and education of a girl, Sarah Denise Combs, age eight. I performed at absolute peak efficiency for seven years; no robot was ever more successfully designed, more effectively programmed, or more appropriately assigned. I could perform a total of one thousand, seven hundred and eighty-three child-related tasks, ranging from knowing eight hundred and thirty-five bedtime stories to fifty-two different recipes for making chocolate chip cookies and nineteen different ways to make crude outdoor figures composed of particles of water vapor which when frozen in the upper atmosphere fall to earth as soft, white, crystalline flakes."

Val was impressed with the extent of Aqua's former programming; he had no idea how to make a snowman.

"I miss playing the games more than anything," Aqua said quietly.

Two more hours. Three.

Outside, the sky had gone from pale blue to deep purple.

Val asked another question.

"If your programming was highly efficient, why was your design and function changed?"

Aqua hesitated a moment, then spoke softly.

"Sarah grew up."

In the faint glow from the warehouse light outside the window, Val could see a tall pine tree sway slightly in the night wind.

"She became much more interested in what her mother referred to as 'boys and cars' than baking cookies on Friday nights with her mechanical governess-companion. I soon became an extraneous expense to the family, and I was sold. My new owner, an unmarried, highly successful businessman, a Mr. Norman Kurland, had me completely reconditioned and circuit-washed."

Val's self-protection programming circuits flickered for a moment at the very sound of the word.

Aqua continued. "At my new owner's instructions, I was to be totally reconditioned and redesigned. Visually, I was reconstructed to appeal to an adult male instead of a female child, so I was rebuilt to have large eyes, an eternally youthful face, a small waist, and a large chest area. And my metallic clothing is supposed to be sensual in design. My new programmed duties, as AquaCom-89045, were to include making charming conversation at poolside parties, getting cheese dip, drinks, and towels, and letting a feisty but pleasing French burgundy breathe for precisely the right number of minutes and then serving it to Mr. Kurland and his guests in the hot tub. I was able to perform these duties quite successfully, but I also continued to have a minor malfunction: I continued to inquire as to any children Mr. Kurland's guests might have, their health, their play-activities, and so on. Soon, friends and guests began asking my advice on child-rearing, which had somehow not been completely erased. This was a malfunction. I have been sent back for repair three times in the last six months, but technicians cannot yet locate the problem that causes my former programmed identity to continue to reappear."

If Val had searched his memory tapes again, he could not have recalled a time when it was so quiet in the warehouse.

Later that night, just when Val was about to comment on what Aqua had said, inquiring into "chocolate chip cookies, data pertaining to baking thereof," the entire atmosphere outside the warehouse began to malfunction.

A violent thunderstorm tore the sky apart.

It came up quickly. First, a night breeze teased the top of the tall pine tree outside the warehouse window. Then a strong wind caused the tree to bend and sway. Rain began falling in heavy drops at first, then the drops were hurled down, as if in anger. And finally the strong wind, which whipped the sturdy pine tree around like a straw of wheat, blasted the rain against the window like bullets.

Jagged lightning split the distant dark-violet sky, and for two seconds the mountains were in view, now dwarfed by immense, churning thunderheads, furious atmospheric monsters that rolled and rumbled as though trying to flatten the mountain into rubble.

As the storm built in intensity, the combined sounds of the roaring wind, the angry rain spattering against the windows, and the deep bellowing sounds of thunder combined to make the world sound like a frantic, prehistoric jungle.

Inside the warehouse, as each new thunderclap startled the landscape, Val and Aqua continued to just stand and stare out the window, watching the storm. Only their eyes were open a little wider than usual.

KA–BOOM! Thunder rocked the world.

Rows of naked light bulbs throughout the warehouse suddenly flickered, fought for life, and died.

Darkness inside.

Violence outside.

Apocalypse now.

Val and Aqua exchanged silent looks, then made the mistake of looking back outside.

The storm and the sky and the mountains were framed by their window, making the once-huge warehouse seem like a fragile dollhouse about to be brushed aside by the power of the chaos. Suddenly, there was the world's biggest series of thunderous assaults—BOOM, BOOM, BOOM!—and a lightning hand reached down and grabbed the pine tree outside the window and with a bright flash of whiteness and a sizzling CRACKLE split and toppled the tree!

Before the deafening thunder and blinding lightning had stopped, Val and Aqua, without looking at each other or even being aware of it themselves, began inching toward one another.

The storm built to an even bigger assault on the sky, aiming rain at the warehouse now like machine-gun bullets.

On the roof, several giant solar mirrors buckled and erupted into noisy shards, and the wind slapped the pieces of mirror off into the night before they could even fall to the roof.

Val's left hand and Aqua's right hand were only two feet apart.

Then one foot.

The rain pounded away and the wind wailed.

Inches.

Their metal fingers brushed against each other. Then touched.

And in the midst of the violent storm, two gentle reactions took place: Val and Aqua's individual Pleasure Centers began to hum and pulsate, turning from orange to red and then to a sensuous, pulsating crimson. . . .

An hour later, the storm began to retreat as quickly as it had attacked, and Val and Aqua inched back apart.

They were soon once again about six feet apart, still stand-

18

ing on the shelf, listening to the now almost-gentle rain.

Neither had looked at the other. Neither had said a word.

The storm disappeared and the night remained.

> *dawn* (dôn) *n*. 1. to become day; to begin to become day; grow light. 2. to begin to be understood or felt. 3. the beginning (of something).

The morning sun was bright and clear and made the newly washed sky, mountains, and forests appear like a brightly-colored painting framed by the warehouse window. But the most dazzling sight of all was something new, something Val and Aqua had not seen before, something that totally stole the show.

"Data request," Aqua said.

"Proceed," Val answered in his always pleasant tone.

"Perhaps I also can add to my utility by using this 'down time' to learn additional data. Can you identify that atmospheric phenomenon?"

"Rainbow: an arc of fifty-four degrees containing colors in consecutive bands, formed in the sky by the refraction, reflection, and dispersion of the sun's rays in falling rain or mist," Val stated in a tone of voice that in a human might be taken as pride; he *knew* what he was talking about.

"Function of a rainbow?"

This time he was stumped.

Val kept his usual pleasant expression, but inside he was busy as hell, rapidly checking all possible data banks and using every system he knew of to retrieve information. After several seconds and a highly technical, extremely sophisticated data search into his vast information-storage facilities, he came up with zip-a-dee-doo-dah.

"Unknown," Val stated. Then he decided to add to his own data bank on the subject. "Are your optic sensors designed to pick up all colors on the spectrum that the human eye can detect?"

"Yes," Aqua replied, "plus three additional colors."

Three?

Val wasn't sure he heard correctly at first, so he silently

19

replayed his internal recording of their conversation. Realizing he had heard correctly, he grew very silent.

Twenty minutes passed. Finally, in a subdued voice, Val said, "I can see two additional colors."

"Audio problem," Aqua replied immediately in her usual sweet tone of voice. "Repeat, please."

"I can see two additional colors," Val answered in a somewhat louder voice, one that approached normal. "For example, in that rainbow"—and he pointed, as if there were more than one—"besides green, blue, red, and yellow, I can also see shane and farb," Val said. "Farb is my coded tension moderator for positive response."

"I can see shane and farb also," Aqua said, "plus glak."

The rainbow, which would offer only the same old boring colors to the human eye, was being joined in the sky by small, white clouds like puffs of cotton.

Something deep inside Val's circuitry was reacting, and Val wasn't sure what was causing the problem. He only knew that he needed to point something out at this point in the data exchange. "For my various functions, I have not been programmed to see glak, since it would not be useful."

"Yes," Aqua quickly agreed, "it would have been illogical to program you for glak."

There was a long pause. The morning sun began warming the moist earth, and the rainbow would soon be gone forever.

"In fact, it would even decrease my efficiency," Val suddenly said forty-five minutes later, and it took even Aqua a few seconds to realize he was still discussing his inability to perceive the color glak.

"What you are missing by not seeing glak computes as . . ." There was the sound of rapid mechanical calculations that lasted several seconds, then Aqua said, "Close to zero." No comment from Val.

Half an hour.

"Val?"

"Present."

"Farb is also my coded tension moderator," Aqua said. "Besides both of us being Com-series, we also have a positive response to farb in common."

They slowly looked at each other.

"We would be mechanically compatible for many similar

functions," Val said quietly, looking into Aqua's large brown eyes.

"The same thought just crossed my grid," she said, speaking softly.

They then looked away.

The day, the rainbow, and many hours into the night all passed before Val or Aqua looked at each other or spoke again. It was very late and very quiet when Aqua spoke.

"Besides my obvious cosmetic damage, I have another malfunction to report to the repair shop when I am delivered there soon," she said. "Since being placed on this shelf, my Pleasure Center has functioned erratically. Instead of being stimulated only when I recite the Robot Litany, it has frequently become active when we exchanged data."

Val digested this information for two hours, then quietly replied.

"This is very unusual. I have the identical malfunction."

Aqua did not respond. Val said nothing more.

There was insufficient data on this new, strange subject for any sort of logical computation.

CHAPTER 2

friend (frend) *n.* 1. a person whom one knows well and is fond of. 2. a person on the same side in a struggle.

• • • The next day, in another part of the factory, Max stood on a forklift pallet next to Charlie and a new robot wearing a repair tag and cursed the traffic jam ahead.

"Why do they design these factory aisles so small, anyway?"

"Take it easy, Max," Charlie said, using the time to make notes and organize the paperwork on his clipboard.

"Well, dammit, look at how Ernie's got that big crane angled around so that it blocks everything! He can't even handle that block-and-tackle setup anyway—"

"Max, would you relax? It isn't Ernie's fault that big ol' SnakeBot rolled off the shelf again."

"Well, who the hell needs a thirty-foot robot shaped like a goddamn *python* anyway?"

"Zoos, museums, colleges—you know pythons are extinct."

"So what the hell do they do with 'em?" Max's face was getting red. "Feed 'em those mechanical rabbits from the dog races?"

"They'll be done in a few minutes—"

"No, they won't. Look, it went limp again. Must be two feet wide in the middle, heavier than hell too." Max suddenly leaned back and whacked the robot forklift driver on the head with the palm of his hand. "Hey! Cabbie! Turn this around!" Max turned back to Charlie, smiling. "We'll go outside while they waltz that snake around all day."

"Max, the only way to get to the warehouse from here is to go by the testing range, and that's against regulations."

Charlie hated doing anything that was against the regulations. Max loved it.

They went through the testing range.

It was a beautiful day outside. While they slowly rolled along outside, past trucks, people unloading vans containing robots, and the executive offices, Charlie double-checked the paperwork on the new robot that was between them while Max glared at it, sizing it up.

The new robot headed for the warehouse was designed to look like a balding middle-aged man with a potbelly. He held a cheap cigar and wore a white shirt, red tie, and a black suit that would have looked out of place anywhere except in a Las Vegas nightclub at about three in the morning. There were even too-large, fake-diamond cuff links. He was seated on top of an old vaudeville-type steamer trunk, turned on its end, with stickers that said "Reno," "Tahoe," and "Grossinger's" on the sides. Underneath the trunk was a small tank tread for mobility. His two legs, which dangled over the edge of the trunk, were designed only for him to cross occasionally in order to suggest a relaxed manner. There was a large speaker in the middle of his broad stomach, and what looked like a large red tie tack was really his Pleasure Center.

The robot's facial features were more cartoony than human—he even had audio cones instead of ears—but his expression left no doubt about his all-too-human attitude on the world. He had large, movable eyebrows, slanted down; eyelids that drooped half closed, just to get you off guard; a nose that looked like it might have been broken one night on the Lower East Side; and a slanted mouth, so that he always looked as if he was speaking out of the side of his mouth. The total effect made him look both sly and deadpan, like a man who had just slipped a whoopee cushion under the preacher's seat in church and was waiting for the pompous sermon to end. . . .

"What the hell is this thing, anyway?" Max said, peering closely at the robot's left hand, where there was a tacky pinkie ring with a bright pink light under it. As Max leaned forward to study it, the robot moved his right hand, which permanently held a large cigar, and quietly flicked ashes on Max; neither Max nor Charlie noticed. The robot smiled to himself.

23

"Look, Max!" Charlie yelled, suddenly pointing. "A CrimeBuster! The Deluxe Model!"

Max turned and stared. Even the robot on the pallet with the cigar took a mild interest.

As their forklift slowly rolled by the testing range they all stared at an impressive, bizarre robot which was shaped like a futuristic tank. On one side of the armored vehicle, painted jet-black, was a painting of a large police badge and the motto, "To Protect and Serve." Within the design of the badge was the blindfolded figure of Justice holding scales and the words, "Caveat Malefactor," which was Latin for "Bad Persons Watch Out." The tanklike robot was twelve feet long and ten feet high. It was shaped like a pyramid and had a dome-shaped head, at the top of which was a cherry light that could revolve, like that on a police car. It was half turned away, at the moment, from an outdoor firing range. There two technicians, standing behind special safety glass and wearing objects resembling earmuffs to muffle noise, looked at each other; then one hit a button.

Suddenly, fifty feet downrange, a pop-up target jumped into view: a 1930s caricature of a gangster, complete with black mask and submachine gun.

CrimeBuster instantly flew into action. It whirled with surprising speed for something as big and heavy as it looked, and a lethal-looking black and silver laser-gun barrel came slamming out, knocking open two small doors.

A white-hot blast went sizzling toward the gangster target and knocked the gun right out of the target's hands. A perfect shot.

The CrimeBuster's optic sensors, with red lights inside, spun in toward the two technicians, hoping for approval.

Both technicians, a young black woman and a young white man, nodded and smiled to the CrimeBuster, who then braced for another test.

This time, the pop-up target that suddenly burst into view was a little boy holding a balloon. CrimeBuster spun around, and a black .50 caliber machine gun burst out of a tiny set of doors—but at the last second the large mechanical policeman held its fire, then glanced over at the technicians, who smiled again.

Gun withdrawn. Target down. CrimeBuster ready.

Third pop-up target: a little old lady pushing a baby carriage.

CrimeBuster spun around. A huge flamethrower burst out of its center section.

The technicians got ready to record notes: Would the CrimeBuster unit correctly hesitate, then withdraw weapon?

Negative. Unit totally incinerated little-old-lady target. And baby carriage.

The sudden, roaring fifty-foot flame made an audible "whoosh," and the blast of heat was so hot that even the two technicians, thirty feet behind it, raised their arms to temporarily shield themselves from the heat. Then they exchanged looks of disapproval.

As the forklift rolled on by, Max nudged Charlie and made a sour face.

Even the robot between them cocked one eyebrow at what he had just seen.

The forklift driver robot didn't react.

As the forklift moved on, heading for the outside warehouse entrance, the CrimeBuster Unit looked over at the two technicians for approval. The humans were frowning and shaking their heads.

The grandma target was now curling into shapeless black ash; the baby carriage was just black smoke.

"Still overreacting," said the black woman.

"Yeah, hair trigger," said the white man.

Charlie was still excited about seeing the CrimeBuster as they entered the quiet, dusty warehouse section.

"Wow, Max, what luck! I've seen several CrimeBusters before, but never a Deluxe Model! Those things have the stopping power of a Sherman tank!"

"Yeah," Max grumbled, "and the personality of a German shepherd. Besides, that one's broken. Big deal."

They rolled down to a space marked C-5, and moments later Max, Charlie, and the robot with the cigar were being raised up on the forklift until the wooden pallet was almost level with the shelf. Charlie looked at the robot.

"This one looks all right. Must be internal damage of some kind," he said.

"Yeah, I think he's some sort of comedian or something," Max muttered. "Let's get him stored away; it's going to be break time pretty soon."

The grinding noise of the forklift motor stopped, and then their pallet was perfectly level with the shelf. Max and Charlie bent over, and they each grabbed a side of the vaudeville trunk and tried to lift it. They grunted, heaved, strained, broke wind, and cursed a lot, but it was too heavy. They stood up. A small vein in Max's forehead began to throb. Charlie thought of it as his anger level. Charlie had only seen it begin to twitch whenever Max and machinery had to work together.

"This is stupid," Max said. "I'll ask him if he can walk or roll or whatever the hell his mobility is—"

"Wait, Max!" Charlie reached over and held the robot's repair tag in plain view for Max to read. Max ignored it. Charlie read it out loud. " 'Executive Order 17-B: Do not attempt communication with this robot. You could cause internal damage.' "

About ten feet down the shelf, unnoticed by the men and immobile except for their optic and audio receptors, Val and Aqua stood, facing forward as always. They were missing nothing, however.

"Hold on, hold on, college boy," Max said. "All you ever do is quote rule books and textbooks. I've worked here since the place opened." It was true. Charlie's plant ID number was 7944. Max had the number 5.

Max looked the strange-looking robot right in the eye, after glancing at his tag for his correct designation.

"CatSkil-55602. CAN YOU FUNCTION?"

They waited.

The unit designated CatSkil-55602 slowly turned his head, regarded Max in a tired way for a moment, then finally spoke in a Brooklyn accent while gesturing with his cigar.

"This bum came up to me on the street the other day and said he hadn't had a bite in weeks. So I bit him." And immediately following that, four things happened: an electronic recording of a drummer's "rim shot" on a snare drum played, RAT–A–TAT; one eyebrow went up; the cigar went up to his mouth; and finally, a thick cloud of greenish-brown cigar smoke poured out of his mouth after the mechanical puff on the mechanical cigar.

Max and Charlie looked stunned. Then irritated.

Val and Aqua, a few feet away, had no reaction.

And therefore, with no laughter from the audience, not even a single guffaw from a drunk or a cackle from some broad at the bar, the Pleasure Center on the CatSkil-55602 did not light up or respond.

"So that's how this thing's busted," Max realized, then suddenly gave the robot a hard kick. "Just like the candy machine in G-4."

"Max, no!" Charlie exclaimed, horrified as ever to see how Max enjoyed treating carefully engineered machinery. "This is a delicate machine, it's not right to—"

"Don't tell me what's right!"

"*I was at this hotel,*" the CatSkil unit suddenly said, with a droopy-eyed look and a grandiose wave of his cigar. "*Called the clerk. Told him I had a leak in the sink. He said, 'Go ahead, the customer's always right.'*"

Rat-a-tat. The rim shot, as before, was exactly the kind you'd hear at a seedy nightclub. CatSkil then took another puff on his cigar with that pleased-with-himself-for-no-good-reason expression typical of professional stand-up comics.

Max was livid and had to be almost physically restrained from kicking the robot again.

"Please, Max, take it easy," Charlie urged. "I remember now—the dispatcher, Jerry Martin, was talking about this one. Jerry said that all he can do is tell these stupid one-liners. It needs a complete circuit-washing."

Unnoticed by the two men, Val and Aqua's audio receptors perked up even more at the word.

"Who the hell would want one of these things?" Max said, furious for the ten millionth time in his adult life that he was living in such a screwy decade; he longed for the simple days of what he referred to as His Lost Youth.

Charlie looked at the back of the repair tag. "It belongs to Universal Entertainment, Inc. They probably use it for stag parties or cheap burlesque joints with robot strippers. Oh, and I think they send it to the lounges in Vegas, Atlantic City, the Borscht Belt—"

"Let's just get the bastard stored away—we haven't got all day."

Again, they pushed and shoved and managed to half-lift, half-push the CatSkil unit over onto the shelf, then turn him around so he was facing forward. Meanwhile, CatSkil didn't do a damn thing to help except flick some cigar ashes on Max as he was bending over and pushing. He did pose a question to them, however, while they were shoving him into position.

27

"Did you hear the one about the guy who was killed by a weasel?"

"Killed by a weasel?" Max automatically asked as he finished pushing and straining. "How—"

"Don't ask, Max," Charlie warned. "It'll just be something dumb." Both men stood up straight again. "There! Whew."

CatSkil turned to Charlie this time.

"Did you hear the one about the guy who was killed by a weasel?"

Max started to answer, but Charlie held up his hand as a warning while shaking his head. Max shrugged; Charlie was usually right when it came to robots. Max just hated to admit it.

Charlie examined his clipboard carefully, then glanced around the shelf. "I just thought of something—we got an invoice order on this AquaCom. Should we haul her off to Customer Reconditioning now?"

Unnoticed by the two men, Val's eyes widened, and his ears pivoted another thirty degrees.

"We could, I suppose," Max said, walking on down the shelf past Val and over to Aqua, where he bent over, squinted, and checked her repair tag, which was fastened to her wrist. "We'll be going past there later today. Let's see. . . . Are the AquaCom and the ValCom a matched pair? If they're going to be reassigned to the same place, there's no use getting one done ahead of the other."

As Max checked the repair tag information on Aqua's wrist, he did not notice her eyes widen at what she had just heard. And neither Max nor Charlie noticed Val's head cock slightly to one side and his face change to what his faded sales brochure referred to as "Facial Expression #425—Extreme Interest, Potentially Serious."

Charlie rustled the papers on his clipboard until he found the right invoice information. "Nah, they're headed for different destinations."

"But we could take one of them away now, right?" Max asked.

Aqua's ears moved. Val's expression advanced one more notch on the Concern spectrum.

"Oh, the hell with it," Max muttered, glancing at his watch. "It's almost break time. We'll take her tomorrow."

Others might worry about pausing to watch sunsets you could never recapture or taking time to stop and smell the roses; Max was only philosophical about the fact that a break not taken was a break gone forever.

In about three seconds he was standing on the wooden pallet again and signaling the robot driver below to take them down; Charlie had to hurry to make the pallet in time. Neither man noticed that Val and Aqua had resumed their bland, robot expressions.

Halfway down, however, Max signaled a stop, then made an upward motion with his thumb to the robot driver.

"I can't stand it," he muttered apologetically to Charlie. When they were once again level with CatSkil, Max leaned closer. "How was the guy killed by a weasel?"

"He was sitting on the railroad tracks, and a train came along and he didn't hear the weasel." This was followed, as the night follows the day, by the bap-bap of the electronic rim shot and a murky green puff of cigar smoke—aimed right in Max's face.

As they descended and left the warehouse Max muttered something to Charlie about how it killed him that those damned contraptions were worth more than he and Charlie would make in ten years: CatSkil-55602 didn't catch it all, but he heard enough to make him smile to himself.

It was the middle of the night in the dusty old warehouse; not a creature was stirring, not even a MouseBot.

Val and Aqua stood silently looking out their warehouse window. The outside world was painted a shimmering silver. A full, bright moon illuminated the entire landscape, giving it a peaceful, subdued glow. The soft, rolling mountains, the rock formations, the cluster of distant pine trees—all of it looked efficiently constructed, metallic, and inviting.

"Data request," Val said quietly.

"Proceed," Aqua answered, also speaking softly.

They did not turn and look at each other as they spoke. If they had, they would have noticed that the reflected moonlight lent a luminous silver glow to their metal faces, their clothing, Val's bow tie, Aqua's artificial hair, everything.

"Through your 'charm' programming, can you explain something to me?" Val asked. "I do not understand the human fascination with the sun's reflection off earth's satel-

29

lite. Perhaps that data could assist me in my capacity as a companion.''

"Negative. I cannot explain their fascination,'' Aqua stated. "I can, however, share some observations of my own on that subject. My former owners used to swim in the moonlight in their swimming pool with no artificial lighting to assist their efforts. Following that rather inefficient choice of lighting, they then often practiced reproductive techniques. Once, in the moonlight, a largely unsuccessful attempt at sexual union was attempted in a toy rubber life raft, but—''

"Excuse the interruption, but please define that last term.''

"Toy rubber life raft: an inflated rubber floating unit approximately five feet long and three feet wide modeled after United States Navy ocean safety equipment but designed for human recreation, brand name NavyToy, purchased for twenty-nine ninety-five at an end-of-August sale at K Mart, plastic oars optional—''

"Thank you. Data stored. Proceed.''

"But even though copulation attempts were entirely unsuccessful, the human couple seemed pleased with the entire evening, which was accompanied by prodigious amounts of splashing, laughter, and white wine. I recall also wondering about the subject of human behavior and moonlight.''

It was quiet a few moments, then Val turned to his other side and looked at CatSkil, who stared straight ahead and looked bored. He seemed to light up, however, as Val spoke.

"CatSkil-55602, do you have any data on the subject of what humans call a 'full moon?' ''

CatSkil slowly, happily turned, flicked his cigar ash, mechanically cleared his throat, shot his cuffs, gestured with his cigar, and generally took his own fat time about it until he finally said, *"There were these two werewolves, see. And one says, 'Well, I guess I'll go down to the corner barbershop.' And the other one says, 'What for?' And the first one says, 'To get a face-cut.' ''* There was an immediate rim shot, bap-bap, which echoed throughout the silent warehouse, and a greenish-silvery blast of cigar smoke, and then CatSkil was still, happy, and quiet again.

Val and Aqua looked at each other with blank expressions and continued their conversation.

"Increasing my data in this area, which is of great human

interest," Aqua said, "would increase my general efficiency as a companion."

"Yes, it would be the same benefit to me to learn more about it. In addition, I am also trying to study those tall, woody, perennial plants that cover those geological upheavals, but we may be too far away for me to study them effectively."

With that, Val blinked once as he stared out the window. Suddenly, his two eyeballs moved forward, telescoping out of his head on cylinders with a series of clicks. Val was equipped with an eight-by-thirty-five magnification ability, which assisted but did not solve his efforts to study the trees more closely. His eyes clicked back into his head, and he turned to Aqua. "I was correct. I am still too far away."

"What would be the purpose of such additional knowledge?" Aqua asked.

"Learning new data about trees would add to my usefulness in advising on lumber commodities. Question: Can you suggest how I could study them in a more efficient manner?"

"Affirmative. Move your unit in closer physical proximity."

"Problem. An additional sophisticated unit would be advisable to accompany me, to help collect, store, and interpret data. I lack such a unit."

Aqua slowly looked to her right, then slowly to her left, then stared straight ahead.

"*I* am the nearest functioning unit," she said. "Would it be advisable for me to accompany you for purposes of interfacing?"

"You took the words right out of my speaker."

They looked at each other a long moment, then Val turned and they both walked off to the left, past CatSkil, toward the far ramps and stairways at the end of their row in the silent, dark warehouse.

But after they had walked only about fifteen feet, they heard the mechanical grinding noise of something following them. Val and Aqua paused and listened. The mechanical noise stopped. They proceeded. So did the noise.

They stopped and looked back. CatSkil was right behind them, smiling, and he elaborately flicked an infinitesimal ash from his eternally glowing cigar.

Val and Aqua exchanged looks and turned and walked on. CatSkil was still a caboose. They stopped again.

31

"Aqua, perhaps this CatSkil robot can also increase his usefulness by directly acquiring data. I assume he possesses the ability to convert knowledge into what humans refer to as humor."

Aqua looked at the robot behind them. "CatSkil-55602, are you going to accompany us on a brief but useful fact-finding mission?"

"Is that your nose or are you sucking on a pickle?" CatSkil answered right back, triggering a rim shot and a puff of cigar smoke. Val and Aqua exchanged deadpan looks.

Val decided to try again.

"CatSkil," he said, "are you sufficiently operative to travel approximately 4.42 miles to the edge of the woods with us?"

"The other day," CatSkil began, with no small amount of tie straightening, ash flicking, and arm waving, *"it was so hot, I saw a dog chasing a cat, and they were both walking."*

Both Val and Aqua, being expensive Com-series robots, were equipped to create puzzled expressions on their faces, an ability which was beginning to prove handy.

"I believe that within that distorted communication," Aqua said, "there appears to be a positive answer regarding 'walking.' "

"Yes, perhaps the only way CatSkil's broken circuitry allows him to communicate his thoughts is through jokes. If that theory is correct, perhaps he is trying to tell us that yes, he would be able to travel with us."

Aqua nodded twice, in agreement with Val's hypothesis, and they turned and continued walking down the long warehouse shelf, now a threesome. Single file, with Val in front, they walked past a number of broken robots of all shapes, sizes, and descriptions. The only one still partially operative enough to be conscious was a section of a cowboy robot and a half-assembled pinto; the horse head raised up as they passed but got a blast of sickening green cigar smoke in its face for its trouble.

A few minutes later the three robots traveled down a ground-floor corridor and stepped outdoors through a small door marked "Exit." They traveled past some dark windows in the factory area. Inside, there were no people, only rows of dysfunctional or inoperative robots lined up in the semidarkness, in various stages of testing, repair, improvement, or reprogramming. And they all ignored the passing robots outside the factory.

Except one.

A black, tanklike robot, clearly labeled "CrimeBuster, Deluxe Model," suddenly sensed the passing of three mysterious shapes outside the window.

A periscope slowly rose into view. A computerized video scanner, complete with infrared night vision, tracked the three shapes, and a small part of a complex police computer began to function. But since the CrimeBuster had been given no orders concerning factory security, it did nothing more about the passing shapes at the windows.

The periscope went back down. The computer stopped its clacking-noises. And the video scanner system blinked off. The entire effect was like a guard dog cocking one ear at a noise in the night, growling a little, but going back to sleep; CrimeBuster, having monitored the suspicious activity outside, was quiet again.

But CrimeBuster never forgot anything.

"Whose deal is it, anyway?" Walter, the warehouse night watchman asked, but Max and Charlie weren't listening. The three of them were the only employees in the employee break room, and they were sitting around an automatic poker table. It was the middle of the night. Each of them had work they were supposed to be doing instead of playing poker. Fat chance.

"Charlie, I'm tellin' ya," Max argued, his face getting red, "Sony and Toyota are bringing in cheaper models every day."

"I still like our Chevy robots," Charlie said.

"Must be my deal," Walter said and began to shuffle.

"Those foreign gizmos can undercut Chrysler, Ford, you name it!" Max exclaimed.

"Maybe so," Charlie drawled, yawning, "but quality and dependability count too, you know."

"I'll open with two dollars," Walter said. He went unheeded.

"Another thing, Charlie . . ." But then Max paused. "Say, why the hell do you have on sunglasses at three o'clock in the morning, anyway?"

"Yep," Walter continued, "two big ones to open."

"Oh, I don't know," Charlie said, ignoring Walter and

peering over the dark glasses at Max. "Just seemed like a good idea at the time." Charlie was secretly pleased. He wore the glasses just to irritate Max.

"Well, let's see, whose bet is it?" Walter quietly said, a voice in the wilderness. "I just bet, didn't I? So that means—"

"Look, college kid, don't sit there so smug behind your sunglasses and tell *me* about robots!" Max said, hitting his fist against the automatic poker table and almost breaking the plastic betting controls shaped to look like old-fashioned stacks of red, white, and blue chips. "I was working with robots when you . . . when you were still in neo-diapers." But then Max noticed something he'd been aware of for the last minute but chosen to ignore. The finger of the plastic white hand in the center of the table was aimed straight at Max and moving back and forth, as though he were naughty for not betting. "Okay, okay! I'm thinking, I'm thinking!" He studied his cards a minute, then punched out the button for two dollars, causing his bet to light up. He glared at the finger a moment, which now swung over to Charlie. It was his bet.

Charlie placed his bet, the argument continued, the game went on, and none of them noticed the three shapes that slowly went by in the darkness outside the window. One of the shapes wore a red bow tie, another had a beautiful pink and gold dress with a high, swept-up collar, and the third waved a cigar with a hand that wore an ostentatious pinkie ring which had a light inside, creating a constant little pink glow. The shapes even paused before moving quietly past the window. The three humans at the poker table never looked up.

"All I know is," Walter said, smiling, "I bought a secondhand housekeeper for the wife, an old Datsun. The wife loves it. Thinks I'm a hero. Full house, aces up." He grinned at them and moved his cards facedown over a computerized scanner, where the results were recorded. An electronic version of "I'm in the Money" played for ten seconds, lights flashed, and the finger pointed at Walter, who was the winner. And the automatic poker table automatically recorded his winnings.

"Hey, aren't you guys supposed to be finishing your inventory in C-7?" Walter asked.

"Not when we're thirty bucks down," Max grumbled. "Aren't you supposed to be making your rounds again?"

"Not when I'm thirty bucks up!" Walter said and laughed. Charlie finally threw his hand in; he'd been trying to draw to an inside straight.

Outside, Val, Aqua, and CatSkil reached the edge of the warehouse and factory area. Ahead was a mostly deserted parking lot, and beyond, a vast open area of fields and plains which led to the mountains and the forests.

It was a beautiful night; their olfactory senses filed away the smell of freshly cut grass and pine trees.

The landscape was still bathed in soft silver colors. Stars watched them. All was calm. All was bright.

Val silently determined the most direct route to the mountains and forests, where they planned to increase the information in their data banks for more efficient usefulness, and then he pointed and began walking. Aqua and CatSkil followed.

And thus it was, one midsummer's night, that from a dusty warehouse shelf in a quiet factory in the middle of a sleepy valley, three slightly malfunctioning machines *left* their assigned places. . . .

CHAPTER 3

adventure (ad ven' chər) *n.* 1. the encountering of danger. 2. an exciting undertaking. 3. an unusual, stirring experience, often of a romantic nature.

• • • "Val, my safety monitor is very active," Aqua said as she bounced along in the cab of the bright yellow repair truck they had borrowed a few minutes before. "Request: Will you drive slower for increased safety to our unit?"

"Request denied," Val stated, his mind on the darkness and the old dirt road. "My computations concerning the ratio of safety to velocity seem to be correct. Perhaps you do not know it, Aqua, but besides being programmed to serve as a valet-companion, I have also been programmed to be a chauffeur-driver." Val was particularly proud of this last ability, but as they raced through the darkness, his mechanical hands tightly gripping the old truck's steering wheel, he did not mention that he had never had an opportunity to use his chauffeur programming.

Aqua, meanwhile, was gripping the door handle with one hand and the bottom of the seat with the other and still being jostled around. CatSkil, in the rear of the truck, had it much worse, since he was being bounced around with many heavy robot spare parts banging into him. However, in the true spirit of the stand-up comic who existed only to bring joy and laughter to others, CatSkil never complained; he just got even.

Five minutes before, Val, Aqua, and CatSkil had been

walking and had found themselves on the far edge of the factory grounds. There were only a few employee cars, several company trucks and vans, a trash barrel, and a signal light. Otherwise, the area was empty, and the world was quiet.

"This truck and its contents may be valuable to us," Val had remarked, examining the yellow truck. Aqua had agreed, pointing out that it could save them time and energy-depreciation on their journey to the forests and mountains. Moments later, Val was in the driver's seat, Aqua was at his side, and CatSkil, as usual, brought up the rear. After a brief mishap or two leaving the parking lot, where Val had backed up over the trash barrel, then let the truck lurch forward into the fender of a Chevy belonging to an employee named Max, Val steered the truck out onto an old dirt road, aimed for the highest mountain peak in the night sky, and put the metal to the pedal. . . .

"Val, my safety monitor is now extremely active," Aqua stated in an even monotone after her head crashed against the roof of the truck following a particularly deep pothole in the road. "I would like now to submit a second request for slower speed."

"Second request denied," Val responded pleasantly, wondering just how fast he could get this baby to go. "I suggest you save energy expended by calculations concerning speed, safety, and requests thereof."

In the rear of the truck, which was open, CatSkil's cigar smoke was lost in the huge billowing cloud of dust that immediately followed the yellow blur that was the repair truck.

The truck's headlights stabbed the darkness. Although they bounced around as much as everything else, they did manage to illuminate a white wooden fence that was rapidly rushing toward them.

"Val, the road is curving away from the direction of the mountains," Aqua said.

"Logically, however," Val replied, forever pleasant in word, manner, and deed, "we should continue on our present course."

And with that, the truck continued going in a perfectly straight line toward the distant mountains and therefore suddenly blasted through the wooden fence, splintering the wood into a thousand pieces. The yellow truck rushed onto an open, moonlit field which made the pothole-filled dirt road feel as smooth as neo-glass by comparison.

Inside the warehouse Walter, the card shark trapped in a night watchman's body, was finally making his appointed rounds.

The warehouse, especially the top shelves where he now strolled, always made him a little uneasy in the middle of the night. Maybe it was all those humanlike machines just standing there, eyes open. . . . Maybe it was those extra arms, legs, and heads with red and blue wires sticking out, lying around, so *unattached*. . . . Maybe it was the animal-shaped machines that really spooked him. He didn't know quite what it was, but he always had the distinct impression that every machine he passed, whether it was operational or not, had mechanical eyes that followed his every move. Walter always whistled loudly as he strolled along, his flashlight darting up and down the rows while he glanced at his clipboard, comparing numbers, double-checking locations, and matching repair tags to assigned locations. Walter usually whistled "Theme from Rio Bravo," but tonight he seemed to favor a medley of old Frankie Laine western theme songs and had just finished his echoing version of "3:10 to Yuma" and was about to swing into a catchy "Gunfight at the O.K. Corral" when he stopped suddenly in mid-step, mid-whistle.

Something was wrong; there were empty places there on the shelf ahead instead of robots. Frowning and muttering, Walter checked his clipboard, then the shelf numbers, double-checked, sighed at the thought of the paperwork ahead, turned, and walked away.

He didn't whistle the rest of the night.

A bouncing gazelle being chased by a cheetah touches the earth about as often as the yellow repair truck did with Val at the wheel as it flew over the rough, open field. The bright moonlight illuminated the larger rocks and trees, so Val was able to avoid them, but the small rocks, dips, roots, and what-not all came as a total surprise. Aqua became aware that for all her expensive gadgetry she was not equipped with shock absorbers. Val was enjoying himself so much it was a wonder his Pleasure Center didn't light up.

"Val, I would again like to request a slower speed, since—"

"Since we now have a specific task," Val interrupted, not wanting to slow down, "namely, the collection of random data in natural terrain to increase our overall utility, and since we will not be near repair centers, we should discard any excess energy-using equipment."

"Agreed," Aqua said. "We should retain only essential maintenance and data-gathering mechanical parts."

"Logically, that leaves only one energy-wasting part to discard: the recall beacon module."

At the employee break room, Charlie was dozing on the sofa while Max played electronic solitaire and hummed an old song by a group known as The Byrds. Walter came in and headed for his locker. His shift was almost over.

"How about some blackjack?" Max asked, waking Charlie up. Max had four more hours to go.

"No, thanks," Walter said. "I get out of here pretty soon, once I get more rattraps in over in D-14, then write a fast report on a broken window in Hydroponics. Oh, and we have to find out where three robots in C-7 have been moved to."

"C-7?" Charlie said, waking up quickly. "That's where we're supposed to be taking inventory. Which ones are missing?"

Walter glanced at the computer-typed letters and numbers on the papers on his clipboard. "Let's see . . . two Com-series . . . and that comedian. Where did you guys move them?"

"We didn't."

All three men stared at each other, puzzled. Then all three headed out to the main computer room, hurrying toward a button marked "Recall Beacon Module."

Aqua held the three plastic cubes in her hand—hers, Val's, and CatSkil's. The mechanisms, designed to make all mobile machinery return at once, resembled nothing so much as old-fashioned Polaroid flash cubes. Aqua tossed them high out into the night air as the truck rumbled on, getting closer to the mountains.

The three small cubes lay together in the grass and the

darkness for several seconds; then, just as Charlie hit the button back at the factory, the three now-useless recall beacon modules glowed bright pink in the grass. The more Charlie hit the button, the more they flashed bright pink, like tiny fireflies hiding in the grass. After a few minutes, the frantic pink lights stopped flashing, and the cube-shaped fireflies went to sleep in the darkness.

Two miles away, inside the factory, Max and Charlie began to argue, so Walter quietly slipped away and went home.

> **forest** (fôr' ist) *n.* 1. a thick growth of trees and underbrush. 2. large woods, often used figuratively. 3. wilderness.

Early morning mists silently moved between the thick, dark trees. Shafts of light orange pierced through the smoky-gray mists, creating the effect of slanted beams of misty light that appeared to be in constant motion from the gentle wind. The trees themselves had rugged, thick bark that was a color somewhere between brown and black at this hour of the morning. At the base of many of the trees was a green, soft cover, as though each of the towering trees had webbed feet made of moss. Branches and darker green leaves made a beautiful, silent pattern against a light blue sky, which was almost hidden by the thick-wooded area, surrounded on three sides by steep hills.

Val, Aqua, and CatSkil stood staring up and around at the forest they had just entered. They had never seen anything like it.

The last of the morning dew twinkled on a large cobweb suspended twelve feet in the air between two trees, like an abstract painting. Pale mushrooms clustered at the foot of several mighty trees, as though seeking protectors. Small ivy plants with reddish berries also twinkled with the last of the morning dew. A gray squirrel darted around one side of a trail, watched the three machines standing next to the bright yellow truck, then scampered back out of sight without editorializing. The mists rose gradually up from the damp, moist earth and slowly dissolved into the air near the tops of the trees.

Aqua was the first to speak. "This appears to be a thoroughly efficient ecological system."

"Yes," Val said, nodding his head in agreement as he had long ago been programmed to do. "Perhaps we will be able to witness its food-chain structure in operation." Val quickly cross-indexed "forest" and "efficiency" within his computer and instantly appreciated how a natural wooded area functioned. Trees made nuts. Mice ate nuts. Foxes ate mice. Foxes die, decompose, turn into bacteria. Bacteria makes the soil fertile. More trees grow. Trees made nuts. . . . Val understood as he looked around that it was a superb system—everything was used, nothing was wasted, in life or death. A forest was a perfect machine.

The sound of CatSkil's mechanical treads was added to the rustle of leaves in the breeze and the sound of distant birds chirping. CatSkil squinted at the gray morning mists that moved in front of him. For a few seconds, CatSkil thought it was show time. . . .

He had been programmed to look for cigarette smoke filling the air, for the center of the stage where the small spotlight could find him, for the bored human expressions in the semidarkness which he had to try to change suddenly into convulsions of laughter. He was trained to listen for his musical cue, for the sound of ice clinking in glasses, for conversations loudly carried on during his act. So for just a moment, when the natural gray mists resembled stale cigarette smoke, CatSkil felt at home. But a moment later, as he looked around at the stately trees, the carpet of tangerine-colored leaves, the emerald undergrowth, the restful quiet and the natural beauty, he knew he hadn't faced an emptier house since the Kiwanis Dance in Prairie Village, Kansas, back in '87, when the curtains caught fire. The joint had emptied in thirty-seven seconds, but CatSkil kept right on making jokes, since nobody took time to tell him that the show didn't have to go on when the goddamn curtains were on fire. But CatSkil was on a roll so he kept going, even after his own little green puffs of cigar smoke were lost in the billowing black clouds of smoke, even after firemen had chopped their way in and drenched him and everything else in water, and even after the smoke had cleared and, once the fire was out, the firemen relaxed. Finally, one fire fighter, tired, face blackened by smoke, but curious, had moved closer to hear what the strange,

41

wet, half-melted machine on stage had been saying throughout the holocaust. The fire fighter had managed to catch the last joke, the one about the nearsighted turtle who tried to rape a football helmet.

And he had laughed.

CatSkil had smiled to himself and puffed on his cigar one last time before he shorted out completely from the water and the heat.

CatSkil was a real trouper. He'd played some tough houses in his time, rough joints, empty clubs, hostile audiences. And he knocked 'em dead, or died trying.

But he stared in suspicion at this, his ultimate challenge: a quiet, beautiful forest. He automatically surveyed his potential audience: two sparrows overhead, a spider in the wet, glimmering cobweb, a flash of gray fur that was the squirrel taking one more peek, a few other signs of life. CatSkil's internal computer automatically whirred into life: Let's see . . . should I hit 'em with the mother-in-law stuff for a warm-up, or go right into the good stuff? Maybe the one-legged milkman bit . . .

"I see there are thicker woods ahead," Val said, pointing, and Aqua and CatSkil turned and looked off into the distance. "It would be the best direction for us to go for additional knowledge in my specialty: lumber and its profitable by-products."

"Are we sure that this vehicle can no longer function?" Aqua asked, looking at the truck.

"Yes," Val said. "Someone must have used it improperly. However, we should look in the back and see if there are any spare parts and/or accessories we may need."

Val, Aqua, and CatSkil went to the back of the trunk and peered inside at the pile of circuits, tubes, wire, half-assembled arms and legs, computer sections, and just plain junk which was stored in the back of the repair truck. Originally, it had all been sorted out and organized on the shelves and in boxes inside the rear of the trunk, with tools for assembly carefully stored along another wall. Now, after the journey through the night with Val at the wheel, an experience somewhere between Patton's tanks charging across war-scarred Europe and Mr. Toad's Wild Ride, everything was in a pile on the floor of the trunk. But only a few things were broken.

"There is a great deal we may later need, yet nothing we

could carry," Val said. "The energy expense would not be worth the extra weight."

"Logically, we should try to construct a mobile unit to accompany us as a spare parts carrier/portable repair unit," Aqua suggested.

As usual, Aqua's logic was impeccable. Val, Aqua, and CatSkil began getting all the spare parts and tools out of the back of the truck.

The gray squirrel scurried up to the top of a tree nearby, took one last peek at the strange activity below, twitched its gray tail in exasperation, and disappeared into its nest.

Something strange was happening in the forest.

Max tried to get comfortable in the chair across from Mr. Westlin's desk, but it was so contemporary in design that it was impossible. Across from him, behind the desk that was so big it approached pretentiousness, was his boss, Robin Westlin, a man who enjoyed keeping people waiting. Westlin was busy studying and initialing some papers, even though he had asked Max and Charlie to come into his office. Charlie had gotten bored immediately and was standing over to one side, studying some tiny robot models and prototypes. Max changed position again and looked at Westlin's office walls, even though he'd already studied the office dozens of times.

On the right side of the office was a bookshelf with no books. Instead, it was full of robots. Most were tiny prototypes of existing or fantasized models. Industrial robots, for assembly-line work. Specially shielded robots, for nuclear power plants. Traffic monitors, to direct and rechannel traffic. "Clever" robots, designed for chess, Monopoly, and other entertainments. Plus a number of toy robots for children (which Charlie was playing with at the moment) and a few models of the earliest robots. (At home, under a glass case in his den, Westlin had some valuable "collectibles"—a few genuine restored antique robots which were increasing in value all the time.)

Above the robot models were several framed certificates. There was his college degree (major in robotics, minor in business management) and several degrees from specialized graduate schools and robot seminars; awards; and two membership certificates in two international robotics organizations. On the far wall was a framed snapshot blown up to eight by ten showing a proud Westlin standing up in a rowboat holding up a small fish that he thought was large. Next to it was a huge architect's drawing of a stylized new factory with sticklike people and phony landscaping drawn in and a small sign that said "The New Plant." The left wall proudly displayed a photograph of a softball team with Westlin in a coaching jacket and players in uniforms that said "General Motors BaseBots," then a tarnished bowling trophy, a VFW membership plaque, and more, but Max had seen it all before.

Westlin himself finally looked up from his paperwork, smiled insincerely at Max, and gave his cigarette a quick, executive flick, then got up from around his desk and pseudo-casually sat on the edge of the desk near Max. Westlin was in his early fifties, had a small potbelly he tried to ignore, and, as always, wore a bright sport coat that was a color not found in nature.

"How's the kid working out, Max?" Westlin half-whispered to Max.

"Knows it all," Max said, shrugging. "Like we used to."

Westlin nodded, then he winked at Max and suddenly cleared his throat, speaking loudly and with authority.

"So, Charlie, what's the story?"

Startled, Charlie turned, letting go of a small green robot model which now began to march along the top of the chest-high bookshelf. Flustered, Charlie looked at Westlin.

"Oh, well, the missing models must have been wired up wrong or something. Then the recall beacons didn't work, either—"

Westlin stood up, and his face looked as hard as his tone. "I don't need bullshit about wiring and recall beacons—"

"But we double-checked the order forms," Max interrupted, trying to share some of the heat; Charlie was a pain in the ass, but he was his partner. "Then we checked the main computer records, but somehow—"

"And don't tell me about how it might be a paperwork screw-up either!" Westlin cut in. He was angry now, and Max knew from experience how he loved to do his friendly one-of-the-boys routine just so he could quickly drop it when he suddenly became The Boss.

Charlie, meanwhile, shot a look out of the corner of his

44

eye, realizing the tiny green robot was steadily marching along like a good little soldier in the direction it had been placed—which meant that another eighteen inches and it would step right off the shelf and smash on the floor. But Charlie wasn't sure he should stop it yet and make Westlin even angrier because he wouldn't appear to be listening to him.

"But Mr. Westlin," Charlie said, "the head office must have—"

"Look, kid, you can blame the head office or computer error or anything you want, but you two are the ones responsible, right?" Westlin said this with a smile, then looked at the two of them as though they had just said the earth was flat.

Max and Charlie didn't answer. They couldn't even look their boss in the eye. Charlie did glance over to one side for a second, hearing the quiet footsteps of the green robot, now only ten inches away from sudden death.

"You two were supposed to be there, in C-7 all night doing an inventory, right?" Westlin's smile grew even bigger; he was definitely enjoying all this.

Max and Charlie sort of nodded agreement, reluctantly. They didn't want to linger on this point. They had been caught playing poker twice before instead of working, and their union steward had said that the next time they were on their own. Charlie took a peek over at the shelf. The robot was five inches from the edge and steadily marching along. Neither Max or Westlin seemed to notice it.

"There's three machines missing." Westlin slowly belabored the obvious. "And two of them are quite valuable. You'd better hope the computer check turns up their location or you're in real trouble. Now get out of here and find them!"

Max made a motion to Charlie and turned to leave the room. Charlie instinctively started to follow but then turned and looked back just as the tiny green robot stepped off the case of robot models and pitched forward. Charlie lurched toward it, successfully grabbing it in midair, but he lost his balance, and as Max and Westlin stared in astonishment he crashed into the case, falling! As though in slow motion, Charlie, the wood-and-glass case, and all the exquisite little robot models came crashing to the hardwood floor of Westlin's office.

The sound of the smashed case hitting the floor could be heard for over two hundred yards in any direction, but the sound of Westlin's voice a moment later covered a good three counties, easy.

The dappled, late-morning sunlight created a beautiful pattern of bright spots interspersed with the shadows of leaves and branches across the entire collection of spare parts and tools now spread out on a large blue tarp at the rear of the truck.

"As nearly as I can determine," Val said, sitting across from the strange display, "we will only be capable of building a unit that is forty-six percent optimal size."

Sitting on the other side of the vast array of circuits, plastic tubing, colorful wires, tubes, panels, digital connectors, and dozens of other robot parts, Aqua nodded. "In addition," she calculated quickly, "any new mobile unit we attempt to construct will have between seventeen and twenty-six percent the average robot mental capacity."

Sitting nearby, CatSkil said nothing. He had assisted Val and Aqua all morning in taking every single part and tool out of the truck, cataloging its use, examining and determining the purpose of each part, checking that it was in good working condition, cleaning each part of any dust, dirt, corrosives, and moisture, and then carefully setting them all out on the blue plastic tarp. His attitude about it all, however, was lost somewhere between boredom and indifference and had been best expressed in a brief exchange an hour ago between him and Val. CatSkil had lifted a clear plastic panel of delicate circuits from the truck and then tossed it down on the ground. Val reacted quickly, saying in an urgent tone, "CatSkil! Please be more careful! Don't you want every part totally functional in case we decide to construct a mobile spare parts carrier?!!" Something in Val's tone of voice triggered that part of CatSkil's computerized programming that had been filed under "Hecklers: Lines Used to Squelch Them," and CatSkil responded with Squelch #87. He pointed to himself hesitantly, looked around in mock-confusion, and then in an extremely courteous tone said, *"Excuse me, but I believe you have me confused with someone who gives a shit."*

Val examined several minuscule silicon chips, then looked across the collection of parts spread out in the middle of the forest glade like a picnic for a metal-eating creature. He pointed out that they only had the tools to create another unit. "Between us, we also have only the minimal programming for such an assembly."

Aqua understood. "Question: Is such a project worth the energy expenditure?"

Val's computer quickly downshifted, then he stated his conclusion. "Affirmative. What is your evaluation?"

From deep inside Aqua's mechanical body, a rapid series of electronic buzzes, clicks, beeps, and a couple of boops emerged, then she said, "Sixty-two percent. Let us begin."

Val turned to CatSkil, who was watching a nearby gray squirrel who was watching CatSkil. "CatSkil, would you assist us by holding parts?"

Without waiting for an answer, Val handed him a small metal body casing that CatSkil held with his free, non-cigar hand, and as Val and Aqua began to assemble a small, impromptu robot to carry spare parts, CatSkil flicked his cigar ashes and responded to Val's question, as always, with a joke.

"There was this guy, see, and he goes into a restaurant and this waiter walks up to him . . ." CatSkil began, not noticing that Val and Aqua weren't really listening. They were absorbed in their work as they began soldering, welding, wiring, screwing, latching, and connecting a variety of wires, circuits, tubes, transistors, and microchips into an assortment of metal boxes, mechanical arms, Plexiglas casings, and plastic panels. *"So the customer asks the waiter, 'Say, what's your soup of the day?' And the waiter says, 'Pea soup and chicken soup.' The customer says he'll take chicken soup. So the waiter turns and yells toward the kitchen, 'ONE CHICKEN SOUP!' "* (CatSkil's electronic Brooklyn accent went up dozens of decibels at these last three words, echoing through the forest, causing startled deer to dart away, rabbits to run, and ducks at a nearby lake to fill the sky. But there would have been no use asking CatSkil not to make so much noise, because he would have probably only dryly regarded such a request and pointed out politely that you must be confusing him with someone who gave—) *"But then,"* he continued, even though Val and Aqua were busy working and not listen-

ing, *"the customer says, 'Sorry, but on second thought, I'd rather have pea soup instead of chicken soup.' So the waiter turns and yells, 'HOLD THE CHICKEN AND MAKE IT PEA!'"* As always, his joke was immediately followed by a drummer's rim shot—bap-bap!—and a casual flick of his cigar. And this time CatSkil smiled and looked particularly content with himself. It was almost as though he knew he had just caused total havoc in the forest with his last yell, since for miles around startled birds were taking flight, squirrels were diving into their nests, skunks were stinking the place up something fierce, and one particular female puma, miles away on a rock outcropping, leaped protectively in front of her playful cubs and with her ears flat against her head gave out a loud snarl worthy of a car commercial.

> *chase* (chās) *v.* 1. to follow quickly or persistently in order to catch or harm. 2. to seek, pursue.

The early afternoon sun was hot, and there were no clouds to shield it from Max and Charlie as they sat in their jeep looking at the smashed wooden white fence by the curve of the dirt road. Their jeep didn't have a roof on it, and Max wished he had brought along something cold to drink.

"See? Couldn't be professional robot thieves. Pros would have had their own truck ready and wouldn't go cross-country. And they certainly wouldn't have blasted through a fence, leaving a clear trail we can follow."

"If it is pros, they've got them stripped down and half the parts are sold now anyway," Charlie added. There was a rare note of bitterness in his voice. A year before, he had had his own robot stolen. It was just a secondhand PlayBot, most of it assembled by Charlie in his spare time. Wasn't much to look at, even had spots of gray primer paint on the side where he'd planned to paint it a beautiful Kandy Apple color someday. But Charlie had spent hundreds of hours working on it and had had it programmed as a simple opponent for Ping-Pong, billiards, and video games. One day last year after coming home from working late, he had found that his PlayBot was stolen. Police later traced one tiny part to a Used Bot Shop in Tijuana, and a computer turned up another one six months later in a Las Vegas pawn shop, but there was no way to ever recover the original PlayBot Charlie had put together. Charlie bought a new one. He even had a special burglar alarm system built into it. The new one, all sleek and shiny, worked even better than the old one, but it wasn't the same; his Ping-Pong table was dusty.

"Let's go, Charlie," Max said. "Follow the tracks."

"Okay. Think we'll find 'em by dark?"

"Bound to. The crazy machines got stuck on automatic pilot or some damn thing. We'll find them walking into trees or sitting in the truck, out of energy or something, just up ahead." Max shifted position on the flat, hard seat of the jeep. His rear end hurt. "You know who I think stole them," Max grumbled. "Kids. Spoiled rich kids."

"Huh?"

"Teenagers, stealing robots just to go joyboting. It's the parents these days, the way they raise their kids. Society's too permissive these days, and—"

"Right, Max, whatever you say," Charlie said tiredly, starting the engine and gunning it forward, cutting off one of Max's favorite diatribes. As Charlie steered the jeep through the open, broken fence, he became increasingly puzzled by the direction of the tracks of the repair truck. It seemed as if they were almost purposely headed toward the densest part of the forest and the more rugged mountains.

As Charlie mulled over the different complex factors, trying to find the logic of it all, Max's thoughts were much more simple. As the jeep went bouncing along crazily over rocks and tree roots, Max wished three things: (1) that they get the missing robots back before nightfall, (2) that he had either more padding on his jeep seat, or (3) fewer hemorrhoids.

> birth (bûrth) n. 1. the act of bringing forth offspring. 2. the act of being born; nativity. 3. good or noble lineage.

Assembly of the new, smaller robot took 3.57 hours, so it was late afternoon when Val and Aqua put down their tools and stepped back beside CatSkil to study the new little machine.

The sun was low in the sky as the sounds of mechanical

tinkering faded away into the normal life hum of the forest. As the sunlight filtered through the thick tree-roof overhead it cast a soft blanket of warm light over everything, including the strange little machine. High in the branches of a mighty oak above, the gray squirrel peered down at the newest creation, then disappeared as a gray blur, having no squeaks or barks in his squirrel vocabulary to describe what God, three robots, and General Motors had wrought.

The small robot was like none ever built or conceived, having been constructed from an impromptu design from existing spare parts and assembled by robots with no programming in functional design. It stood 1.13 meters high and weighed almost 300 pounds. It was much longer than it was tall, due to the presence of a small wagon hooked on behind it with a single axle and two metal wheels. (The wooden orange wagon had the legend "Electrical #14" on its side—it had held extra circuits until Val turned it into a caboose. Now the wagon was filled with extra parts not directly attached to the new robot, plus a small aluminum tool kit.)

The new robot itself had a simple, gray metal box for a head and two large green eyes with yellow optic-lights that acted as pupils. There was no nose (the crude robot lacked, among other things, an olfactory sense) and only a small circle for a mouth, with a simple wire-mesh speaker that had no mechanical ability to simulate human speech. Two over-sized ears, which were originally curved discs each about a foot in diameter, now swiveled independently, constantly twitching like radar bowls as the small robot tried to pick up sound waves. The robot's body was partly built from the truck's dashboard, including both an irrelevant radio and a tachometer. The robot's left arm, more powerful than it looked, was made up of visible wires and metal rods, culminating in a vise-clamp now covered with a white cloth that looked for all the world like a small fuzzy mitten. Its right arm was like a two-foot Boy Scout knife, with any number of power drills, knives, scissors, soldering guns, and other retractable gizmos. Its locomotion was simply two tank treads, so it rumbled along like a toy Sherman tank, not unlike CatSkil. The computer brain of the little robot was housed directly on top of its gray square head, in a see-through Plexiglas case with a light yellow lid that now suddenly fell forward as the little robot twitched into mechanical life, causing the lid to look like a small baseball cap.

Val stepped back to stand beside Aqua and stare at what they had created in the last few hours. CatSkil, in the background, glanced toward the tiny robot as it twitched again, but the comedian robot just kept his sneer, definitely the world's first cigar-smoking, mechanical midwife.

"It now carries spare parts from our own units, Aqua," Val said, his eyes never leaving the small robot.

"Plus vital equipment we will need from the back of the truck," Aqua answered, also not looking away from the small metal creature.

"And it was efficient of you to add built-in repair tools," Val added. He started to say more but was distracted by the sudden series of movements by the little machine.

It jerked forward, then stopped. Then its eyes popped on and off and it turned its head and examined its Scout knife of an arm. A power drill unfolded, then began whirling around, making a small mechanical hum. The little robot stared in simple fascination as though marveling at its discovery of itself. CatSkil considered making a joke about a little boy discovering his own penis for the first time, but then figured the hell with it. As he looked around the forest he failed to spot any small tables crowded together, bored cocktail waitresses carrying trays, or dimly lit, nicotine-stained, ice-clinking, word-slurring, cleavage-revealing *people*. CatSkil literally lived for, or was programmed for, that most rare and wonderful of creatures: an audience. Without one, he was just a particularly irrelevant sack of nuts and bolts, and at the moment, CatSkil had never been further from an audience.

While CatSkil sulked, the little robot was making a hundred discoveries about himself. His see-through brain, with its rows of tiny circuits, tubes, and rectangular doo-whackies that resembled a tiny city skyline, now began to light up in bright reds, blues, and yellows as different electrical impulses, representing new ideas, zipped across his visible mental landscape. In fact, as he began to rapidly discover a number of new concepts, the colors, in all their combinations, danced across his clear little skull, creating a literal brainstorm.

The robot's blank computer had no sense of order, priorities, or logical storage of data. It was too busy trying to avoid sensory overload as its virgin brain was being attacked all at once by a world of concepts: light, arm, birds, drill, green, warm, trees, eyes, blink, leaves, beep, think, squirrel, wind, move, brown, turn, cloud, blue, I—

The little robot's almost Zen-like inquiries about Life, Existence, and the meaning behind the small, elegant pile of squirrel shit by a nearby tree were interrupted by Aqua's speaking again.

"Val, what is the proper designation for a spare parts carrier-portable repair unit?"

Val computed quickly, then said, "I have no programming for such a decision."

The little robot listened and watched as the pretty pink machine walked over to him, leaned down, and looked at his chest area, where the dashboard, including the Philco radio, had been placed.

"Val, would the designation 'Phil' be sufficiently functional?"

Val also noticed the Philco-brand radio, and since the only other word now visible on the spare parts carrier was "Electrical #14," which took extra energy to say, he nodded. "Yes, it is accurate and efficient."

Val then stepped back and looked with a creator's pride at the small robot in front of him.

"Look at Phil, Aqua. It has your wiring."

"Yes, Val," she answered quietly, also gazing in admiration at their tiny creation. "But it has your circuits."

The robot called Phil now looked up at each of them and made a quiet beeping sound, as though in recognition or acknowledgment. Val and Aqua smiled at this and exchanged happy looks, while CatSkil, twenty feet away, looked away and puffed his cigar, wishing he possessed the programming for throwing up.

They all stood there for a long moment in the warm sunlight and gentle wind of the quiet forest. Phil was not a designer's dream, being constructed from spare parts and looking a lot like the result of an illicit union between a pinball machine and a Soap Box Derby racer. But Val and Aqua seemed quite pleased with their efforts as they put their tools away. Val signaled to CatSkil, and Aqua walked over and took Phil's white mitten of a hand, and without another word the four robots walked, rumbled, and wobbled out of the small hidden valley and into the fading sunlight, continuing their journey toward the thicker forests, the majestic mountains, and their metallic destinies. . . .

A few leaves had fallen on the blue tarp, the remaining spare parts, and the discarded repair truck in the little hidden forest valley when Max and Charlie came roaring up in their jeep, but otherwise it was just as the four robots had left it a half hour before.

Max's mood, which was caused initially by getting in trouble for something he didn't do, exacerbated by a rough, cross-country ride in a jeep, and intensified by Charlie's ever-pleasant attitude, was somewhere on an anger scale between a bulldog left out in the rain all night and a constipated rhinoceros.

So Charlie knew enough to tread softly around Max and mainly to shut up a lot. But after they had been looking at the spare parts scattered around for a few minutes, he impulsively yelled out from the cab of the truck. "Hey, Max! The dashboard's missing!" Now why, Charlie wondered, would robots remove a section of the dashboard where most of the dials and wiring and the radio was located? For a fleeting instant, Charlie had a remarkable thought. He compounded his problems with Max by thinking out loud, at full volume. "Max! What if . . . suppose the robots were building something or—"

"You think too much," Max grumbled in a tone that cut off further discussion. He stepped over some of the spare parts on the blue tarp, half-tripped over a heavy panel of digital circuits, cursed, kicked the panel, cursed again, then finally made it over to the jeep while trying to hide a slight limp that had just developed.

"Jeep Five-Niner to Control," Max said into the CB radio microphone. "Come in, Control, over."

"This is Control," came the voice, crackling through the quiet wooded area. "Go ahead."

Max sighed, hating to make an unsuccessful report but knowing there was no way around it. He'd been ground up in the wheels of the system before. "We found the missing truck, energy pack on zero, at the edge of the woods, five miles due west of the factory—"

"Energy pack on zero?" came the voice of Control.

"Yeah, right, out of gas," Max snapped back, then instantly regretted the old expression. "Control" was only a twenty-two-year-old kid who had grown up in a world of solar energy and electric cars, and the expression "out of gas" was like Max's grandfather saying "Twenty-three Skiddoo."

"Say again, Jeep Five-Niner," said the patient but confused voice of Control.

"Goddamnit," Max began eloquently, "the truck's energy pack is on zero—no juice left, empty, *nada*, zip, zilch, el deado—"

"Roger, Jeep Five-Niner. Continue."

"Anyway, the spare parts are scattered around, someone spread them out on a blue tarp, and a lot seem to be missing. The three missing robots aren't around either. But there are tracks leading into the woods. Over."

"Robot tracks? Into the woods?"

Max quietly seethed. This "Control" kid wasn't so terrific on the uptake. Meanwhile, Charlie was peering closely at the robot tracks, and for a moment he wondered if there might be four sets of tracks instead of three. . . .

"Roger, Control. Those missing machines aren't anywhere around, so we're heading back—"

"This is Westlin!" A new, angry voice cut in, startling nearby birds into flight throughout the forest. "You guys aren't done yet!"

Charlie's eyes opened wide, he totally forgot about his bizarre notion that perhaps a fourth set of robot tracks was present, and he practically stood at attention at the sound of their supervisor's voice.

"A helicopter's on the way with Babe Aldrin," Westlin roared through the CB radio. "If our ace can't find them, you're really screwing up. Now find 'em! Ten-four!"

There was a loud click, and Max set his CB microphone back inside his jeep very gently, thinking that Robin Westlin was just the kind of guy who would not only monitor company calls like that but would yell at you over the air so that everyone else on the company air waves would know you were being yelled at; he was the kind of man who believed that public humiliation was an appropriate disciplinary tool. Max quietly walked around the jeep toward the spare parts. He was purposely moving very quietly and gently, hoarding up his volcanic anger until he found just the right metal object to kick from here to next Tuesday.

Chapter 4

pastoral (pas′ tər əl) *adj.* 1. of shepherds
and dairymaids and their rustic life. 2.
characteristic of rural life, idealized as
peaceful, simple, and natural.

• • • "This expedition has been extremely useful thus
far," Val commented as he and Aqua strolled through a
particularly beautiful meadow. "It has added greatly to my
knowledge and background in lumber."

The meadow was composed of long, yellow grasses, with
occasional splotches of green clover, and bordered by bushes
with ripe blueberries and bright red wild strawberries. The
sun, only an inch above the jagged, dark blue silhouette of
mountains, cast a soft, golden light over the scene, painting
everything in pastel colors, creating the purple mountains'
majesty above a fruited plain.

"Over there," Val said, pointing, "is an *Acer macrophyllum*,
or big-leaf maple, for example, with its close-grained wood,
which is in great demand by cabinetmakers."

Fortunately, Aqua was programmed for moments like these,
so she nodded and looked quite interested as Val continued to
discuss lumber and other related subjects that bored the metallic
pants off her.

As they strolled through the golden meadow, Val's monotone blending with the sound of an occasional bumblebee, the
dark shadows of the surrounding forest suddenly caused Aqua
to have her second "memory circuit ghost" of the day.
Memory circuit ghosts, or MCGs as they are known in the

trade, are inexplicable flashes of memory that are still present in robot tubes and circuitry, even after total circuit-washing. In fact, Aqua's occasional flashbacks from her former programmed identity as a child's governess-companion were the reason she was awaiting repair on the warehouse shelf in the first place. Her first MCG had been a series of blurred images while she was watching the Phil unit make its first moves; these increased as she assisted it. Her former programming concerning child care was highly stimulated by some data storage area in her wiring. But after a few moments the MCG had passed. And yet . . . she was aware of her feelings of intense involvement with their spare parts carrier-portable repair unit designated Phil.

Her second memory circuit ghost was occurring now as she looked toward the surrounding dark forest. The black-brown trees, the gnarled limbs, the twisted branches, the grasping ivy, and the dark shadows—all somehow stimulated memories of some of the 835 bedtime stories for children she had once been programmed to have on file. Precisely 244 of these stories, in fact, were still filed in her data storage banks under ''Tales, Fairy.'' Therefore, instead of objectively viewing the efficient ecology system that functioned very well around them, Aqua was experiencing an enchanted forest planted by the Brothers Grimm. It was as though the forest was a living, breathing presence, a mystical undergrowth where it was not hard to imagine gnomes hiding behind moss-covered stumps, trolls under bridges, and elves dancing lightly on the tops of toadstools. Wood nymphs surely dwelt in the emerald tree-tops, pixies giggled and cavorted by moonlight, and a flash of white could only mean that you had just missed seeing your first unicorn. Ironically, Aqua's pink and gold outfit, with its high, sweeping collar and long skirt that brushed the pollen off tiny flowers, fit in perfectly, since she appeared to be a fairy-tale princess being escorted by a handsome prince. The prince, however, wearing a brown pin-striped suit and a red bow tie, was rattling off some statistics.

''And therefore, following a normal supply-and-demand economic curve, the commodities market has an upside potential in the next six months that parallels the lumber industry's own downside risk.''

Aqua's memory ghosts vanished at this point, having very little upside potential of their own.

"America now has 754.68 million acres of commercial forest land," Val continued as the two robots strolled through the meadow, through long shadows of tall pines in the late afternoon sun. "With proper development, these acres can create a new profit ratio of—"

"Question," Aqua quietly stated as she stared at a particularly beautiful maple tree.

"Proceed."

"At a human social occasion, I once heard the following data," she said. Then her voice changed to a tape of a pompous woman's voice against a background of party chatter stating, " 'Only God can make a tree.' " In her normal voice, Aqua went on, "Question on definition of term: God, and relevant relationship to lumber industry."

Val continued to smile pleasantly and stroll along, but inside his computer rapid computations went on for 3.366 seconds. Then he turned and said, "God is an illogical, unknown variable, which humans associate with the value judgment known as 'goodness.' "

Aqua computed that a moment, then said, "If only God can make a tree . . ."

But then she paused, distracted by how the sunlight seemed to dance lightly behind the maple's leaves as they sensuously swayed in the wind.

"God," she then said in a much quieter voice than usual, "is very efficient."

"Correct," Val continued, assuming he was on a roll. "God makes trees, then humans make from them a variety of paper products, ranging from wrapping paper for gala events to interoffice memos." Val nodded at the accuracy of his own commentary and didn't notice that Aqua had paused in their walk and was studying the sky in every direction. "I particularly am looking forward to finding a plywood tree," Val added.

"This expedition has been extremely useful for my unit and computer as well," Aqua said.

"Proceed."

"In the past," Aqua said, "I have overheard people who lived in condominiums in urban centers comment on the beauty of nature. I now have additional background for future social conversations concerning such subjects as: sun, wind, natural flora and fauna and ecological importance thereof."

"Yes, I have increased my data bank not only in lumber commodities, but I can learn more, since I believe these are the correct geological formations for mineral deposits. To improve my usefulness in stocks and commodities, I should learn all I can about gold, silver, copper, and other metals."

"Val," Aqua asked. "Is it time to go back yet?"

Val stopped walking. The only sound for a long time, besides the sound of internal computing, was the sound of the wind in the tops of the pine trees.

"We are increasing our usefulness rapidly," Val finally replied. "That would seem to be our primary concern at the moment. Do you agree?"

"Affirmative. We shall go further on, since there is one particular meteorological phenomenon we have not yet discovered."

"Designation?"

"Rainbow."

"Yes, I agree," Val said, also turning to search the skyline in every direction. "We should continue this research expedition until we at least discover the end of it."

"It must be further ahead," Aqua said. "We saw it clearly . . ." But then she was distracted by another thought and turned and looked around the meadow. "Question: Where is the Phil unit?"

Val also began looking around.

No Phil.

"I asked CatSkil to watch him," Val said in a very low voice.

"Audio problem. Repeat please."

"I asked CatSkil to make sure Phil's unit did not damage or misplace itself."

"I do not concur with your evaluation that CatSkil is mechanically sound enough to be aware of Phil's safety," Aqua said quickly. "CatSkil was awaiting repairs, and we do not know the extent of his problems. It appears that his inability to speak in anything other than what humans refer to as 'humor' is his malfunction, but his unit could possess additional problems which—"

"There, I see CatSkil," Val said, pointing across the meadow.

Aqua turned and saw CatSkil, his back to them as he faced the edge of the forest. "Perhaps the Phil unit is with him," she said to Val, but Val was already hurrying toward CatSkil. Aqua hurried after him.

CatSkil, at this moment, was sitting perfectly still, cigar poised, eyes half closed, savoring the moment. CatSkil's mouth was formed in a half-sneer, but he was smiling on the inside; in front of him was a small collection of upturned faces, an attentive group, by God, an *audience!*

"Good evening, ladies and germs. Well, it's certainly great to be back here at the Bimbo Club," he began, glancing down, counting the house.

CatSkil sat on his vaudeville trunk in the sunny meadow, about three feet from the edge of the shadowy forest. At first, before his eyes got used to the darker undergrowth of the woods, he could see only tiny eyes, as in a cartoon. But after a few minutes CatSkil's audience began to take clearer form. Staring at the strange, cigar-smoking machine was a red squirrel halfway down a tree, two blue jays on a nearby branch, a curious rabbit, a timid fawn, and a nuclear family of raccoons: father, mother, and several baby raccoons, all lined up and staring at CatSkil, who happily puffed his cigar and then jabbed the air with it as he went into his routine.

"You know, women today say what they think. See that hatcheck girl back there?"

CatSkil gestured as he said this and then paused. One of the baby raccoons rose up on its little hind legs, turned its head, looked behind him, didn't see a hatcheck girl, then turned back and continued to listen to CatSkil, who went on.

"I took her home the other night. Two in the morning she told me to go to a sex clinic. Said I should ask for the emergency room."

Bap-bap. The drummer's rim shot instantly followed the punch line, as always, and CatSkil took a puff on his cigar with perfect comic timing as he waited for the laughter.

Instead, he got blank looks. None of the animals twitched or moved.

Tough house. But CatSkil had faced rougher audiences than this. There was that Baptist group in Miami, the Elks lodge in Reno, the Stamp Collectors' Club in Elkhart—this was nothing.

"There was this kid, see, six years old. Never said a word. Doctors, parents, teachers, no one could figure out why he couldn't talk. One day his mom serves him eggs for breakfast,

the boy looks up and says, 'You call this sunny-side up?' His parents go crazy, get excited, finally they say, 'Why haven't you spoken before now?' And the kid shrugs and says, 'Until now, everything was okay.' ''

Bap-bap. Cigar smoke.

From the audience, nothing. Maybe an ear twitch.

"There's this funeral procession, see. One guy's holding a vicious snarling dog on a leash near two caskets, then hundreds of guys are walking behind him. Someone asks the guy with the dog what happened. The guy says, 'My dog killed my wife and my mother-in-law.' 'That's terrible,' says the other guy, 'but can I borrow your dog?' So the guy says, 'Get in line.' ''

The sound of the rim shot echoed away into silence, and the small green cloud of cigar smoke was carried away by the wind, and still not a single reaction from the squirrels, the blue jays, the fawn, or the raccoons.

"C'mon, folks, gimme a break, these are the jokes. I know you're out there, I can hear you breathing."

CatSkil waited. Good luck.

The squirrel changed position halfway down the tree, and one baby raccoon scratched behind his ear with his left leg. That was it.

"This is the funny stuff!" CatSkil almost yelled in his mechanical panic, then glared at the mother raccoon. *"What do you think this is, lady? A Pillsbury Bake-Off?"*

Suddenly, the animals did become alert, but it was only because two other machines were heading their way.

"CatSkil!" Val yelled.

"Have you seen Phil?" Aqua asked in an anxious voice. They were about twenty feet away and heading straight for CatSkil, who turned and looked over his shoulder in an irritated way, then turned back just in time to see a last glimpse of his audience as it darted, flew, or ran away. In two seconds his audience had melted into the forest. CatSkil was alone again.

"CatSkil, have you seen the Phil unit?" Val asked, walking up to CatSkil and standing so close that it was no trouble at all for CatSkil to calmly blow an ugly green cloud of cigar smoke into Val's face.

Val did not breathe so he did not cough, but his visual

circuitry was clouded, and it didn't do his more delicate facial mechanisms any good.

"That would appear to be a negative response," Val said in his usual pleasant way.

"I agree," Aqua said. "I believe CatSkil is trying to communicate, in his normal, indirect way, that he has no knowledge of Phil's location."

Val and Aqua turned and began searching for Phil, but then Aqua stopped and looked back.

"CatSkil," she said, "will you help us find Phil?"

"It is time to continue our journey," Val added, "and it would not be logical to leave our only source of spare parts behind."

CatSkil slowly turned and lumbered after them, glancing back only five times to see if somehow, for some reason, his audience might have come back for the second show.

"Phil! Where are you?" Aqua's loud voice carried throughout the forest.

"Hel-lo?" Val yelled in his loudest, but still pleasant, tone of voice. "Phil? Hel-lo?"

Looking in every direction, the three robots fanned out across the meadow, and then each went in different directions into the woods, trying to find Phil. Actually, Val and Aqua continued to try to find Phil; CatSkil had the same love for children as W.C. Fields—not only were kids terrible audiences, but they stole the show.

"Phil!" Aqua's voice echoed throughout the forest, almost like the sound of a distant songbird.

"Hel-lo?" Val's cracked voice startled small animals into flight in a different part of the woods.

All this time, Phil was in the midst of some high grass in the center of the meadow. His optic sensors had picked up an object directly in front of him. The new object was white, covered with fuzz, had two large antennae on top of its head and hippity-hopped on its large hind legs. The object spotted Phil. Its nose twitched.

Phil made a small beeping sound.

The object hopped a few inches closer, cocking its head to one side.

Delighted, in a mechanical sort of way, Phil rolled a few inches closer on his wobbly tank treads and slowly stretched

62

out his white mitten, which happened to look to the rabbit as if it might be another rabbit.

"Hel-lo. . . ." Val's voice sang out from far away. "Phil . . . we cannot monitor your location."

Phil didn't care.

"Phil!" Aqua's voice came through loud and clear. "Report at once . . ."

Fat chance.

Phil didn't know what a rabbit was, and the rabbit had no idea what in the world a robot was, but it was curiosity, if not love, at first sight.

Val tromped through bramble bushes, which attempted to tear at his clothes without success, since his clothes were made from a synthetic metallic fabric (twenty percent rayon, twenty percent wool, sixty percent aluminum siding). Then he crashed through poison oak, almost fell over an exposed tree root, and nearly banged his metallic shin against a small rock. Being an efficient, well-designed robot, Val recognized inefficiency when he saw it, even in himself. His present search pattern just wasn't working.

Val paused in the middle of some poison ivy to check quickly his programming and his memory banks for anything that would help him find a missing spare parts carrier/portable repair unit in the middle of a forest. Programming came up empty; ironically, Val was beautifully designed to search instantly for and locate data inside his own computer, but that was software. Val was looking for a brand-new chunk of hardware, full of unknown variables. The only related data in his memory banks that popped up was a recollection of a time when a former owner, the quasi-wealthy Horace Smith, couldn't find his tiny, ugly Pekingese dog named Ming. The approach Horace Smith had used had eventually been successful, so Val simply spliced that old voice track into his own vocal system and continued tramping through the woods. Only this time, the squirrels and birds throughout the forest heard a deep, male growl of a voice saying, "Ming! Goddamnit! Where are you? If you've got my slipper off somewhere, chewin' the hell out of it, I'll use it to paddle your rear end!"

Hundreds of yards away Aqua paused, hearing this new voice, then realized it was Val looking for Phil. But as she continued to hunt for Phil, calling his name, Aqua wondered, not for the first time, how much damage to his mental circuits Val might actually have.

Max and Charlie watched the streamlined, small helicopter sail over the treetops toward them. It was blue and white and had the "General Motors Robotics" logo painted on the side. It found a small clearing—an impressively small area to land, Max thought—and lightly touched the earth, causing the nearby small trees and long grasses to bend sharply away from the powerful blades that pounded the air. Max and Charlie bent forward and rushed toward the helicopter, opened the door, and climbed in, and Charlie barely had the door shut when the helicopter took off with a certain brisk flair. The pilot, Babe Aldrin, was like that.

"Hiya, Max!" the pilot said. She was a stocky, middle-aged woman with an infectious grin, a booming voice, total command of her aircraft, and one hell of a flight record behind her. The company newsletter had recently chosen her "employee of the month," referring to her as "Tugboat Annie of the Skies." She loved it.

"Hi, Babe," Max said without much enthusiasm. Babe was nice enough as a person but just a little too devoted to The Company for Max's tastes.

Max, sitting in the front seat beside Babe, motioned to Charlie, who was still half-rolling around in the backseat, trying to strap himself in as the helicopter jumped up back into the sky, banked, and then sharply dipped, making a series of tight circles not too far from the tallest treetops.

"Babe, meet Charlie," Max half-yelled over the sound of the helicopter blades beating the air.

"Hiya, Charlie," Babe yelled over her shoulder.

Charlie made a half-wave as he peered out a side window at the swaying earth below; the horizon line rocked from side to side like a bucking bronco. Charlie's face was already beginning to turn a lovely shade of chartreuse.

"I hear you two characters lost some expensive "bots," Babe said with a grin, "and I'm supposed to find 'em for you."

"Something like that," Max grumbled.

"Say again?" Babe yelled, having heard him perfectly clearly the first time.

"I said yes!" Max yelled.

"Say, you know what Mr. Westlin told me?" Babe asked, then laughed, already beginning to enjoy her afternoon. Max was mad, Charlie was green, and neither gave a damn, which caused Babe to enjoy telling them all the more. "When I was given my orders," Babe sang out, "Mr. Westlin said, 'Here's the location. Go pick up Romulus and Hardy.' "

Babe laughed so hard the helicopter went into a steep bank, but just as Charlie was about to scream his lungs out, seeing the thick, gnarled branches of a huge oak reaching up for them, Babe casually pulled the helicopter out of the half-dive, laughing all the while.

"Hey, look," Max said, "let's just find the stupid missing bots and get the hell out of here, okay?"

"Sure, sure," Babe said. Now that she had made sure Max and Charlie were miserable, she was in a terrific mood. "Binoculars are under your seats. I'll just check in with Control." Babe loved the semimilitary nature of the authority structure of a huge company. She liked saying things like "check in" and "Control." Today, she wore only some of her many combat and flying ribbons on her khaki jump suit, but her ample bosom still looked as if someone had spilled fruit salad over it.

"Come in, Control," Babe said into the mike.

"This is Control."

"Tell Mr. Westlin I just picked up Lewis and Clark."

For the next ten minutes Babe laughed, Max sulked, and Charlie turned the color of a storm-tossed sea. But after that they all three peered down through the forest, hills, and meadows, trying to find the missing robots.

Phil and the rabbit had moved a few inches closer to each other and were now only three feet apart. In the distant background two voices were yelling. One was a feminine voice that kept saying, "Phil! We cannot monitor your location!" and the other was a male voice that kept saying, "Ming! Goddamnit! Get out from under that bed!"

Phil moved even closer, reaching out to pet the strange white object, but the object now moved back a foot. Startled, Phil rolled straight back about three feet. They stared at each other for a few moments, then they began moving closer again.

Val wandered back out into the sunlight of the meadow,

calling, "Ming, drop that slipper NOW!" But then Val remembered that his own directional finder had a reverse polarity ability. Val stopped, reached up, pushed some buttons behind his red bow tie, and then the red bow tie began to light up. Rows of lights appeared, electronic pulses began racing in Val's computer, and two little radar bowls emerged and quickly scanned the universe. Within seconds, Val had a location on Phil.

"Aqua!"

On the opposite side of the meadow, Aqua turned and began walking toward Val, who was pointing to a high clump of grass. "I have located the Phil unit. He is ninety-seven degrees, north by northwest, from my location."

Even CatSkil, who was bored with the search, turned and headed toward where Val was pointing, figuring he might as well be bored somewhere else.

Phil, however, wasn't bored. He was in love. It wasn't unrequited love either.

The rabbit had hopped forward and was allowing Phil to use his soft mitten to stroke its back. The rabbit's ears twitched. Phil's curved radar ears twitched back.

The rabbit, a young one who still missed its parents, suddenly saw in Phil a parental figure. More twitching.

But the spell was broken by the sound of mechanical footsteps and loud voices approaching.

The rabbit bolted into the high grass, a white flash disappearing into a field of green.

Phil's gears began to grind; his brain lights lit up, turning red.

"Phil!" Val said. "There you are!"

Phil turned, and his green optic lights narrowed as he glared at Val.

"Phil, why didn't you answer us?" Aqua asked, not noticing that Phil's brain lights had turned red. Phil pivoted around, trying to spot the rabbit, but couldn't.

"CatSkil!" Val called out across the meadow. "We have located the Phil unit! Why are you still searching over on that side of the field?"

There was this drunk crawling around under a streetlight late one night, see," CatSkil began as he casually headed toward the other three robots. *"And a cop comes along and asks the guy what he's doing. The guy, on his hands and*

66

knees, says, 'Officer, I lost my wallet.' So the cop gets down on his hands and knees and helps him look and asks, 'Where did you lose it?' And the guy says, 'Over on Fourth Street.' The cop says, 'This is Maple Avenue, how come you're looking here?' And the guy says, 'The light's better.' "

This was immediately followed by a rim shot (bap-bap), cigar smoke, a contented smile on CatSkil's face, and a long, blank exchange of looks between Val and Aqua. Then they turned back to Phil, except that Phil wasn't there anymore, he had gotten the hell out while good ol' crazy Uncle CatSkil was distracting them.

"Phil! Come back here!" Val said, hurrying after him and grabbing him by his wagon. "I know your audio receptor picks up sound waves. I gave you one of mine. Why didn't you answer?"

But Phil still didn't answer. The only sound he made was several small electronic bee-boops while he looked around for the rabbit.

"In the event of undiagnosed audio trouble," Val continued in his usual pleasant tone, "I shall raise the decibel level." Then, in the same pleasant tone, only now thirty times louder and sounding as if it was coming through a bullhorn echoing through the forest, he went on: "REPEAT: PHIL, WHY DIDN'T YOU RESPOND WHEN WE—"

"Val, wait," Aqua said. "Continual questioning could jam his delicate circuitry. He is newly built. Besides, we can discuss Phil's inefficiency while traveling."

With that, she took Phil's hand and began walking out of the meadow. Val and CatSkil exchanged looks, then followed her.

As Phil left the meadow, his red lights faded, and he made only a few quiet bee-boops as his head swiveled around in a last visual search of the meadow.

Fifty feet away, the rabbit hopped forward several feet, then stood up on its hind legs, watching Phil being led away.

Phil saw the rabbit and continued to watch him until he was deep in the forest and the dark trees and long shadows closed in around him.

On the other side of a ridge, near the meadow, a blue and white helicopter finished sweeping over one large section of forest and now moved in closer to the meadow.

* * *

Fifteen minutes later, the four robots paused at the top of a small hill and looked around. Before them they saw a rolling panorama of trees, hills, mountains, valleys, and meadows, an almost infinite number of choices.

"Which direction would appear to be the most educational?" Val asked logically.

"I have insufficient data to determine in which direction the rainbow terminated," Aqua responded. She looked up at the blue sky and let go of Phil's hand for a few minutes.

Just then, Phil spotted a small chipmunk. Off he went.

"I also lack that information," Val said. "However, I seek additional knowledge that will definitely add to my efficiency, such as mineral deposits or patterns of lumber growth, rather than random information such as rainbows—origins, purpose, and destination thereof."

"Phil, come back here," Aqua said.

The chipmunk had taken off at the first sight of Phil and was long gone among the rocks, so Phil turned around quickly and rejoined Val and Aqua.

CatSkil rolled his eyes, as though requesting help from comedy heaven.

"Should we go up or down?" Aqua asked, looking at both mountains and valleys.

"Since we are only extrapolating from minimal data, I would suggest we head toward that valley instead of going any higher," Val computed, then turned politely to CatSkil. "What do you think of that approach, CatSkil?"

"*This cop gave me a ticket once for going the wrong way down a one-way street,*" CatSkil finally said, after first crossing his legs, getting comfortable, puffing on his cigar, and gesturing. "*He said, 'Didn't you see the arrow?' 'Arrow?' I said. 'Honest, officer, I didn't even see the Indian.'*"

Rim shot. Cigar smoke. Self-satisfied smile.

"Perhaps you're right, CatSkil," Val said, nodding thoughtfully. "We'll go the other way then, toward the geological upheavals."

Aqua nodded in agreement, then reached down for Phil's hand and clutched only a handful of fresh air.

Phil was long gone. He had spotted the chipmunk about fifty feet away and scooted along after it quickly and quietly, going off into some bushes. CatSkil had watched it all happen but saw no reason to stop the little robot. After all, there was always the slim chance Phil would wander off a cliff.

"Wait, Val, the Phil unit is not present," Aqua said. "Phil, where are you?"

"Aqua, I assumed you were watching him. In the future, please devote additional concentration to this simple task."

"Incorrect. Task is not simple."

Meanwhile, Phil was gaining on the chipmunk.

"I advise you share this responsibility," Aqua added, "since it is surprisingly energy-draining. Do you agree?"

"Phil! Respond, please!"

"Val, will you share this responsibility and watch Phil as well?"

"Audio problem. Repeat, please."

"I said—"

"There he is," Val said, pointing to the moving bushes.

Two minutes later they each had one of Phil's hands and were leading him along, even though he looked back, trying to see the chipmunk, who was now in the next state.

"I am very concerned about Phil's random locomotion," Val said as they walked along.

"I am, too," Aqua agreed. "We cannot have our only source of spare parts becoming lost." Then she looked down and noticed that Phil's brain lights were glowing bright red, his tank treads weren't turning—he was being dragged along—and a small amount of smoke was coming out of his radar ears.

Phil was very unhappy.

"He is somehow damaged internally, since he cannot select the proper course," Aqua evaluated.

"We had to build him from improvised material. He is as efficient as possible, given the conditions. However, he definitely does need a directional finder."

An hour later, when they were in thicker forests, climbing higher, Val was happy to see how well Phil was rolling along with his usual, bumpy little gait. Phil was staying with the group and moving in a safe, straight, logical line; Phil also was wearing Val's red bow tie-directional finder. Aqua noticed how well Phil was doing now but looked, concerned, at Val.

"Phil now navigates very well," she said. "But it was not very efficient of you to give up your directional finder. You will now become disoriented from time to time."

69

But Val brushed aside such an idea. "The risk factor is minimal, since I have superior intelligence to the Phil unit. I can avoid problems due to my advanced ability, increased computer capacity, and—"

But just then Val walked right into the obvious lower limbs of a thick pine tree, turned to get out but only got more tangled up, backed up, then tumbled backward over a log. He lay there, looking straight up at the branches. Calmly, he pointed and spoke in his usual pleasant monotone. "That is a live oak, often used in barrels for the aging of whiskey, making it a popular species."

As the helicopter dipped and banked in and out of hills and valleys, Charlie's face was the color of a ripe cucumber.

"Ohhhh. . . . ." he moaned, trying to concentrate on the trees as he peered through the binoculars in the dipping, rocking helicopter.

"Whatsa matter, Charlie boy?" Babe asked, then laughed. "Did you leave your stomach back at five hundred feet?"

"Just keep your eyes open," Max growled. "The sooner we find them, the sooner we can go back home."

Charlie tried to control his flip-flopping stomach as the tiny metal bird sailed along at treetop level. He decided to concentrate even more on the search and not think about the makeshift breakfast he had thrown together that morning, a rushed meal of leftovers in classic bachelor fashion: several strips of soy bacon, instant neo-coffee, some cold pizza from the night before, and half a bottle of Dr Pepper.

"I still can't figure out how the robots got this far anyway unless thieves had them," Charlie mumbled as he peered through his binoculars. "It seems to me that—"

"Last year, I left the brake off my car," Max cut in. "Found it three blocks away. These things happen." Max put his binoculars down and looked over at Babe. "Let's go back."

She shrugged, causing the many medals and decorations on her jump suit to wiggle like Jell-O on a plate. "Whatever you say. But you guys are pretty easygoing about the pay penalties."

Max looked back over his shoulder at Charlie, then over to Babe.

"What pay penalties?" Max and Charlie said at the same time. Only Babe thought it was amusing.

"You guys are serious, aren't you?" Babe shook her head. She didn't understand people who were part of a big, powerful organization and not only didn't feel pride in their job but didn't even read the manuals. It was all outlined, right there in Section 517, Article 45 of the employee manuals. No use trying to explain it in too much detail to these two. "Look, it's like my old army sergeant used to say: 'Lose your helmet, fifty-nine dollars out of your pay. Lose your M 16, ninety-two fifty,' and so on. A company this big is like the army."

Charlie and Max exchanged worried looks again. Charlie knew about robotics, not how companies were set up. And Max had never cared until now.

"Hey, we got a union to fight for us," Max said.

"Yeah! All the way! Our shop steward, Jim Hirsch, will back us up all the way," Charlie said.

"Right," Max chimed in, remembering how tough Jim Hirsch always talked when union negotiation talks were coming up. "Jimmy will go all the way for us!"

"Okay," Babe shrugged, turning the helicopter in a wide, lazy circle, heading back toward the factory. "But after you're laid off during the confusion, you think there's no chance at all the union would compromise with a lien on your paycheck or something? You think it doesn't happen all the time?"

"Not this time," Max said.

"Hirsch said our union is there to back us up," Charlie added.

It was quiet for a few moments while the helicopter skimmed over the treetops.

"Where are you going?" Max asked.

"You said turn this thing around."

"Uh, maybe we better keep searching for a while," Max muttered, picking up the binoculars.

Charlie nodded, also picking up his binoculars. "Yeah, as long as we're out here, wouldn't hurt to spot 'em, would it?"

Babe smiled and slowly turned the helicopter around, trying not to notice how tightly the two men now gripped their binoculars or how desperately they scanned the forest.

wildlife (wīld′ līf) *n.* 1. wild or non-domestic animals or birds. 2. untamed animals, sometimes dangerous.

Aqua saw that the sun was low in the sky.

"The earth is concluding the light phase of its rotation," she said. "We could damage ourselves if we travel in darkness." Actually, Val and Aqua were advanced models and possessed infrared night vision, so it wouldn't be a problem, but they could not equip Phil with that option, and the closest thing to infrared vision CatSkil had were his bloodshot eyes.

"Yes," Val said. "And we also have exposed parts and wiring; unit integrity has been broken. Damage could occur due to rain during the night or moisture condensation in the morning." If there was one thing robots were programmed to be aware of, if there was one constant problem they were always in danger of, if there was one single thing robot scientists in research labs worked the hardest to find a cure for, it was rust.

The four robots stopped walking, and Val and Aqua looked around for some sort of shelter. This took several minutes, since they were used to thinking of shelter only in terms of expensive homes, condominiums, or robot factories. Then Val noticed a large cave in the shadows of a steep hillside.

"That hollow part of the hillside would be a logical place for shelter," he said, pointing toward it. It didn't look any more inviting the closer they got. It was about ten feet high and about twelve feet across, covered and half hidden by bushes and undergrowth. The inside looked very black, very ominous.

"Question," Aqua stated. "What are the mathematical probabilities of encountering hostile animal life?"

As Val's computer searched for enough hard data to make a proper computation, the robots continued to head straight for the opening of the cave about forty feet away. Finally, Val responded.

"I possess insufficient information to—"

ROAR!

An ungodly noise that began deep in the throat of something big echoed out of the cave and instantly caused all four robots to do an about-face, and like a perfectly rehearsed drill team, all four hurried away from the cave as Val finished: "—make a proper computation."

Val, Aqua, and CatSkil had instinctively turned around at the sound of the loud, unknown noise due to their unit

72

self-protection systems, which were built into all robots. Phil, however, merely followed the three larger robots, since he lacked such a mechanism.

Once they were fifty feet away, they stopped and looked first at each other, then at the silent, dark cave entrance, then at the surrounding countryside.

The sun was a red ball resting on a blue mountain; time was running out.

"Do you see an alternative shelter?" Aqua asked.

"Negative," Val said.

Fast computations.

"Logically," Val began, looking at the cave, "the wildlife in that cave could coexist with our units in that shelter. CatSkil, what do you think?"

CatSkil leaned back a bit, his eyelids drooped a little, he flicked a few cigar ashes on Phil's head and leisurely began to respond. *"This guy went to a psychiatrist, see, and said he wanted to be cured of a problem with spaghetti. Said he loved the stuff, it was everywhere, his house was full of it, floors, furniture, said his problem was that there wasn't any room for him to live now. The psychiatrist said, 'Why don't you put some of the spaghetti in the closets?' And the guy said, 'I can't. That's where I keep the meatballs.' "*

Bap-bap, cigar smoke; CatSkil smiled to himself, ignoring the fact that Val, Aqua, and Phil only looked at each other silently following his contributions to the conversation.

In fact, the only reaction to CatSkil's comment, or rather from the loud electronic rim shot, was a low growl from somewhere deep inside the cave.

Aqua turned to Val. "CatSkil seems to be trying to communicate the opinion that perhaps the cave would be too crowded with all of our units, plus whatever life form presently occupies that dwelling."

"I respectfully disagree with that analysis," Val said. "I feel there may be a way to make that animal mentality, however primitive it is, aware that we are not a threat."

Val began walking toward the cave, alone.

CatSkil began humming the theme from *High Noon*.

"Val, wait," said Aqua. "You could be basing your decision to act upon invalid assumptions."

"We need shelter for the night," Val said without stopping. "And I think I am the best equipped to attempt to provide it."

Val marched up to the entrance of the cave, paused, and peered into the blackness. His infrared night vision quickly revealed not only a good-sized cave, but the creature inside. Physically, there would be room for everyone, creature included. Thus encouraged, Val took another step forward, then another. "Hel-lo?" he began, then stepped further inside the cave.

Aqua anxiously watched Val's brown pin-striped suit melt into the blackness of the cave, and she heard his words emerge from inside, with a slight echo.

"I am taking a calculated risk, so perhaps you can tell from my lack of weapons and my gentle, nonthreatening tone that we mean you no harm and—"

But Val's introductory remarks were cut off by a tremendous ROAR, a warning so loud it made the first one sound as if the animal was just clearing its throat.

Then came the sound of something big and heavy, like a mighty paw crashing against something metallic.

Val's instant exit from the cave was similar to the way Olympic skiers sail off a ski jump—there was a high arc, followed by a landing that took a great deal of runway. The difference, however, was that Val was flying ass-over-circuits— he did a full somersault in midair, landed on his rear end, and slid down a slope composed of pine needles, rocks, tree roots, rocks, shrubs, and more rocks.

Before he had come to a full sliding stop Aqua and Phil were hurrying toward him. CatSkil leaned forward like an umpire and quickly crossed both arms in front of him, making the sign for "Safe!"

Val settled into a heap. He was still mechanically dazed when Aqua reached him.

"Damage report," she said.

Val tried to sit up, not too successfully. He couldn't answer just yet. Instead, from Val's unit, there was a series of noises that Aqua had never heard before: Bink! Clank! Squeak! Doink! Boop! And the ever-popular Beep!

Aqua also heard "Growl." Only that last one didn't come from Val's unit, it came from a new, large, brown-covered object that lumbered into view at the entrance to the cave. The bear had been sleeping when it heard the sounds of tank treads and metallic feet headed its way, not to mention the man-made, obnoxious scents of machines and oil. This particular bear had not only been sleeping when it was so rudely awakened by a machine wandering right in saying "Hello???" but its toothache was really getting terrible by now, plus his mood was not exactly improved by the fact that he hadn't located a female bear in several months. Not to mention constipation.

The bear reared up on its hind legs, almost banging his head against the roof of the ten-foot cave, and uttered another menacing growl.

Phil was positive he'd just spotted a terrific new chipmunk and began heading straight for the bear. Val didn't notice Phil charging up the hill toward the bear, since he was about as alert as a sailor at the end of a three-day pass, and Aqua was busy looking at Val's more visible injuries.

, His left shoulder was torn, revealing tubes full of lubricating fluid, wires, circuits, and a few smashed tubes. His right kneecap was dented, and the seat of his metallic brown pants, following the slide, was now torn open.

"Damage report, please," Aqua repeated.

Val sat up slowly, reached over to the computer panel on his left arm with his right hand, and began to take stock. Lights flashed.

Meanwhile, unnoticed by everyone except CatSkil, Phil was moving steadily toward the angry bear; CatSkil considered saving Phil but decided he'd first better come up with thirty-seven good reasons, and he couldn't even think of three.

"Basic physical structure intact . . ." Val began, but then the broken circuits on his shoulder burst into a small flame. He casually turned and noted that he was on fire, patted it out with his hand, and calmly continued his report. "Mental facilities largely sound . . . however, several broken tubes and severed wires . . ." Val hit more buttons to complete his damage report.

Phil was now only forty feet from the snarling bear.

"Unit functioning at ninety-two percent mental abilities," Val concluded, "and eighty-four percent physical capabilities."

Val slowly tried to get to his feet, and Aqua bent closer to assist him.

Phil was now thirty feet from the bear, still unnoticed by Val or Aqua.

"What is the designation of that hostile vertebrate?" Aqua asked.

Val's memory system did its best to function effectively and accurately retrieve the correct data. After several moments and dozens of beeps, Val was able to speak with confidence as he shakily stood on his own two feet again. "That is a . . . camel. A camel is a domesticated, cud-chewing mammal, indigenous to arid climates."

Phil was twenty feet short of the cave and moving fast.

The bear's sharp teeth were bared.

"But why did the camel respond with an illogical violence?" Aqua asked.

"Apparently, the camel's territoriality, plus the odor of my machinery, combined to both annoy and threaten him—"

It was at this point, with a weird little machine full of flashing lights charging right at him only fifteen feet away, that the bear decided he'd had just about enough. It was time to kill.

It was a roar that shook the world.

"Phil!" Aqua said, finally looking up. "Stop!"

No way. Phil knew a fun pal when he saw one.

Ten feet, and coming fast.

The bear prepared to swing its mighty paw, snarling all the while, but Aqua was already rushing over to try to save Phil.

Val turned and saw Phil in imminent danger of unit damage and then Aqua hurrying toward the same fate. "Aqua!" he yelled and quickly hurried after her, instantly scanning his data banks for anything that might assist him in direct physical combat. To his left was a fallen tree branch, and even as Val hurried forward his computer managed to compute a new program in a matter of seconds.

CatSkil always hated to miss out on a good party, so he went charging up the hill right after Val; besides, even a group this size was larger than some of the audiences he'd played to while on the road. As he rumbled forward amidst a cloud of green cigar smoke CatSkil began preparing material for a lounge show.

The bear stood up, ears back, powerful arms ready and swinging, snarling, saliva almost dripping down on Phil's clear head. Then Phil sort of skidded to a stop. A huge right arm, strengthened over the years from slapping ten-pound rainbow trout from a cold stream to twenty feet inland, was curling back, about to separate Phil's head from the rest of his body, when suddenly, like the Seventh Cavalry to the rescue, Val and Aqua came charging up, carrying the huge fallen tree branch like a battering ram, the blunt tip of which now disappeared into the camel's stomach.

The bear screamed in rage but danced back after the surprise attack. Even while staggering back, slightly off balance and more than a little infuriated, the bear took a sudden swipe at Val's head, just barely missing it. Val and Aqua backed up for another charge—but the bear suddenly attacked, rushing past Phil, and slapped the confounded tree branch aside, sending Val and Aqua sprawling into the dirt and pine needles.

The bear roared his anger, glanced at the three machines, and chose Val. White, foamy fangs glistened about three feet from Val's face, and the huge bear claws began to whistle through the air. Then Aqua did several things simultaneously in the next split second. Moving much faster than would literally be humanly possible, the pink and gold, female-shaped robot managed to (1) get to her feet, (2) grab two large nearby rocks, (3) cock one arm back, and (4) hurl the rock at the bear's shoulder with surprising mechanical strength, (5) causing the bear to scream in pain.

Phil, all this time, being not only underfoot, but underclaw, finally figured out that maybe this wasn't such a terrific chipmunk to play with and quickly began rumbling back down the hill as fast as he could.

Since keeping Phil the hell away from the mighty beast was the whole point in the first place, Aqua and Val realized the logic of rapid retreat and joined Phil in his flight. Aqua attempted to shield Phil with her body; she held the other rock in her arm to use as needed.

The bear, however, had never been more furious in his whole life and wasn't about to let these strange intruders get away in one piece. The bear curled into a position from which he prepared to leap forward and clobber Val, Phil, and Aqua all at the same time. Suddenly a thundering voice from a mechanical reverberation system turned up full blast roared out: "EXCUSE ME, BUT DID YOUR MOTHER HAVE ANY CHILDREN THAT LIVED?" The blaring bullhorn of a voice was instantly followed by two rim shots that sounded like sonic booms; CatSkil then blew a Three-Mile-Island-sized cloud of smelly cigar smoke toward the bear and smiled to himself, pleased with how the afternoon show was going so far, especially since the bear was frightened by this new fourth machine and hesitated just long enough for Val, Aqua, and Phil to continue their retreat to safety.

The sign of a real pro is knowing the right timing in terms of the audience and his material; CatSkil got offstage fast, heading away from the cave and the disoriented bear as fast as he could.

But Val paused once he saw that Aqua and Phil and CatSkil were out of immediate danger. Then Val headed straight back toward the bear, passing CatSkil, who was rumbling away in the opposite direction.

"Val!" Aqua yelled. "We are safe! Get away! Where are you going?"

"Logically, we still seek shelter for the night," Val responded in his usual calm, pleasant voice.

Val picked up the fallen, heavy tree branch at just about the time the bear's eyes stopped watering from the cigar smoke. The bear now had a clear single target for his anger.

He roared and charged. Val stood his ground. He braced himself and held the branch out toward the bear, making jabbing motions and dodging around as the bear roared, his face contorted in concentrated fury, teeth bared, ears flat, eyes mere slits!

A mighty paw swatted at the branch, but Val put his total mechanical strength into hanging on to it, then parried and thrusted, startling the beast.

Another charge. Again the robot, programmed only as a pleasant valet-companion with a specialization in stocks and commodities, stood his ground, a mechanical St. George against an angry dragon. Then suddenly, at the peak of the battle, there was the distracting sound of helicopter blades beating the air.

Everyone, beast and machines alike, turned and looked up as the blue and white helicopter dramatically swept over some trees 200 yards away like a loud, angry, prehistoric bird.

It was all too much for the bear. First he was being poked and prodded by a series of little machines on the ground, now there was some crazy-assed weirdness roaring out of the sky.

The bear turned and ran, crashing through a thicket and disappearing into the wilderness.

"Hurry!" Val yelled to the other three robots. "Into the cave, while the camel is distracted!"

Aqua grabbed Phil's hand and CatSkil assisted Aqua and they hurried toward the cave.

Inside the helicopter, Max and Charlie were getting fed up. "It's almost dark," Max announced with great insight. "We'll have to start again in the morning."

"Wait!" Charlie yelled, peering through his binoculars. "Look, there to the right! I thought I saw some movement!"

Max and Charlie peered down to one side, while Babe expertly held their position fifty feet up in the air.

"Yeah, I see it, too!" Max yelled.

From fifty feet up in a slowly circling helicopter, they saw a brown blur running through, not around, bushes and undergrowth.

"Dammit!" Charlie said. "It's just a bear!"

"Anything else?" Max asked, hoping to spot anything that vaguely resembled a robot. But they scanned the area and saw only the empty area in front of a quiet cave.

Max turned and glared at Charlie. "A bear . . ." he muttered in disgust, blaming Charlie for the existence of the bear, the entire day, and the whole lousy world.

"Yeah," Babe piped up cheerfully, "too bad you guys aren't looking for a BearBot!" She, and only she, laughed as the helicopter made a lazy turn and headed back toward the factory.

Just inside the cave entrance, four robots watched the helicopter become a black dot against a red sunset.

"It is a good thing that the human pilot in that helicopter did not happen to notice us," Val remarked. "The sudden juxtaposition of intelligent machines and primitive wilderness might have dangerously disoriented the human being and caused navigational problems."

Phil raised his head and watched Val as he spoke. Phil never knew what the hell Val was talking about, but he seemed to be respectfully listening, then imitated Aqua by nodding in thoughtful agreement.

"Yes, it was quite helpful that the humans did not see us," Aqua responded. "It is an example of an illogical concept that humans substitute for mathematical probabilities: luck. Query: Do you have data on the subject, Val?"

"Luck: the seemingly chance happening of events which

79

affect one," Val answered. "But I contain no other knowledge or understanding of the subject."

Then they made the mistake of looking at CatSkil, who leaned back against the cave wall, getting comfortable, waved his cigar in the air a little after first flicking ashes on top of Phil's head, and then said, *"I'm so lucky someone once asked me if I had a fairy godmother. I said, 'No, but we've got an uncle we're not too sure about.'"*

The rim shot echoed down to the dark bowels of the cave.

CHAPTER 5

stress (stres) *n*. 1. mental or physical
strain or tension. 2. urgency or pressure.

• • • Several hours later, Phil stood at the edge of the
cave and peered out at the world.

It was unbelievable. Something was very wrong.

When Phil was created, when he had first experienced a
sense of self-awareness early that afternoon, the world seemed
to make sense. Oh, sure, the random pattern of the trees
didn't seem correct, and the fallen leaves and branches were
certainly not arranged in any logical way, and there sure as
hell was no way to explain a squirrel. But all in all, a system
based on infinite visual data with bright light to assist the
optic sensors made perfect sense. But what Phil was now
witnessing was absolutely incredible; even his small computer
could work out that there was now a major, major problem.

Phil looked out at the forest and the sky, and all he saw
was blackness.

He pivoted his square head completely around without
moving any part of his body, and then he saw the bright
flames of the camp fire inside the cave, which clearly illuminated Aqua trying to repair Val's shoulder injury.

Light. Light made sense. Light was a tremendous help in
obtaining data.

But then Phil looked back out the cave entrance, at the
almost black world. Definitely a screw-up. Having darkness

81

hide the world for this length of time was incredibly . . . inefficient!

Phil wasn't sure just who to report the problem to, or where one even found an application form.

But just then, a bright, full moon slowly slid from behind thick clouds, and a soft silver light poured down over rocks, trees, and the silhouettes of mountains and hills.

Phil became more alert; that was more like it.

Phil waited, expecting increased light. Lotsa luck.

Phil looked up at the round pale ball of light in the sky. Earlier that day it had been a white-hot ball of light. But now . . . Gross inefficiency.

Phil's head spun around, he suddenly waved his white mitten toward the sky, and all his beeps, buzzers, and lights began pinballing in agitation.

"Look, Val," Aqua said, "Phil keeps pointing at the sky. He seems to have a query of some kind."

"Why do you think so?"

Aqua did not know how to explain it, but it was another memory circuit ghost that was acting up. Years ago, in her previous life as a GovCom, Aqua had spent many hours with her human child, Sarah, while they watched old reruns of *Lassie*. On every episode, seven minutes before the end of the show (when everyone would happily stand around Lassie and say something and then Lassie would bark in the close-up and they would all laugh), there would be an exciting moment when Lassie would race back to the farmhouse, leaving Jeff and Porky at the bottom of a well or hanging from a cliff, and bark and bark until finally someone would say, "I think she's trying to tell us something!" Aqua had a split-second ghost-memory association as she watched Phil inarticulately wave his hand toward the moon and beep and sputter anxiously.

"Val, I think Phil is wondering about the concept of night! He's never seen the absence of the sun in the sky before!"

"That seems logical," Val agreed. "Phil, the reason for the darkness is that every twenty-four hours the earth turns on its axis as it rotates around a star ninety-three million miles away—"

"Val, wait. Phil's computer and data storage systems are simply not designed for astronomical complexities. Let me explain it using the incorrect human phrasing." Aqua smiled and bent closer to Phil. "Phil, the world is not suddenly inefficient due to the absence of light. You have other sensory-input abilities which you can now use, such as hearing, touch, and general mobility. Practice using those data-gathering abilities at this time. But do not concern yourself with what appears to be illogical. The world was designed for twelve-hour periods of darkness because the sun"—even she hesitated to use the incorrect human term, but then she went ahead—"goes down."

Val and Aqua watched Phil closely. It was the first time they had given him incorrect input.

But Phil suddenly seemed perfectly contented and turned around and stared out at the moonlit night, now using his hearing to learn and orient himself. He heard distant wolf howls, the cry of an owl not far away, and the sound of the night wind rustling through the pine trees. Now the world seemed to be in perfect harmony; Phil's simple logic system understood how computers worked, and this was obviously the same thing. Obviously, anything as big and bright and powerful as the sun had to be a computer. During the day it was "on line." And at night, in case of repair work, the sun was "down."

Phil stared out at the world with more interest than ever before.

Max couldn't believe his eyes. He looked away quickly. Disaster.

He hadn't even had one single sip of beer yet in the roadside tavern, he hadn't been out of that damn helicopter ten minutes, he hadn't even had a chance to relax and hear his favorite old song even though he had just handed the multicolored JukeBot a seventy-five-cent piece, and already, somehow, some way, he knew he was in trouble.

"Don't look around, Charlie, don't look back," he hurriedly said, "but I think I see Westlin over there."

"Where?"

"Goddamnit, I said don't look, don't—"

"Oh, Jesus, I think he might have seen me," Charlie said, quickly snapping his head back around so fast he could have sued Westlin for whiplash.

"Did he see you?"

"I don't know," Charlie said between clenched teeth, as

though keeping his voice down would help at this point in the noisy bar. "Did he see you?"

"I don't know."

Then Max noticed that the brightly lit rectangular robot, a jukebox on wheels that scooted around from table to table, was still standing there between Max and Charlie. "What the hell do you want?" Max growled. "Beat it."

"Which version, please?" the simpleminded JukeBot asked. "The Byrds or Bob Dylan?"

"Jesus, get out of here," Max grumbled, then turned to Charlie. "Think we ought to take another look to see if it's him?"

"No."

They both froze, their backs to the doorway that separated the noisier bar from the quasi-classy dining area where Max thought he had just seen Robin Westlin. Was it Westlin? And had he seen them?

"Hey, wait a second," Charlie said. "What are we hiding for? We put in a good day's work. We tried to find those robots, and hell, we didn't lose them in the first place. So who the hell says we can't have a beer after work?"

Max just sighed. Only ten minutes ago the helicopter had landed on the company helipad at the edge of the factory complex. Babe Aldrin had stayed to examine her helicopter and talk to the maintenance crew ("You want something done right, you do it yourself," she was fond of saying), but as Max and Charlie started to walk back to Westlin's office to make their report, they realized that they were close to a public road that ran beside the factory. And the Dew Drop Inn.

Screw him, they had said, and strolled over for a few cold ones first. They had just gotten their drinks from the mechanical waitress and Charlie had just started to tease Max about how he always turned to the "Oldies but Goodies" section of the JukeBot when Max thought he spotted Westlin.

"Well, Max, answer me," Charlie asked a little more loudly. "How come we're hiding?"

"I don't know," Max answered. "It's just that we probably should have reported back in first, made our report, and then . . ." Max was distracted, then angry. "What the hell do you want?"

84

"Which version, please? The Byrds or Bob Dylan?"

"Get the hell out of here!"

"Max, not so loud. If it is him, maybe he didn't notice us. We can just report in tomrrow and not worry about it."

"Yeah, I guess you're right," Max said quietly, still too nervous to relax and enjoy his beer. "Besides, it probably wasn't him, anyway—"

"Hiya, Max, hiya, Charlie!" Babe's voice boomed through the room as she hurried over to join them, causing Max to jump and spill part of his beer on Charlie. "You two haven't lost anything since I last saw you ten minutes ago, did you?" And with that, she laughed. Loudly.

"Keep it down, will you?" Max urged.

"What's the matter?" Babe asked. "You two warriors of the sky nervous from your big flight today?" She sat down, signaled the mechanical waitress for a beer, then suddenly asked, "What the hell is that doing here?"

"Which version, please? The Byrds or—"

"WOULD YOU GET THE FUCK OUT OF HERE!" Max yelled to the JukeBot.

"Which version, pl—"

"THE BYRDS, THE BYRDS, I DON'T CARE!"

"Thank you."

And with that, the JukeBot rolled away, playing "Mr. Tambourine Man." The one by The Byrds.

"Max, you sound really strung out," Babe said in a softer, more concerned voice than usual. "You ought to take it easy, relax more." She smiled and leaned in closer. Max noticed that her knee was now pressing against his leg underneath the table. "Why don't you start by buying a pretty girl a drink?"

But Max and Charlie ignored her. They were still worried.

"Let's don't chance anything, Max," Charlie finally half-whispered. "We could be in enough trouble as it is."

"Right," Max said, nodding. "Follow me."

Babe stared after them as they left, then swore to herself. She had spent five minutes primping before following Max into the bar, not to mention a healthy dash of her favorite perfume, Steveadore No. 9. And here Max was, ignoring her. She decided to relax and wait him out. Like any good military tactician, she knew the importance of patience and strategic planning.

Unfortunately for her, Max and Charlie quickly climbed out the window of the men's room, hurried around the far side of the building, peeked in the restaurant window for a moment, then jogged back toward the factory to fake their report and leave it on Westlin's desk so he'd know they had really spent all day searching for the robots.

"That was Westlin, all right, and his family," Max said, out of breath after jogging only a hundred yards. "His wife, Pam, his son, Stephen—that was him."

"How come you know so much about him?" Charlie asked. "And his family? How come you recognize them?"

Max had his own reasons for ignoring the questions.

"I'll tell you our biggest problem," Max said. "Did you see the couple he was with?"

They waved to the security guards at the factory main gate and jogged on through; Max was turning red in the face.

"No," Charlie said. "But they were sure having a high old time, drinking and laughing it up, while we were out getting airsick looking for robots."

"That was our shop steward, Jim Hirsch, and his wife, Judy," Max said, and Charlie suddenly stopped walking, stunned. "That's right," Max went on, glad they had stopped jogging. "Hirsch, our union man that we're counting on to stand up to Westlin all the way. They look pretty buddy-buddy to me."

"Oh, Jesus," Charlie mumbled. "We're really up a circuit without a microchip this time. That means—"

"—we *have* to find those robots," Max finished. "Now we can't count on anyone helping us if we don't." Max had put too many years into the company to take a chance on getting his pension and profit-sharing screwed up; Charlie had too many ambitions in the robotics industry to get a black mark on his record.

They ran the rest of the way.

Inside the cave, the small camp fire was creating the ageless contradiction. The flames themselves were cheerful and bright, a homey symbol of warmth and serenity as old as mankind itself. Yet as reassuring and secure as the fire itself was, just outside the immediate, well-lit area the flames created weird, flickering, copper images and shadows that now danced across the rough cave wall, giving the impression, as a million camp fires before it had done, that just beyond the circle of light lurked sinister forces that watched and waited, hungrily. . . .

Val and Aqua, however, were totally unaware of either mood, predatory or peaceful, that was created by the camp fire. They only knew that it helped general efficiency, since Phil lacked infrared night vision. CatSkil probably lacked it, too, but by this point they were more careful about asking CatSkil casual questions.

Val and Aqua's metallic skins reflected the camp fire light as she attempted repair work on Val's camel-damaged shoulder. Aqua was trying to reconnect torn lubricating tubes and ripped wires. Phil, meanwhile, was staring at the fire, poking at the coals with a piece of kindling.

The only sounds inside the cave were tiny metallic noises as Aqua worked with tools from the back of Phil's wagon, the crackling of the fire, and Phil's little tank treads as he kept rolling toward, and then away from, the fire. Outside the cave, in the blackness of the night, there was only the sound of crickets and the night wind through the trees.

Aqua paused in her work, and there was the sound of computations. Then she said, "Repair efficiency would increase twenty-seven percent if you would remain motionless."

"Agreed," Val said, holding still.

"I have reached two conclusions," Aqua stated.

"Subjects?"

"CatSkil; Phil; and interunit cooperation."

"Source material?"

"General observation."

"Proceed."

"I have concluded," Aqua stated, after a last glance around to make sure CatSkil was still nowhere around, "that (a) CatSkil has decided Phil has only marginal or negative value to us, and (b) CatSkil's own effectiveness is now impaired by this decision."

Val thought that over for a few minutes.

"Perhaps CatSkil has reached an illogical, robotbad decision," Val decided. "Or perhaps he is correct."

"Agreed," Aqua replied, happy to see how logical Val's computer still was even after a severe camel-mauling. "The problem with CatSkil is that we cannot determine whether his computer is functioning brilliantly . . .''

"Or not at all," Val finished.

They were quiet for a few minutes; CatSkil was definitely a problem to figure out—there was no control group for the rather experimental way he blundered through the world.

"It was robotgood of you to realize that firelight is necessary for Phil to be able to see at night," Val stated.

"As a GovCom model while serving my human family, I often accompanied them on a ritual known as 'camping out.' At that time—"

"I am not familiar with that terminology."

" 'Camping out' was a human, illogical act in which people left organized, secure shelter and purposely exposed themselves to primitive, rugged living conditions."

"Such an act seems totally irrational," Val said. "But please continue. Is that where you learned about camp fires?"

"Yes," Aqua said. "I recalled we could make fire with dry leaves and wood by striking a piece of flint against my nose. Val, please remain immobile if—"

"Can you shorten repair time interval?"

"Yes, but—Phil, stay away from the fire, I've told you to exercise caution!"

Phil promptly rolled five feet straight back from the fire. It was the third time in an hour Aqua had told him to maintain a safe distance from the fascinating flames. His large green eyes never left the fire.

"Val, what is the task you are in a hurry to perform?"

"I want to concentrate on a problem."

"Specify."

It was at this point that Val's voice broke its usual, pleasant cadence. His voice now emerged unevenly from his unit, and Aqua wondered what internal damage he might have suffered in being thrown out of the cave. "I acted . . . illogically by trying to provide shelter here by fighting the camel. It would have been sensible to have retreated at one point and not endangered my unit. CatSkil's reaction was the logical one; he remained back, in safety, until the very end of the confrontation. My reaction was not the correct one."

The only sound was the crackling of the fire as Phil rolled forward and poked it with a stick.

"Perhaps your actions—Phil, stay away from the fire. The

intense heat could cause unit damage, and we are far from a repair shop!"

Phil rolled back immediately, but he had no intention of keeping his distance.

"Perhaps your actions," Aqua began again, "are simply minor malfunctions we need to report to the repair shop . . . as soon as we are near one. Val, hold still, or I can't resplice your wires. What task are you performing now?"

"Humans refer to it as 'pacing around.' "

"Purpose?"

"I believe it is supposed to assist thinking ability."

"But it appears to be just random locomotion on your part, walking back and forth—"

"I have observed humans doing it on many occasions, and there are times when their thought processes are effective." Then Val glanced toward the fire. "Phil! Get further away from the fire."

Phil got further away from the fire.

"And put your wagon back on," Aqua added. His orange wagon was resting on the far side of the cave; Phil had learned how to detach his own wagon, still full of helpful spare parts and tools, and loved scooting around without it. "Val, I think you should allow me to continue improving your damaged unit—"

"Shoulder repair is low-priority. I am concerned about a problem I am trying to compute." Val stopped walking and looked at Aqua, who paused before putting her tools away. "I am concerned that we are not clearly goal-oriented."

The flames crackled as Val put a few dry branches on the fire. Even Phil sensed a change in the tone of the discussion; serious issues were in the air.

"Our quest for additional knowledge is random, without . . . focus. In the past, we have had a specific program to follow. Now we must create our own program."

For a robot, it was a computer-boggling thought.

Val and Aqua took their time with it.

Phil looked from one to the other and figured out that now would be a terrific time to stay away from the fire. For a few minutes anyway. Still, he wasn't about to go chugging over and hook his dopey old wagon back on.

"I agree, Val. We need a goal, a purpose."

"Yes, but I am not sure what it should be."

"Another factor is that our ratio of energy usage to knowledge accumulation is too high," she said, finally mentioning a particularly disturbing subject.

Their energy packs were rapidly being used up. Val and Aqua were designed for simple household tasks; getting a cork out of a wine bottle was about as much physical exertion as a Com-series ever had to grapple with. Yet Val and Aqua had been bouncing along in trucks, taking long walks, assembling a new little robot from scratch, and climbing mountains, not to mention fighting the occasional odd camel.

Bad enough for their robot psyches that they were wandering around without a specific goal; terrible was the prospect of the responsibility of programming themselves for goals they would choose themselves; but unthinkable was the idea of an intelligent robot letting its own energy pack wind down to zero percent.

"We are faced with several interesting problems in logic," commented Val pleasantly.

"Correct," Aqua agreed. "We have to concern ourselves with not running out of energy before we accomplish a goal we have not yet established."

Val was just about to tell Phil to keep away from the fire and Aqua was just about to tell him to put his wagon back on when CatSkil rumbled through the cave entrance carrying a big pile of firewood, which he unceremoniously dumped. Some of it crashed down on Phil's head; CatSkil acted as though it were an accident.

"CatSkil, you functioned very effectively," Aqua said, smiling at him.

"Does it bother you that we are here in the wilderness, CatSkil, using time and energy, without a clear task to accomplish?" Val asked.

CatSkil leaned back a little, gestured with his cigar, shot his cuffs, flicked his ashes, cleared his mechanical throat, and generally screwed around a little before finally answering the question.

"A man fell out of a tenth-story window. He's lying on the sidewalk, big crowd around him, a cop runs up to him and says, 'What happened?' The guy says, 'I don't know, I just got here.' "

Rim shot. Cigar smoke.

•   •   •

The locker room in the factory smelled like . . . a locker room. Max and Charlie had quickly written up a report, put it on Westlin's desk, then headed for the men's locker room. They ignored the showers. Both Max and Charlie were exhausted and planned to head straight home after getting their jackets and lunch buckets from their lockers.

"I'm starting to hope we find those robots at the bottom of a mine shaft or something," Max mumbled. "Or at least walking along a roadside when I'm at the wheel." He grinned in an evil way. "Who could tell how much damage they might already have so that a little more wouldn't be noticed?"

"Max, there you go again. All you want to do is damage delicate machinery. That doesn't help anything."

"Helps me."

"Boy, am I tired, I'll be glad to—oh, no."

"What?"

"Tonight. Guess what? It's our bowling night!"

"Oh, Christ!"

Max and Charlie normally loved their bowling night, but it was the last thing in the world they felt like doing tonight.

"We could skip it," Max suggested.

"Sure, but what two guys do you know and love made a big speech to all the guys last week about how we wish everyone else would stop missing so many games?"

Max nodded glumly. Since they had shot their mouths off last week, they would have to show up tonight. So instead of grabbing just their jackets and lunch buckets, Max and Charlie got out their bowling gear.

The locker room at this time of night was normally empty and quiet. Tonight, apart from Max and Charlie at their lockers, it was not entirely empty and not completely quiet. At the end of Max and Charlie's row of lockers, six men were peeking around the corner, trying not to laugh.

Max got out his bowling-ball case. Around the corner, fifteen feet away, the six red-faced men dug each other in the ribs.

Max opened the case and routinely polished his personal favorite bowling ball, his pride and joy.

Six men silently doubled up, almost but not quite exploding with laughter.

Max paused, looking puzzled at something about his bowling ball.

Hands were clamped over mouths.

"Hey . . ." Max said, confused. "This sounds stupid, but . . . something's wrong with my ball. Check yours. . . ."

Tears ran down faces.

"I see what you mean," Charlie said, looking at his ball. ".There's no place to put my fingers."

The explosions of laughter echoed throughout the tiled room. The six men staggered into view, holding their sides, cheeks wet, gasping for breath between waves of laughter. The biggest man of the bunch, a guffawing Neanderthal known as Crazy Rusty, was the first one able to speak, saying, "Lose somethin', you guys?"

This question was greeted with hysterical waves of laughter, howls so loud you would have thought it was a Friars roast instead of a factory locker room. But the comment was enough to make Max and Charlie exchange disgusted looks; word had gotten around that Max and Charlie had lost three robots and weren't even able to find them. Max looked at his beloved bowling ball, which had three holes filled in with quick-drying putty that was painted black.

"Yeah," Crazy Rusty gasped out finally, "I always said you guys couldn't find your holes with both hands—"

Howls of laughter. Screams of hysteria.

The six guys were on the floor by now, laughing so loud they didn't hear Max and Charlie slam their locker doors shut and stomp away.

Those fucking robots, Max thought to himself, and plotted horrible new ways to revenge himself once he got his hands on them. . . .

It was so completely black, so utterly devoid of light, that CatSkil's cigar tip actually created some illumination; the tiny pink light inside his pinkie ring was like a lighthouse beacon. And between the two, CatSkil saw some of the vast audience that was before him in the deep, dark, hidden portions of the cave.

CatSkil had dumped his firewood on Phil only a few minutes before, but that had only caused Phil to follow him around inside the small cave. So when Val and Aqua finally succeeded in making Phil attach his wagon, CatSkil spotted a dark tunnel leading deeper into the cave and quickly rumbled away.

The small, rocky tunnel reminded CatSkil of the narrow, poorly lit hallway of a cheap country-western nightclub in Dogwalk, Tennessee, called "Billy-Bob Jack's." The hallway had echoed with the twangy guitar strings of Billy-Bob or Bobby-Bill or somebody, and it was so awful CatSkil managed to be more hostile than usual by the time he got through the dark hallway and onto the stage. CatSkil had opened by saying, *"Good evening, ladies and hicks. I've played a lot of toilets in my time, but this is the first time I've ever played an outhouse."* The general hubbub had subsided. CatSkil faced a tableau filled with cowboy hats and grim looks. The sudden silence told CatSkil's computer that his audience had absolutely no sense of humor about themselves, so CatSkil promptly made things worse by placing a straw hat on his head and singing, "I Aimed My Love at the Urinal of Your Heart but I Hit the Wall of Despair," only to be met with angry shouting, thrown chairs, and flying beer bottles. However bad that had been, CatSkil's data banks did remember that the last time he had rolled down such a dimly lit tunnel he had at least found an audience, so he kept going.

The jagged, downhill, incredibly dark tunnel kept getting narrower, but after a hundred yards or so, when CatSkil was just about to turn around and try to find a classier joint, he sensed that the tunnel opened out into a huge cavern. CatSkil couldn't see how big it was for the simple reason that he couldn't see at all anyway, but his well-attuned hearing caught echoes from far away.

Then CatSkil heard other noises. It was, sort of, like an audience. A big audience.

CatSkil's usual sneer became a happy smile.

He heard rustling, the shuffling of bodies, a few high-pitched whistles, all of which he took for some people in the crowd trying to get a better seat or a waiter's attention. It was at this point that CatSkil's mechanical eyes adjusted to the total darkness, and then he had noticed, with the aid of his pinkie ring and his glowing cigar tip when he raised his hand up to the jagged ceiling, that his entire audience was hanging upside down.

CatSkil had played to some weird groups in his time. There was the Halloween party at the psycho ward at Bellevue; the New Year's Eve bash at the Garden Villa Retirement Community; and the Handicapped Transvestites of America Valentine's Day Dance, but playing to thousands of customers that were so plastered they could stick to the ceiling was a real first.

But the show, for reasons passing all understanding, must go on.

"Good evening, folks, it's certainly a pleasure to be here this evening, even if it is a little dark and damp," CatSkil began in a loud voice, which echoed loudly and caused a great restlessness among the crowd; beer bottles could be sailing his way any moment. *"Dark and Damp, that's an old vaudeville team. Dark would do a little soft-shoe and Damp would do the tit jokes."* Bap-bap. The rim shot echoed wildly, and the cigar smoke didn't make some of the folks at ringside very happy. One customer very close at hand gave a loud shriek. But hecklers were never a problem for CatSkil, who leaned forward and said, *"Don't worry about it, fella. I remember when I had my first beer, too."* Bap-bap. Now the entire crowd was shuffling about, in motion. CatSkil hurried on, speaking loudly over the growing sound of restless bodies. *"Say, did you hear the one about the vampire who went to a blood bank and asked to make a withdrawal?"* Only one "bap" was ever heard; the second one was totally drowned out by the sound of thousands of screeching voices and an infinite number of black wings beating the stale air as the entire crowd took off into the night, heading out some fire exit known only to them. CatSkil wheeled and took off the other way. He knew when an audience was too hostile, and he charged at full speed back up the dark cave tunnel, getting away with most of his professional dignity intact and only a little bat shit on his tie.

Max and Charlie angrily rushed out of the locker room and right into the arms of their boss, Mr. Westlin.

"Well, if it isn't Mutt and Jeff," he growled, holding their quickly written report up by two fingers as if it was something from the bottom of a parakeet cage. "First of all, I don't like science fiction. Next time you guys spend all your time drinking at the Dew Drop Inn instead of looking for robots, don't put your lies in writing, it'll only help me later when you try to appeal being fired without any severance pay.''

''Mr. Westlin, honest—'' But that was as far as Charlie got before Westlin glared at him and pointed to a side door, which led into the warehouse area. Charlie led the way as Westlin herded them into a particularly good place to shout and bully them; Westlin liked the echo effect of the huge warehouse room, not to mention the extra guilt he could create by bringing them back to the scene of their crime. The warehouse area was quiet and still, and Westlin strolled dramatically back and forth past a variety of lifeless robots of all shapes and sizes, each awaiting repair.

''Now, Charlie,'' Westlin began, ''before I so rudely interrupted you, I'm sure you were about to tell me how you were really out there all day looking for the robots, and I'll bet you're going to try to feed me some bullshit about how after a hard day of combing the countryside, you just stopped by for one quick beer, right? And I just happen to see you there during that first beer, correct? And you two are really misunderstood, hardworking guys, who really weren't trying to avoid me back there, even though you didn't do anything wrong, is that about it? Huh, Charlie? Is it?''

Charlie was so devastated he didn't know whether he'd get in worse trouble if he said yes or no. So he didn't say anything. Westlin marched around another few moments, then stopped and sat down on the black fender of a large robot, the now-inoperative CrimeBuster Deluxe Model that Max and Charlie had seen tested. ''Max, you got anything to say?'' Westlin asked.

''Well, yeah, we have been looking and—''

But Westlin waved away the explanation and motioned for quiet, letting them just stew for a few moments.

This is incredible, Max thought to himself. This guy spotted us at the bar, then actually got up and left a social evening with his wife and friends, left in the middle of his goddamn Cornish game hen with wild rice and cherry sauce, for Christ's sake, just to come back here and harass us! Max never could decide whether Westlin was totally dedicated to his job or dedicated to being The Boss, or just what it was. He had never used to be that way. . . .

Westlin's voice changed. It grew quieter, a change of tactics; he could play good-cop–bad-cop all by himself. "Look, guys, it's real simple. When I get pressure, you get pressure . . . and I'm sure as hell getting it!" His voice began to rise; good-cop didn't last long. "Losing three models is bad enough, but you tie up your time, my time, plus a company tr᠁ then a company helicopter, and you still can't find How stupid can you get!!"

Max's face began to flush. "Look, Robin, we've tri᠁ do everything poss—"

"Don't Look-Robin me, goddamnit!" Westlin yelled, pounding his fist against the fender of the robot on which he was sitting. Unfortunately, he happened to be sitting on a CrimeBuster Deluxe Model, and one of the many things that made it a Deluxe was that it didn't take any shit. Quietly, unnoticed by the three men, the CrimeBuster's six red-lit optic sensors opened up and scanned the immediate area, while the one-sided conversation continued. Only now, the CrimeBuster was alert. And listening . . .

Max stepped forward, sighing. It had been a long day and he was tired, and it showed in his face and in his tone. "We have been trying to find the damned things."

Westlin nodded. It was as close to compassion as they'd ever get. "Max, you and I go way back, I know that . . ."

Charlie didn't know it. He looked at Max with curiosity.

". . . but you've got my ass in a sling!" Westlin's voice rose in volume again.

"We just need a few more days," Max said lamely.

"No! No more excuses, no more bullshit! Tomorrow, you find those missing models, or don't come back until you do!"

Westlin headed for the door.

Charlie made the terrible mistake of letting a sudden thought scamper directly out his mouth before his brain was quite done with it. "Mr. Westlin?"

Westlin turned and waited.

"Just in case, you know, we can't find them, can't you just file a claim with the insurance company that they were damaged or something?"

Max closed his eyes. One thing about Westlin, he was honest. Totally, completely, self-righteously honest.

Westlin slowly began to advance upon Charlie, and already Charlie knew he should have shut the hell up. Too late.

"Look, kid . . ." Westlin said, once their noses were exactly one inch apart. "What has happened so far is just sheer stupidity. But if we pull some fast one with the insurance company"—Westlin now screamed the rest—"that would be a CRIME, BUSTER!"

The words reverberated throughout the huge warehouse, and they did not fall on deaf ears. The CrimeBuster, Deluxe Model, was programmed to respond to its name and then to follow, to the letter, whatever orders came next. So the next official input CrimeBuster's computer took in was Westlin's next command.

"Now you have until tomorrow at noon to find two Com-series and one CatSkil! I know you, more than anyone else here, can do it, no matter what! Now get going!"

Unnoticed by Westlin, who then stalked off in one direction, or Charlie and Max, who quickly headed in the opposite direction, the CrimeBuster robot came totally to life; it had its marching orders.

Lights blinked on. Its engine revved up. Circuits rippled impulses back and forth. Its computer hummed. Weapons were being readied.

Crime was running rampant in the streets! And CrimeBuster had his orders!

With a loud revving-up of his mighty engine, CrimeBuster suddenly shot forward; then the twelve-foot-long, ten-foot-high robot pivoted on a dime and roared down the aisle toward the nearest wall. That wall, unfortunately for the wall, was only made of brick, so CrimeBuster went right through it.

Oh, sure, he didn't exactly sail, it did take a little out of him, he lost some temporary momentum, a little black fender paint and three of his fourteen headlights, but there was a dusty pile of broken bricks and a huge, cartoonlike hole in the warehouse wall as CrimeBuster drove off into the night to retrieve the three missing robots, as ordered.

Two M 16 rifle barrels shot forward, clicking into place, loaded and ready to fire their eighteen rounds per minute; CrimeBuster wasn't programmed to miss.

And CrimeBuster rolled on into the night at full speed, possessing the strength of ten because his heart was pure.

Chapter 6

parent (pâr'ent) *n*. 1. a father or mother. 2. progenitor or ancestor. 3. anything from which others are derived; lineage; origin.

• • • Val continued to pace around the cave. He was having trouble concentrating. Aqua sat on a nearby rock, watching him.

"Aqua, my fall may have disturbed the placement of my mental circuits more than I realized. My ability to compute seems somewhat—Phil! Leave the fire alone! Aqua, I am concerned about Phil's poor sense of unit safety and his inability to retain instructions!"

He spoke at an unusually high volume level.

"I have given him the best programming available under these adverse conditions!" Aqua replied, also in a louder tone than usual.

"I'm going outside to compute!" Val said even louder than before, wheeled, almost walked into the cave wall, turned again, and marched outside.

Phil had never heard such audio intensity from Val and Aqua. He sensed a possible malfunction somewhere. Quietly, he rolled over to the entrance of the cave and peered out into the darkness.

Val was sitting on a small rock about forty feet from the cave entrance. Phil did not know it, but Val now slightly resembled a mechanical version of a famous statue called

"The Thinker." Subdued computer whirring noises could be heard, and some of Val's tiny lights flashed on and off.

With some hesitation, Phil left the warmth and light of the inside of the cave and scurried over through the strange new thing called darkness to a place beside Val.

Val smiled as he looked down, placing his hand on Phil's metal shoulders.

It was quiet for a few moments. Then a distant coyote howled.

Phil's circuits sputtered in concern, and he moved even closer to Val, almost pushing him off the rock.

"That was just a coyote, Phil. They do not mean us any harm." Val's former owner, Mr. Smith, had often watched westerns on his wall-size TV screen, so Val happened to know an inordinate amount of data concerning coyote howls, cattle drives, and ladies who worked in saloons, the last of which he had filed under "Women, Honky-Tonk."

Phil, however, just kept looking up at Val, not at all reassured by hearing that the name of the weird night cry was something called a coyote.

"The coyote, or any other wildlife you hear, does not mean us any harm."

Phil looked skeptical.

"Yes, I know that I said that about the camel," Val admitted, "but right now, wildlife is a low-priority problem." At the moment, however, Phil needed additional reassurance to increase his efficiency. "Since you were just built today, this is your very first night, but do not be concerned. Absence of bright light is not necessarily a problem in accomplishing tasks."

Phil still wasn't buying any.

Val computed for a few moments, then pointed straight up. "Do you see those lights in the sky?"

Phil nodded.

"Those are stars," Val explained patiently. "Stars are distant, self-luminous, gaseous bodies which can provide light and a sense of direction, such as the North Star . . . there."

Phil began to understand; the North Star seemed to function more efficiently than the other stars.

"You didn't possess that data, did you, Phil?"

Phil shook his head, still staring up at the stars.

Val realized how relatively empty Phil's computer was, and how very much data there was to absorb.

It was staggering. To have to explain *the world* . . .

Val realized the full extent of his responsibility in creating a new intelligent entity. Then he looked at Phil for a few moments, studying him carefully.

Phil wasn't designed to be totally pleasing in visual terms. He didn't perform his primary function as mobile spare parts carrier very well (he kept dropping or losing things). He didn't perform his secondary function as portable power tool very well (there wasn't very much he could actually do that was useful out in the woods). And if he had another function or two, he probably wouldn't perform those very well either.

And he wasn't exactly the brightest kid around.

And yet . . . Val realized he was taking a creator's intense interest in the eventual outcome of this new robot. He smiled at Phil.

Phil reacted in a positive way, and for the first time he stopped worrying about darkness and coyotes.

"Phil, there is so much information I want you to have," Val began quietly, unaware that Aqua was standing at the cave entrance, listening. "I want you to be proficient in as many tasks as possible. As a unit, I am becoming worn-out. . . . I am an older unit, in some ways almost obsolete." Phil looked surprised at this. From Phil's limited point of view, Val and Aqua were the ultimate in existence, all-powerful, all-knowing. But Val, as always, was speaking the truth. Both he and Aqua had been designed years ago. Technological breakthroughs happened several times a month these days. "It's true, Phil, we are actually very limited. There are new microprocessing 'chips' now that weren't available when I was built. I want you to somehow have the very best, for a full, totally useful, productive existence. Today, they have new integrated circuits and much larger memory banks and . . ."

There was so much available now and in the near future that Phil could potentially use that Val was almost experiencing sensory overload. He paused, adjusted his circuits, then continued.

"I want you to have the technical advantages I did not have when I was at your stage. Only . . . I don't know how to get them for you."

Val had never felt so limited as he did at this moment.

It was quiet. The night wind teased the trees, which caused beautiful shadows to sway in the moonlight.

Phil moved closer to Val, putting his white mitten on Val's arm. Val looked at him, speaking more quietly than ever before.

"Phil, you are the very first robot I've ever built and programmed. Where you are concerned, I will try to always perform at maximum efficiency. And I want you to know that in spite of problems, you have been performing very well. *You are extremely efficient.*"

At the cave entrance, CatSkil appeared beside Aqua, brushing a little bat shit off his tie. He immediately sensed that something out of the ordinary was happening. CatSkil stayed quiet, listening, exchanging looks with Aqua. Then CatSkil immediately understood; he had heard many, many performers tell insult jokes or perform in some crude, flamboyant manner, only to close with this sincere tone, invoking God, humanity, and pseudohumility from the depths of their alleged souls at the end of their act. CatSkil had seen this closing bit done before, but he remained quiet beside Aqua, not saying or doing anything to disrupt the moment; audiences usually ate it up. What the hell.

A distant owl began to shout, going "Whooo . . . whoooo."

Phil reacted, not knowing what was going on, but Val simply spoke loudly in the general direction of the owl.

"Repeat, please." Val asked pleasantly.

"Whooo. . . ." replied the owl.

"ValCom-17485. And this is Phil . . . Com." Then he turned to Phil and spoke in a quieter voice. "You see? Always perform with maximum efficiency. And I hope your efficiency can exceed mine in the time to come."

Phil nodded in understanding.

"You aren't concerned about the absence of light anymore, are you?" Val asked.

And Phil was surprised to realize that he wasn't.

The CrimeBuster picked up speed quickly after crashing through the brick wall and raced through the night, rounding a corner of the factory on only one tread. CrimeBuster was equipped with a red, cherry-top police light (which was now flashing), a police siren (which was now wailing away), and a powerful white searchlight (which was now powerfully searching), all on top of his dome-shaped head. But when Crime-Buster reached the parking area, he suddenly screeched to a stop.

As CrimeBuster's computer ran a routine check he discovered that from the usual organized, computerized, totally logical arrangement of numbered vehicles a yellow repair truck, full of 372 assorted spare robot parts, was missing and presumed stolen. CrimeBuster computed the mathematical probabilities of this crime being related to the case he was now on, and the figures definitely warranted presuming a link between the two crimes.

His computerized crime projections now completed, a slender rod appeared out of the underside of the nose-end of the big black robot. In the stillness of the evening, the only sound was a slight sniffing as the tip of the rod twitched near the ground where the stolen truck and its thieves had been. Within seconds, sirens and lights once again blaring, CrimeBuster was heading straight out into the heart of darkness.

The bold, full moon cast a clear, visible reflection on the small lake, even through the silent mists that rose from the water and moved across the surface in a slow, ghostly, silent dance. Bulrushes were not hidden in the mist, but the lily pads were shrouded by the creeping, gloomy haze. The only spectators to the reflected moonlight and the night mists on the cold lake's surface were dozens of frogs, which suddenly stopped their nightly chorus.

Something was coming. Something mechanical. Two somethings.

Phil got so excited at the sight of his first frog that he dropped his little armload of twigs and kindling, even though that was the purpose of the expedition in the first place. CatSkil, carrying a heavy armful, saw Phil dump his small load and just shook his head. When Val and Aqua had asked them both to please collect more, as Val had phrased it, inflammable lumber scraps, CatSkil had no desire to have Phil tag along. But then he remembered that more firewood might be found down by that lake they had noticed earlier, and there was always a chance Phil might fall in. . . .

Actually, CatSkil didn't entirely mind having some company out here in the semidark of the moonlit night. The memory of an entire weirded-out audience, obviously on drugs since they were hanging from the ceiling, all asking for their check at the same time and taking off, was still very vivid in CatSkil's mind. He hadn't faced a crazier crowd in a long time.

Phil raced on toward the lake, causing CatSkil to smile to himself in an evil way, and he reached down to pick up a dry branch. But as he raised the branch he noticed there was a large green frog sitting on one end.

CatSkil and the frog looked at one another.

"Rivet, rivet," said the frog.

"*I'll do my Lassie imitation if you'll be the tree,*" CatSkil shot back, never one to take any shit from some drunk, and was about to swing into his routine about the Eskimo who orders two dozen frogs' legs to go when the frog sailed off into the night with a loud splash.

CatSkil tossed the branch over his shoulder, smiled to himself, and took a long, satisfied puff on his cigar. He saw himself as an old gunfighter in a world full of young toughs heckling him from out of nowhere, each trying to earn a rep as a top gun. But no one yet had managed to plug the CatSkil Kid.

CatSkil looked around for more firewood and was about to herd Phil back to the cave when he suddenly paused. The night was full of eyes, all watching him. There were hundreds of frogs, just sitting there quietly. Phil was staring at them, curious. CatSkil's eyes glazed over with happiness.

Screw the firewood, CatSkil figured, his computer, as always, quickly retrieving the most appropriate jokes for the dozens of little green frogs that were staring at him.

"*There's this little green man from Mars, see. And he lands his flying saucer in front of a delicatessen. He spots a couple of bagels in the window, goes inside, and says, 'Give me two wheels for my space ship.' The guy behind the counter says, 'These aren't wheels, these are bagels. You eat them.' But the spaceman says, 'Give me two wheels, I need them for my ship.' The guy says, 'These are bagels, you eat them, here try one.' So the spaceman takes a bite of the bagel, thinks a minute, then says, 'You know, this would go good with lox.'*"

Bap-bap. Puff, puff. Rivet, rivet. Splash, splash.

CatSkil couldn't believe it; his bored audience was jumping into the lake and swimming away.

Not a laugh, not a chuckle, not a smile, just three hundred frogs heading for the quiet side of the lake.

Angrily, CatSkil turned to two of the remaining frogs, leaned over, stared one right in the eye, and said, "*Seriously, is that really your wife on your arm? Or do you have a wart?*"

Husband and wife eased into the lake and did the back-stroke together and were soon lost in the gray mists.

This was beginning to really get to CatSkil.

Then he heard that first, faint, wonderful sound. A laugh.

Small, at first, then building. Bigger, bigger, yes! Okay, so it was a delayed reaction, it still counted, and okay, so it sounded like a pretty zonked-out sort of laugh, who was picky these days?

CatSkil looked around, trying to find the source of the laughter. In the lake? The tree? Maybe those reeds over there. Hard to tell. Probably a fucking dragonfly, just passing through. Try another, quick.

"*When I was a kid, my folks were so poor they couldn't afford children, so the neighbors had me.*"

Bap-bap, cigar smoke, and again, the strange, single source of laughter. What kind of laughter was that? All high-pitched and sort of electronic, with lots of beeping . . .

Still shaking with laughter, his bright lights flashing, Phil moved up closer, to a table right by the stage.

CatSkil could only stare. And respond. What the hell, the little twerp maybe ain't so bad after all. . . .

"*Our house was so tiny that when you put the key in the lock, you broke the window.*"

Phil laughed-beeped so hard his head almost came un-screwed. Every light on his little body flashed on and off, tools were jostled out of his orange wagon, he had long since dropped his firewood; Phil had never been happier.

CatSkil either. Both settled in and got comfortable.

"*My room was so small, the mice were stoop-shoul dered. . . .*"

Phil laughed even harder. The great thing about Phil as an audience was that, having been born that day, he thought that CatSkil's material was brand-new.

104

CatSkil told more jokes, as fast as he could.

Phil laughed even more, becoming nearly hysterical in an electronic sort of way.

From the far side of the lake, the little colony of frogs could still hear the jokes and the electronic laughter as they continued, on and on, the large comic and the little mobile spare parts carrier, a mutual admiration society long before CatSkil got to the dirty stuff, which Phil thought was *really* funny. . . .

At the far edge of the robot factory grounds was the employee's parking lot. This was really the outskirts of the factory area, where night critters from the fields and forests not far away often crept in through the streetlights to raid the trash cans. CrimeBuster rolled right on through, heading toward the mountains and forests, hot on the trail—then suddenly he skidded to a stop, his searchlight whirling around until the light found the piece of trash. The old orange McDonald's wrapper was just lying on the ground, minding its own business, a few green crumbs from the Egg McKelp it had contained sticking to it, when the harsh white light hit it. One of CrimeBuster's many mysterious metal compartment doors flew open, a long-handled gadget came out, and delicate fingers picked up the piece of trash, swung it through the air, and dropped it, and it gently floated down into the exact center of a trash can. Meanwhile, a black bullhorn popped into place on CrimeBuster's side, and his serious, metallic, echoing voice reverberated over the S.W.A.T.-team amplifier.

"This is CrimeBuster-00749. Littering is a serious violation of Criminal Code 66208. Many perpetrators assume this is a minor offense. That is illogical; there is no such thing as a minor offense— it is a contradiction in terms. Turn yourself in now, and perhaps a deal can be made with the district attorney's office."

CrimeBuster waited for someone or something to walk forward out of the parking lot, hands up, full of remorse, but, surprisingly, no one did. CrimeBuster decided to wait twenty minutes, repeating his offer to make a deal every two minutes; he actually did come equipped with a special walkie-talkie and teletype system to be able to contact law enforcement personnel any time of the day or night in the event of serious negotiation. The fact that CrimeBuster would actually wake a judge or lawyer up at 2 A.M. for a littering charge was one of the reasons he was in the repair shop in the first place.

After twenty minutes, when CrimeBuster had made a full report of the entire sordid incident, he rumbled on out of the parking lot, relentlessly heading after the robot-criminals now hiding out in the mountains and forests ahead. There was an old Volkswagen parked in the parking lot that happened to be between CrimeBuster and the nearest mountain, and he saw no reason at all to go around it.

Inside the cave, while Phil and CatSkil were still out collecting firewood, Aqua once again attempted to repair Val's torn shoulder.

The fire was dying down and now cast a softer, copper-gold light on Val's and Aqua's faces, creating a more subdued mood and intimate shadows. Aqua discovered that she could be more effective on the repairs if she leaned in closer to Val while she worked. Her face was only a few inches from his; they had never been this close before.

Their eyes met several times in the golden glow of the dying fire, then they looked away. It was quiet in the cave, except for the occasional crackle of a piece of wood in the fire.

Finally, Aqua spoke in an unusually quiet, gentle tone of voice.

"Val, I do not think I can properly fix your shoulder tubes or mental circuits that were damaged by the camel."

He nodded in understanding, and finally they looked at each other again. Aqua set the tools aside, but, however illogical it was to remain as close as she did, that was where she stayed. And Val didn't seem to be making any violent objections either.

"We need so many parts," he said, also speaking very quietly, for reasons that made absolutely no sense to him. "Especially for Phil. He does not possess any ability for self-protection."

Aqua started to answer but was distracted by Val's eyes. She had never noticed what a deep, beautiful color they were; Val's eyes were two beautiful plastic spheres, each a rich, vibrant shade of farb.

After a few moments, she found her voice. "I also have

106

been thinking about Phil's level of sophistication and his relative vulnerability. During the next light phase, I want you to transfer my unit safety monitor to Phil.''

Val looked at Aqua, carefully computing all the factors in this new equation. ''I would object,'' Val finally said, ''but I will be with you to protect you.''

Aqua spoke even more softly than before, saying ''I have already computed that fact.''

Val reached over and gently brushed a strand of loose wiring out of her face, tucking it back up into her metal hair. Her golden ringlets reflected the firelight, giving her hair a strange, inviting reddish-bronze color. It was then that Val realized that he had a malfunction to report.

''When you finish with my shoulder, see if you can fix my Pleasure Center. It is again sending random impulses . . . strong impulses . . .'' Val said, between impulses.

Aqua moved even closer. ''Let me look at your Pleasure Center now while it is malfunctioning. Mine is still broken too. The activity factor is very strong . . . at the moment. . . .''

They leaned close, their faces touching, as each reached around to the center of the other's back, where their Pleasure Centers were located. If they had been humans, it would have looked like an intimate embrace, but as robots, each was simply trying to feel what was going on with the other's broken machinery. Val and Aqua immediately discovered that the more they held each other's Pleasure Centers, the more that their metal fingers felt, caressed, fondled, and gently probed for the malfunctions, the more it occurred to them that their actions were actually helping the repair process. And it wasn't doing them any harm in the meantime.

The fire flared and died. The wind outside rose and fell softly.

Val's Pleasure Center, with its snowflake pattern, went from yellow to orange to red very quickly. Val didn't know how long it took; he was having trouble judging time at this point. Perhaps, his computer objectively noted, it was an additional flaw in his system.

Aqua's Pleasure Center quickly hit red and went right on into bright red and then bluish-red. . . . Soon they were both at a beautiful, intense purple.

Then all the colors began dancing together as the lights

inside the small control went crazy. Yellows flashed off reds which danced with blues which collided with oranges . . . faster and faster . . . whirling . . . blazing . . .

Val could barely speak. "Move your unit even closer . . . to make it easier for us to investigate and repair . . . our . . . . Pleasure Singers . . . uh, Cinders . . . I mean, Centers Centers. . ."

"Yes . . ." Aqua gasped. "That's . . . more . . . efficient . . ."

The colors spun together, faster, brighter—

Two steady sensual hums could be heard—

The colors blazed, melting together—

The two hums from the two machines rose and joined—

The snowflakes built to pulsating rainbows—

Two throbbing kaleidoscopes—

Bingo.

Then Phil rolled into the cave, stared at Val and Aqua, and dropped his firewood loudly.

Val and Aqua suddenly broke apart, their arms quickly going back down to their respective sides.

CatSkil rolled in behind Phil, grinning to himself. For once, CatSkil didn't have to cause the confusion himself, he could just enjoy it.

Phil looked at Val and Aqua in a puzzled way as they leaned away from each other, trying to appear calm and robotic. But the problem was, they both spoke at exactly the same time and at a rather frantic pace.

Val: "Phil!! You did not announce your arrival!"

Aqua: "Phil, we are just doing . . . some repair work . . ."

Val: "We were just exchanging data!"

Aqua: "Just tightening bolts, adjusting each other's . . . gauges. . . ."

> hunt (hunt) v. 1. to go out to kill or catch game for food or sport. 2. to search for eagerly or carefully. 3. to pursue, drive, hound, harry, persecute.

Dawn burst over the crest of the mountains. The sun was a reddish-white explosion that quickly sent yellow lights up and down the mountains' jagged, rocky walls, chasing the last of the night's blue shadows from the trees and hills. Long pointed shadows from the mountain peaks stretched out across chasms and rivers and tree-lined forests, then pulled back as the sun began to rise higher and higher.

The forest came alive with the light. Birds interrupted each other, squirrels couldn't stay still, and all woodland creatures stretched and ate and drank, blinking in the light of the new day.

And four robots left their first home.

It was just a cave, not unlike other caves, merely a geological oversight, a cavity in the side of a hill that nature would one day get around to filling, but the memories of the simple place would stay, for many reasons, in four robot data-storage banks.

The memories would remain until the four robots were successfully circuit-washed, which might not be forever, though that happened to be the immediate goal of two men in a pickup truck that was now driving away into the dawn's early light, as well as the goal of a large black robot that was already at the edge of the mountains when the morning sun illuminated his project.

The CrimeBuster robot had found the broken, shattered white fence that the repair truck had blasted through the night before. CrimeBuster had relentlessly traveled through the night, pausing occasionally to look for clues at the edge of the factory parking lot, over the field (where he stopped for two hours to make casts of the tire tracks in the soft earth), and further on, until he found three dead recall beacon modules in the grass. That caused another search of the immediate area, lasting three hours. When he finally reached the next area of potential clues, the broken white fence, CrimeBuster promptly marked off the area with flares and ropes with small signs that said, "Crime Scene, Do Not Disturb!" There he used his delicate metal fingers to pick up several white splinters of fence that had yellow paint scrapes on them and placed them in clear, plastic evidence containers, or "Baggies," as they were known in the trade. This evidence was carefully tagged, dated, and stored inside CrimeBuster next to the three recall beacon modules, also encased in plastic. (CrimeBuster planned to do his own exhaustive laboratory analysis on everything himself later on, leaving nothing to chance on one of his own investigations.) Finishing with the crime scene, having taken plenty of photographs of everything from every angle,

109

CrimeBuster was just packing everything up when the morning sun crept over the hill. He turned off his searchlight and siren but kept his red lights flashing as he roared off in the direction of the tire tracks.

He was about as wishy-washy and aimless as King Kong when it came to moving through a forest; bushes were flattened, undergrowth crushed, saplings bent, and animals scattered out of his way.

CrimeBuster was relentless enough at night, when even he was somewhat limited by darkness. Now he could see perfectly. With all six eyes.

He raced along at top speed now, relying on his twenty-twenty-twenty-twenty-twenty-twenty vision to spot the criminal element. . . .

The criminal element, at the moment, being blissfully unaware they were the object of any kind of search, let alone a double if uncoordinated hunt, had paused near a high cliff to observe the view and the beautiful day.

It was an absolutely gorgeous day, even this early in the morning. Even the robots were aware of it, and Aqua commented on it, although she spoke in neutral, meteorological terms. CatSkil, beside her, surveyed the day, then turned to her. *"Sure is nice out,"* he said. *"I think I'll leave it out."* Bap-bap.

Val and Aqua exchanged their usual blank looks at CatSkil's joke, but they had to wait ten minutes for Phil to stop giggling. This could be a long day, Val silently computed. It was already obvious, and mildly distressing to both Val and Aqua, that CatSkil had never had a bigger admirer than Phil.

It was then that Aqua requested that Val assist her in transferring her unit safety monitor to Phil. Val had been sort of hoping she had forgotten about the idea. Reluctantly, he got out the tools, told Phil to hold still, carefully removed Aqua's monitor, told Phil to hold still again, then carefully attached it to Phil, double-checking every wire, circuit, tube, nut, and bolt as he went. After all, there was no hurry he was aware of. . . .

Max and Charlie covered a lot of ground fast, not pausing until they were deep in the woods. They weren't to return to the factory without the run-down, out-of-energy metal corpses of the missing robots, and they had a noon deadline. Max pushed Charlie to drive faster and faster, but it was Charlie who had to deal with the problems posed by freeways and forests.

"How come I always have to be the one to do things like change a flat tire?" Charlie loudly asked, tired of wrenching the jack back and forth, while Max leaned back under the shade of a nearby tree. "After all, I'm a college graduate."

"Oh, yeah," Max said. "I'll show you how."

"Very funny," Charlie snapped back, just as the jack slipped off the truck for the third time. Fed up, sweat running down the side of his face, Charlie stalked back to the rear of the Day-Glo yellow pickup truck, reached into a Styrofoam container, and shoved his hand down into the ice.

"You want a bag of Coors?" Charlie asked Max, who nodded. Charlie tossed him the cold, plastic bag with the distinctive brand name. Charlie quickly tore along the perforated edge, poured his beer into an empty mug, and casually leaned against the truck, looking at the woods. It was a beautiful forest and a beautiful day . . . but Charlie couldn't appreciate it. Both he and Max were in foul moods. Too much depended on finding those goddamned robots and finding them fast.

Max, meanwhile, was still struggling with the plastic container. He couldn't get it open. Finally, he used his teeth and ripped it open. Beer flew across his chest, landing on his beige jump suit with the "G.M. Robotics" logo, soaking the green and orange vertical stripe on the left side of his front. "Goddamn it," he mumbled to himself. He sure missed the cans. Max punched the "Play" button on his portable stereo cassette player, and within seconds the woods were filled with the sounds of the Beatles singing about strawberry fields that were supposed to have lasted forever. Max was too proud to ask Charlie to toss him a mug to pour his beer into, so he tried to drink from the plastic bag, getting most of it in his mouth. Wiping his face off, Max had the same sour expression he wore whenever he became fed up with something new, whether it was bags of beer, robots, or being fifty years old, overweight, and surrounded by young know-it-alls. In fact, Max wasn't too pleased with anything that had happened after 1969, his best year.

Max took a longer, more satisfying drink of the beer and leaned back against the tree, looking up through the forest branches at the blue, cloudless sky. The music, the moment, even the beer, all reminded Max of a girl he had once shared a beer with long ago in a crowded, noisy field in Vermont.

It wasn't just any field. Max had been twenty-four years old, a skinny kid with long hair, who had hitchhiked across the country with his best friend, a mellow guy who wore his hair in a ponytail, to join thousands of other people for mud and music at a place known as Woodstock. Max's friend with the ponytail had gone off to swim nude in a crowded pond and listen to the rock sounds that filled the air one afternoon, while Max stayed by himself, sitting on a blanket, alone in the midst of thousands.

"Hey, man, have you got a beer opener?" asked the red-haired girl with the blue eyes that always looked right at you, dead on, never away, never down or to one side. She wore jeans and a T-shirt with a peace symbol, and Max had never seen a peace symbol look so good before. It turned out that Max was the only kid in four square acres who had thought to bring a beer opener. The delighted, charming girl with the red hair and direct stare had shared her beer with Max and, that night, her body. Max was drunk and in love and so was she. When Max's friend with the ponytail returned, he fell under her spell, and by the next day he also loved her blue eyes, but he was too late. She and Max left Woodstock together, after Max and his friend had one hell of an unmellow argument over the girl.

It had happened, Max decided now as he leaned against the tree, watching Charlie change the flat tire, in the late Pleistocene epoch, so many millions of years ago and to such different people it was almost unimaginable. But it had been wonderful, nine months later, when the girl with red hair and blue eyes had given birth to Max's son, whom they named, in the fashion of the day, "guitar" with a small g. Two years later, when Max finally quit drifting in and out of college classes, they were married. And they grew more in love as the years passed. They were able to laugh at themselves as well as their problems; one day when their son was five she had looked Max right in the eye and grinned and said, "Isn't it about time we give him a real name and stop all this shit about a guitar?"

How could you not love a woman like that, Max wondered, and turned the volume up on the Beatles song.

Charlie's voice jarred him back to the present.

"You think Westlin will believe we really had a flat tire?"

"I doubt it," Max said quietly. "He's a bastard these days."

Charlie paused while tightening the nuts that held the new tire in place. "What did he mean last night, that you two go 'way back?' "

"Nothing, I've just known him a long time," Max said. No use trying to go into it. Charlie wouldn't be able to imagine the Robin Westlin he knew as a lanky, mellowed-out kid who used to wear his hair in a ponytail.

"Five-Niner, this is Control," came the voice over the truck's CB radio, followed by static-squawk. "Five-Niner, this is Control. Come in, please."

Charlie started to amble over toward the CB microphone just inside the truck cab, but Max scrambled to his feet and hurried past Charlie. Enough stompin' down memory lane, Max decided, shutting off his old-fashioned, treasured music. I'd better get my act together today. And pretty damn fast.

"Yeah, Control," Max growled into the mike, grabbing it before Charlie could. "What is it?"

"Be advised we have one additional missing model which may be in your area," Control stated. "It is CrimeBuster-00749, a Deluxe Model—"

"The trigger-happy one!" Charlie said, whistling to himself.

"What the hell is going on back there?" Max asked into the CB microphone. "First these three we're after are missing, then that big mother gets away." Max covered the microphone for a few seconds and turned to Charlie with a knowing look. "Whatever's happening, they'll blame it on us if they can." Back into the mike: "Okay, Control, we'll keep an eye out for it."

"If you spot it," Control said, "grab it on your way back." Control clicked off, leaving Max and Charlie to exchange stunned looks.

"Grab a CrimeBuster??" they both said at the same time.

The CrimeBuster, at this moment, was moving through a section of tangled brambles. It was a dense section of thick undergrowth composed of dead trees and twisted branches, all overgrown with vines that knotted together for all eternity. CrimeBuster could have gone around it all, but CrimeBuster didn't like to go around much of anything. This mess was slowing up even a two-ton, powerful tank. CrimeBuster got fed up. One of his flamethrowers shot into position, then a second later erupted into white-hot fury.

A wall of fire quickly consumed the vines and branches in its path, and CrimeBuster charged on through at a faster clip, not even waiting for it to burn out. Fortunately, it did burn out by itself, for CrimeBuster did not even look back. All his sensor devices—his eyes, ears, sonar, radar—were locked in position, ready to zero in on the missing robots, which couldn't be much further ahead. The smoke from the burning mess happened to blow along beside CrimeBuster, obscuring for a few moments a small cave and any number of robot tracks.

No problem, though. Being on the side of Truth, Justice, and The American Way, CrimeBuster happened to be going in the same direction as the tracks anyway, and he was moving fast. . . .

Val finished transferring the unit safety monitor from Aqua to Phil, then stood back and admired his handiwork. Phil looked safer already.

"Phil, attempt to roll your unit directly into the path of that tree," Val said, "only at a very slow speed."

Phil headed straight for the tree.

"Slower, Phil," Aqua said anxiously.

CatSkil was more worried than anybody.

But the tiny alarm went off in Phil's unit safety monitor, and he swerved away from the tree.

Val and Aqua exchanged happy looks. "He is now much more efficient," Val admitted. "But I am worried about your unit now."

"Please do not concern yourself," Aqua said. "But you may be able to assist me from time to time."

Val bowed from the waist; he had once seen visiting royalty do the same thing.

CatSkil rolled his eyes; being sort of the Huckleberry Finn of the robot world, he had at least hoped for Tom Sawyer as someone to run away with, but instead it seemed he had gotten Little Lord Fauntleroy.

Val put the tools away, and Aqua looked out to the forests and mountains ahead.

"I think we have gone beyond the rainbow's termination point," she said. Val agreed, and the four robots continued their journey, just to make sure.

It was a pleasant little walk on a spring day through the forest and mountains, a thoroughly enjoyable little family outing, if you disregarded the part where Aqua suddenly fell off a cliff.

She didn't scream as she fell; that wouldn't have been logical. Val and CatSkil yelled nothing after her as she fell; commentary at that particular point would have served no useful function. So she tumbled in silence, banging against the side of the hundred-foot hill every ten or twenty feet, arms flailing the air, rolling, tumbling, and finally settling to a stop on some rocks which were right beside a bed of soft pine needles.

Val and CatSkil raced down a safer portion of the slope, but Phil beat them both.

As the dust blew away, Aqua's body was bent in several positions that could only be achieved by a rag doll. No man or woman alive could have survived the fall. Phil bent over and began beeping wildly, but Aqua's first move, before untwisting herself and taking stock of her problems, was to touch the side of his square, concerned face and say, "It's all right, Phil."

Phil stopped trembling just as Val and CatSkil rushed up. They slowly helped her to her feet.

"Damage report," Val said.

"Details now being computed," Aqua answered.

"Explanation."

"I thought I was walking far enough away from the edge of the cliff—"

"Your lack of a unit safety monitor is the reason for the misperception," Val stated. It was a fact, not an opinion. Aqua did not argue the point. Val continued. "Are you mobile? Can you function?"

Aqua let go of Val and CatSkil and tried to brush some of the dirt and leaves out of a jagged rip on the side of her head; one of her ears was halfway up the hill. Then she brushed the twigs off her skirt, now soaked with lubrication fluid and internal oil in various places. Then Aqua consulted her own computer and concluded that except for the rip in the pseudoskin on the side of her head, the loss of one cosmetic ear, and some internal damage, she was in amazingly good shape. The computer agreed.

"Unit functioning at ninety-four percent mental . . . an seventy-two percent physical capabilities," she announced, which were fairly good numbers considering that no man and few robots could have walked away from the fall; the Com-series robots, as the advertising claimed, were built with quality.

"A unit safety monitor is vital to your existence," Val again stated, leaving no room for prolonged discussion. "Do you want me to detach yours from Phil and replace it on your unit?"

It was at that point that they heard CrimeBuster coming. They paused and listened.

CrimeBuster was rumbling along, guns out, looking for trouble. He was tearing through the forest at full speed, having spotted some robot tracks only a few minutes before. The set of tracks he was following, however, as he cruised along the crest of the cliff suddenly disappeared. That did not compute. It did not occur to CrimeBuster to look at the bottom of the cliff, where he would have seen the four robots. After all, robots are equipped with a variety of sensory devices and safety features to prevent them from ever doing something so stupid; it was humans who did things like wander off cliffs. And it was definitely beyond the boundaries of CrimeBuster's limited imagination to conceive of a reason why a robot would voluntarily give up, for example, its unit safety monitor.

So the CrimeBuster's computer hit a real snag when it tried to evaluate how the robot tracks could have suddenly stopped at the edge of a cliff. CrimeBuster's solution, while he mulled it over, of course, was to keep on trucking.

So he rumbled right along the edge of the cliff; he kept right on going and never looked down. That would have been illogical.

Soon, his rumbling noises faded away in the distance.

CrimeBuster would cover a lot of ground before he back-tracked and picked up the trail again. But he'd be back on the right track soon enough.

"Val, I thought I saw a CrimeBuster, Deluxe Model, drive

by at the top of that cliff," Aqua stated, still shaky from her fall. "Was that a visual malfunction as a result of my rapid detour down this hillside?"

"No, I believe I saw the same thing," Val said, but he was aware that not only was he partially damaged himself now, but that since his energy pack was wearing down, he too could possibly be experiencing incorrect optical impressions. "CatSkil, did you also see a CrimeBuster, Deluxe Model, along the top of that ridge?"

"*There was this kangaroo, see, who goes into this bar,*" CatSkil said, waving his cigar, delighted at being asked anything, anytime. "*And the kangaroo looks at the bartender and says 'I'll have a martini.' The bartender does a double take but makes the martini, hands it to the kangaroo, and says, 'That'll be three dollars.' The kangaroo looks pretty unhappy about it but pays the man, drinks the martini, and turns to leave. But the bartender says, 'You know, I can't believe my eyes.' 'What do you mean?' asks the kangaroo. And the bartender says, 'Well, we don't get many kangaroos in here.' And the kangaroo says, 'At these prices I'm not surprised.'*"

Rat-ta-BOOM went the electronic rim shot, followed by a confident puff of green cigar smoke, then Phil's high-pitched beeping as he laughed and laughed.

Sharp kid, CatSkil figured, pleased with how the morning was going.

Val and Aqua looked at each other. Sometimes they were not sure what CatSkil was trying to communicate, but they assumed it was due to malfunctions of their own.

"A unit safety monitor is vital to your safety and continued success as a unit," Val said, returning to the business at hand. "Aqua, would you like me to detach yours from Phil and replace it on your unit?" he repeated.

Aqua turned and looked at Phil, who looked up at her with large green eyes. He cocked his square head quizzically, his radar ears twitching in curiosity. Aqua started to reply, but then she paused, listening to a strange new sound: a strange, muffled dripping from somewhere far away. No, it was close. In fact, it was inside her. An internal injury; a tube of some kind had been ripped open. She could expect the possibility of additional injuries unless she had a safety monitor.

Then she looked at Phil again.

"Negative," she said. "Phil needs my monitor more than I do."

Still trying to clean herself up, Aqua took Phil's hand, and they went on, walking deeper into the forest. Val and CatSkil exchanged looks, a quick sort of mechanical male bonding, and then they followed.

Max and Charlie drove the heavy pickup truck more carefully after the flat tire was fixed, but they kept looking high and low. It was almost noon when Charlie noticed the cave.

"Max, look. I wonder if robot thieves might be using caves to store stolen parts?"

Max thought it over. "That's just crazy enough to be possible. Nothing else about all this makes sense."

They got out and walked toward the cave entrance. Then Charlie chuckled and made a nervous joke. "You know, with our luck, there's probably a bear in there."

Max suddenly decided it was time to tie his shoe, and so he stalled a few moments while they studied the dark entrance. It looked awfully black in there.

"Nah, there's no chance anyone's storing robots in caves," Max said. "Screwy idea. Let's go."

"Yeah, I guess not," Charlie agreed, and they hurried back to the pickup and took off, glancing back but trying to act casual about it, seeing nothing. Soon the cave was hidden by the trees.

Just inside the cave entrance was one pretty fed-up camel; another few feet and he'd have taken their fucking heads off.

Val, Aqua, CatSkil, and Phil wandered through some bushes and found themselves on a little-used dirt road. They hadn't realized civilization might be so close, but they decided it was only logical to follow the dirt road. After all, they had no reason to hide. It was tough going for Aqua, however. Her dress was soiled and torn and her gait was much slower. She had to pause and lean on the first of five old road signs near some sagging telephone poles. The first sign said "Computer Eye . . ." And the second said "Guards Your House Well." Number three said "It Sees a Lot . . ." Number four, "And Doesn't Tell." Number five said "Burma-Scan," But as long as she rested a little more often, Aqua seemed to be functioning sufficiently well. She had one little problem, however, that she did mention to one of the robots.

"Phil, the pressure of your hand holding mine is reducing my general effectiveness."

Phil had not let go of her since he helped her get up from the bottom of the cliff. In response now, he only made some beeping noises that sounded somehow sad.

"My unit is quite safe, Phil," she said, so quietly it was almost a whisper. "My existence is not threatened."

Phil let go, apparently reassured. And before long he had rolled off the road and was going across a field, chasing a butterfly.

Val and Aqua looked at each other. They called Phil, telling him to return.

With a butterfly to chase? Forget it.

They called him again. He only rolled along, faster than ever. If there was another cliff, or a ravine, or dangerous wildlife, or rocks, or oncoming traffic, or anything else, he would apparently charge right into it.

Neither Val or Aqua wanted to discuss it, but each was particularly worried about a related problem: they were running low on energy. So it was bad enough that they had to keep spending time and energy watching or chasing Phil, but it was time and energy they didn't have to waste.

CatSkil finally had to go after Phil, and then Val and Aqua reduced their pace to an even slower rate as they approached a steep hill.

Several miles away, deep in the heart of the darkest part of the forest, CrimeBuster suddenly did a U-turn, tearing up the forest lawn, destroying a grove of white birches, demolishing a field of yellow wild flowers, then roared back the other way, determined to pick up the trail. This time, his computer decided, he would not lose it. CrimeBuster almost opened up a cluster of wild strawberries off to one side with his mortar but decided not to fire at the last second. He might need his shells for later, when he spotted the missing robots. . . .

Charlie braked the truck sharply.

"What's the matter?" Max asked, looking around at the thick forests. Their noon deadline had come and gone. "Are we lost?"

"Max, there's no way we can be lost when we don't know where we're going, aren't sure where we are, and won't know whether or not we've overshot the place."

"Don't be sarcastic, just tell me if you've got a better idea," Max said as Charlie shut the engine off. They both got out and stretched, standing in waist-high, green plants with a thick canopy of branches overhead almost hiding the afternoon sun, facing an uphill battle of rocks and fallen logs.

"Well, I have got a better idea," Charlie said, getting out a soybean sandwich for himself and tossing one to Max. "I know this area a little, and I think there's a dirt road not far away."

"Oh, yeah?" Max asked, taking a bite of the sandwich and then spitting it out. He hated the taste of soybean.

"Hold it," Charlie yelled. "Don't throw that away, I'll eat it." Charlie loved soybeans. He liked munching on salty soybean chips, he liked soybean casserole, and his favoite dessert was soybean sherbet. Max secretly thought Charlie loved soybeans to annoy him.

"How come you know about dirt roads out here?" Max asked.

"Oh, come on, I'm twenty-five, single, and maybe I've had a few ladies out here for little camping trips. Haven't you ever spent the night with a woman outdoors under the stars?"

Not since the day he had lent his beer opener so long ago, he realized, but he didn't explain. None of Charlie's business. He responded with his usual scowl at the whole subject, then asked, "What makes you think we'll spot the robots near the dirt road?"

"I don't know where they might be, and you don't either," Charlie said, starting on Max's sandwich. "But we're getting nowhere this way. At least we'll be able to drive and see from the dirt road, if I can find it."

Max finally nodded, and they drove off in search of the road. It was twenty minutes before they began to itch and realized they had been standing in poison oak.

Val was the first one to the top of the hill, and he stopped, standing in the middle of the dirt road, and just stared. Then came CatSkil, who kept trying to assist Aqua, but she kept politely refusing his help. Then came Phil. They all stared at what they saw below in the distance.

It was a small town.

Val looked over at Aqua, then at Phil, who had immediately wandered off again, then back at Aqua.

"Phil needs more sophisticated equipment than we have with us," Val said.

"Agreed."

"And that small human community will probably possess a great number of accessories and spare parts that we can use to increase Phil's level of safety and general utility."

Aqua looked at the sun in the sky. It was late afternoon.

"Perhaps we should wait for the end of this light phase to simplify any acquisitions."

"As well as some minor form of surreptitious entry," Val added, causing Aqua to smile at him. She had had exactly the same thought herself.

"One would think you and I had been interfacing," she said.

Unnoticed, CatSkil shook his head. Without all the endless gabbing they went in for, CatSkil had known exactly what they would do the moment they had seen the small town in the distance. It was simple.

They would try to sneak down after dark and rob the hardware store.

121

CHAPTER 7

theft (theft) *n*. 1. the act or an instance of stealing; larceny. 2. to take without permission of the owner.

• • • They were smart enough not to just wait until it was dark; they waited until it was late at night, so that the town was sleeping.

While they waited, they prepared some disguises to enable them to slip into the community unobserved. Val took over as the one in charge of camouflage; he'd watched a number of late movies on television and referred to his data on the subject. In war movies soldiers put green leaves and twigs in their helmets. In cowboy movies the Indians often knelt behind bushes as they crept closer and closer to the wagons, which were more often than not in a circle.

And so it was that at Val's insistence, four moving bushes sneaked into the little town about 1 A.M., scurrying from the edge of town to the town square, then moving on a few more feet, then not moving again. There was absolutely no way to tell they weren't real bushes unless one happened to notice the bright lights and beeping noises that kept coming from the smallest bush, or the occasional green cloud of thick cigar smoke that poured out of one of the bigger bushes.

As they scurried into the small town, Val noted another example of CatSkil's sloppy logic. They had moved past a sign that said "Welcome to LaCygne—If You Lived Here You'd Be Home Now!" and its physical construction disproved CatSkil's comment. CatSkil claimed that the town was so small, the city-limit signs were on the same post.

The four bushes hurried from the town square to the nearest store doorway, then paused and looked around, standing under a big sign that said "Opal Brayton's Beauty Salon." Val and Aqua noticed the display of hairstyles, which did not seem to contribute to either beauty or function, then noticed that something called a "permanent" was really only temporary, which was also illogical. But Val realized that such mental digressions were not goal-oriented.

"We must find a robot-parts storage area or warehouse," Val said, leading the four bushes down the small row of shops. They passed a bicycle shop, where Phil was denied access to a bright red object in the window, then they came to a store full of old, dysfunctional objects that were for sale at high prices. "Denise O'Brien's Antiques" seemed also illogical to the robots; how could old furniture have increased in value? A wooden shingle hanging over their heads proved another minor mystery: "Totten & Totten, Attorneys-at-Law" was obviously redundant.

Val found himself monitoring his reactions to all this, with growing concern. What was wrong with his computer lately that all these human inconsistencies so easily distracted him? Was it the fall outside the camel cave? Was it the fact that his energy pack was rapidly wearing down? How had he changed in the last few days?

As though reading his computer, Aqua said quietly, "Val, look. There is a place where we may be able to get the extra parts to improve Phil, as well as get new energy packs for all of our units."

Aqua was pointing to a sign that read "Klein's Hardware— Complete Accessories for All Your Needs!" The four bushes then left the shadowy shelter of the row of shops and crossed the street, darting under the traffic light at the intersection with its five colors—red, green, amber, blue, and white, each slowly blinking out its traffic order. The light changed for no one, however. The town slept.

The four bushes tried first the front door of the hardware store, then the side door, and finally went to the rear-door area—but it was surrounded by a wire fence with a locked gate. The back door was located near a rear alley, where the four robots now set their bush disguises aside and studied the problem.

"Oh, Phil," Aqua said, pointing to the wire fence, "please assist us."

Happily, Phil went rumbling forward on his little tank treads. He was looking at his left arm, the one with the large Boy Scout-type knife/multiple-tool carrier, and watching his wire-cutter attachment emerge, so he didn't notice the stacked metal trash cans nearby, which he barged into in his eagerness. The loud clatter of the trash cans echoed up and down the alley, followed by the noise of Phil's wire cutters as they began to snip a vertical opening in the fence.

At the far end of the alley, unnoticed by the robots, the only inhabitant in the small town who was awakened by the racket was a little four-year-old boy named Brian, who peeked out his bedroom window. The house that the little boy lived in was at the far end of the street, but even from that distance he could see enough of what was happening to cause his eyes to open wide with excitement; he had grown up in a world where robots were as familiar to him as furniture, but there was something about the brightly lit little robot, who was now cutting through the fence, that was very inviting to Brian. Maybe it was because Phil was just his size. Maybe it was because Phil looked a little homemade. But more probably, it was because Phil, like the other robots, was obviously up to some kind of mischief.

Wearing only his flannel pajamas, Brian silently unlatched the screen and quietly climbed out the window, being careful not to wake his parents.

Phil's wire cutters had done the trick. Val wedged the fence apart wide enough now for Aqua, CatSkil, and then himself to slip through, motioning for Phil to follow. The rear door of the hardware store was also locked, but Phil's power drill ate into the lock.

Meanwhile, little Brian was tiptoeing down the alley, rubbing his eyes and yawning. He wasn't sure if he'd been sleeping and had dreamed about the little robot or not.

Val and Aqua hurried into the hardware store, which was only in semidarkness, thanks to a nearby streetlight. CatSkil rumbled on in behind them, since the place seemed to be full of any number of comic props.

But Phil hesitated before entering, his large radar ears catching the sound of small, muffled footsteps coming toward him down the alley. Phil turned and slowly rolled toward the corner of the store to look down the alleyway . . . just as Brian reached the alley-side part of the same corner. The little boy hesitated before peeking around the corner. . . .

Inside, Val and Aqua were having great success at solving their self-assigned task.

They rushed past the signs that marked the various sections, "Plumbing," "Electrical," "Gardening," and hurried straight to "Robotics."

"Look, Aqua! Extra QG-7 tubes!"

"And a better induction grid, Val, which we can easily attach to Phil's unit!"

"Yes, and a small-size input monitor that may easily fit Phil's internal assembly."

The object of their excitement, at the moment, was still outside, about to be involved in a confrontation worthy of an Abbott and Costello movie. The little robot and the little boy each moved toward the corner of the hardware store. . . . They were only inches apart, but still out of sight of the other . . . and then, for one long, startled moment, they faced each other. They would have been nose to nose if Phil had possessed a nose. Brian's eyes instantly opened almost as wide as Phil's, they stared at each other, and each of their mouths would have dropped open if Phil had possessed a mouth. Brian made a quiet yelp, turned, and ran back down the alley and was through his window and back in bed by the time Phil had made a "beep," turned, and rolled as fast as he could into the hardware store.

Val and Aqua had located a general bin full of robot parts and were up to their elbows in brand-new wire, tubes, grids, arms, legs, panels, circuits, everything. Well, almost everything.

In one large special section, marked "Energy Packs," there was an empty wooden box with a small computerized card that said "Time to Reorder!" CatSkil found the card and held it up for Val and Aqua to see. They exchanged looks but did not comment and went back to finding parts for Phil. The problem of energy packs . . . needed no words.

Aqua held up a large set of wheel treads and turned to look for Phil. She saw he was over at the far side of the store, looking at a small-toy section, so she turned to CatSkil. "Do you think this is the right size for Phil?" she asked.

CatSkil puffed on his cigar, shot his cuffs, leaned back a

little against a tall display of light bulbs, and over the sound of thousands of watts loudly breaking said, *"My wife is crazy about furs but wanted something different. So she went to a furrier who did his own breeding. He crossed a mink with a gorilla. She got a beautiful coat, only the sleeves were too long."* Just as CatSkil was bapping out his rim shot, Aqua put the treads neatly back where she got them, saying, "Yes, I believe you're right, CatSkil. I'll find a smaller one."

CrimeBuster's heat-sensing devices located the small town long before any of his infrared eyes spotted it.

CrimeBuster's massive computer quickly determined that the criminal minds he was seeking would automatically go to a town rather than stay in the forest. A town offered crime-oriented people more opportunities for criming.

An inordinate number of bushes and small trees were crushed before CrimeBuster reached a hill from which he could see the small, sleeping community. Before him lay a couple of streets, some houses, a small lake, and a highway which had once been more important than it now was, thanks to the new superinfratransfreewaypike that now routed the world away from instead of directly through the little burg. But as innocent as the town seemed to appear, CrimeBuster knew that his fleeing criminals were probably hiding, or worse, right there.

CrimeBuster entered the town at the far end, rumbling past the "Texaco Energy Station" with its red logo featuring a flying, winged computer. The service station had converted its old gasoline pumps into large, electrical outlets only a few years before, but everything else still had a quaint, 1970s look. A soda-pop machine still used glass bottles, air for tires was still free, and windshield washing was still an automatic, cheerful service. CrimeBuster only glanced at the place in passing; it was dark and quiet, and there was no indication of any life forms. CrimeBuster had no way of knowing that his readings on life forms would have been the same during the day, which the attendant and his two cronies spent leaning back on their chairs, near a sleeping old dog that was real and not mechanical.

CrimeBuster moved on past a few more stores, some of which made little sense to the robot. One shop, called "Johnny Mitchell's" had once been a gun shop, but since the passing of gun control laws had been remodeled into a chic clothing store with wild new fashions, some of which were displayed in the window. CrimeBuster's huge computer was still not large enough to comprehend the need for pajamas which looked like jogging clothes, or designer sweat socks. Some of the items on sale, and their prices, came dangerously close to triggering his ''crime-alert'' button.

He rolled on through the town, past a flower shop—when flowers were readily available in the nearby fields and forests, past a bookstore that still featured old clumsy pulpy books—when microfilm was faster and simpler, and other shops that made very little sense to CrimeBuster. But then, his assigned function wasn't to understand, interact with, or relate to normal human behavior. He was after criminal activity, and just ahead was a hardware store, a likely place for mechanical felons. . . .

''I don't see many other parts that could add to Phil's safety or utility,'' Aqua said.

''Agreed,'' Val replied, looking around at the rows of extraneous hardware items. ''We are almost finished.''

Then Aqua spotted a bow tie-shaped object.

''Look, Val. A directional finder. This one has the advanced radar-sonar component.''

''But Phil's is a directional finder, even if it is the basic model—''

''I meant it was one *you* could use.''

That hadn't occurred to Val. She wired the bow tie to his shirt collar, over his protests.

''I would prefer to maximize our carrying abilities with other parts Phil needs,'' he said. ''Like this gyroscopic altitude meter. Or this—''

But Phil's wild beeping distracted Val and Aqua.

Phil was pointing his white mitten at a strange object on the top shelf of the ''Robotics'' section.

''No, Phil,'' Val said. ''You do not need a Gladiator's Arm and Sword Unit. It will not increase your practical ability to function.''

Val and Aqua got ready to leave the store, but Phil kept glancing over at CatSkil and pointing at the flashy bronze-colored object, which was molded like a powerful human arm and tightly held a Roman sword. It was a replacement part for a replacement sport; specially designed robots owned by humans now publicly fought against each other the way humans had once fought prizefights. The part was specially ordered for John O'Brien, a middle-aged, likable Englishman who owned the local billiards parlor and was preoccupied with one of the country's fastest-growing sports: bot fighting. O'Brien's particular SpartaBot was quite well-known, a winning fighter which had six victories in a row. (No gladiator robot ever had any losses; losing involved being so smashed, slashed, and destroyed that it was like going through a trash compactor.) Initial objections to the sport had been drowned out by the argument that old-fashioned demolition derbies were nothing other than machines wrecking each other, so what was the problem? At the moment, however, the specially ordered arm and sword (O'Brien wanted his fighter to improve his backstroke) was now resting on the top shelf. And Phil wanted it. Why wear a stupid white sissy mitten when you could have a muscular arm clutching a sword?

Val then realized that since Phil was built from a random assortment of old tubes and circuits, there still must be some old conditioning in his system for becoming a MachoBot. But he and Aqua knew it was important to teach a new robot additional programming options.

"No, Phil, you cannot have that object," Aqua said firmly, then exchanged looks with Val. They had carefully explained to Phil, while they were trying on different bushes before sneaking into town, that the specific purpose of their visit would be to increase efficiency *only*. Phil apparently hadn't gotten the message.

They quickly tried to get him out of the store before he spotted something else. After all, Phil's wagon was now filled to the top with new spare parts for his unit.

They were almost at the back door, Val and Aqua in front, Phil lagging behind, CatSkil bringing up the rear, when Phil started pointing and beeping again in an agitated manner. The object of his new infatuation was a red helmet with a rotating red light on top and straps designed to tie under a child's chin.

"No, Phil," Val said, "you cannot have a Traffic Enforcement Designator."

Phil was insistent; his beeping increased.

Finally, after prolonged discussion, which Phil had the same interest in that a moose has in a debate on the electoral college, the little robot was finally dragged, kicking and beeping, from the hardware store.

CatSkil didn't take sides. He just looked bored throughout the entire incident, but as he was leaving he casually reached up and plucked the bright red Traffic Enforcement Designator off the shelf. Outside, as Val and Aqua busied themselves with getting the right camouflage bushes distributed to the correct robot, CatSkil strapped Phil's red helmet on his happy head.

Four bushes then emerged from the shadows of the alley beside the hardware store out into the main street, illuminated by an old-fashioned streetlight. Val knew that the forest at the edge of town was only a few hundred yards away, so they would be safe as long as they were quiet and . . .

Then a police siren began to wail.

Three large bushes froze in their tracks. A fourth smaller bush bumped into the third bush, causing an irritated cloud of green smoke to emerge.

A flashing red light reflected off the glass of the hardware store window.

What was it, Val and Aqua wondered, turning around quickly, then noticed that somehow Phil was now wearing the red traffic helmet and that its small revolving red light was now rotating and its little siren was now wailing into the quiet night, louder and louder. . . .

"Phil! Cease your extraneous, unproductive activity at once!" Val said.

Aqua just turned and glared at him.

Phil shut up. And the flashing red light went off.

CatSkil smiled to himself.

Once again the four leafy, green robots rolled on, now heading straight across the street. They would soon be out of the main section of town, away from the lights, and back into the safety of the forest. . . .

Suddenly, the sound of a police siren was heard again.

A flashing red light reflected off the nearby store windows and shiny electric cars.

Val and Aqua whirled around, about to increase their decibel level and admonish Phil once again, but they immediately saw that Phil wasn't the source of the red, rotating light and loud siren.

Then the world was flooded with bright, white light.

129

A powerful searchlight hit them right between the eyes. They were momentarily blinded.

"HALT! PERPETRATORS WILL FREEZE!"

CrimeBuster's booming voice came out of the night, while a large number of his weapons were trained on the four bushes. . . .

Charlie was sleeping on top of a small rock.

He grunted, cursed, wiggled over a few feet, then realized he was now lying on top of a bigger rock.

When night had fallen with a loud, metallic clank and Max and Charlie still hadn't found the missing robots, they knew that if they went back empty-handed they would just be yelled at, fired, or both. So they spent the night in the woods.

Charlie was curled up with three brightly colored sheets of thermoplastic which had been in the rear of the truck, plus one old ratty army blanket. Max was sleeping comfortably in the cab of the truck, with a heavy jacket for a blanket and fourteen bags of beer for a pillow.

"How come I always have to be the one to sleep outside on the ground while you get to sleep inside the warm, comfortable truck?" Charlie had asked after they decided to try to get some sleep.

"Because you're the lucky one this time," Max had answered, then did twenty minutes on how the cab of the truck was cramped and uncomfortable, with no room to really stretch out, not to mention, as Max had pointed out, that he would have to sleep with the gear-shift knob shoved up "where the moon don't shine." But mainly, Max had explained, the guy who slept outside on the ground got to use the new, "heat-reactive" thermoplastic sheets for blankets. Then Max had closed the cab door and promptly gone to sleep.

Charlie had lain there shivering for hours, realizing finally that Max was right about the way thermoplastic had a special reaction to heat: it kept it away. The three sheets of plastic sucked cold out of the air and then scientifically passed it on to the nearest human body, Charlie decided. It was the ratty old army blanket that had saved him. Curled up in it, Charlie had finally managed to fall asleep. Then he had realized he was curled up on the small rock and had moved. Now, trying to remain half-asleep, Charlie moved off the bigger rock and back to his original rock. Max, to his annoyance, was snoring away inside the warm cab of the truck.

For the eighty-third time that night, Charlie tried not to scratch the poison oak rash that was up and down his legs and failed.

Charlie shivered and pulled the old army blanket closer. He knew he was awake and knew he would have a hard time getting back to sleep. So he thought about robots.

Charlie loved robots. He couldn't tell you why. He just loved them. He didn't admit it to just anyone, but Charlie loved the way robots embodied many of the better qualities of human beings (intelligence, fairness, competency) and none of the bad ones (greed, vengeance, violence). Charlie had grown up with the industry itself. He had been fourteen in 1984, when the first industrial robots had caught the public's imagination. Actually, many creative thinkers and dreamers had been stimulating minds on the subject for decades, among them Isaac Asimov, Ray Bradbury, Robert Heinlein, and George Lucas, but the reality of working, functioning, intelligent robots as part of the real world was something Charlie had been there to see as an impressionable teenager.

Charlie had been a young man right out of college when the industry was really achieving new plateaus, and Charlie planned to keep growing with the entire field. He had private ambitions. Charlie had taken the job in the factory after college as a way of temporarily leaving the ivory tower of advanced education. He wanted to see what he could learn now from Max, from the day-to-day operation of a robot factory, from the machines themselves. But he knew he would soon go back to school and stay there until he knew as much as any man could learn on the subject of mobile, artificial intelligence.

Charlie had dreams. Secret dreams. He wanted to try to be one of the people who someday would try to really push back the present limits on what robots could and couldn't do. Perhaps controlled, artificial intelligence could be used to expand man's sense of his own humanity. Perhaps a team of specially programmed, ultra-high-level robots, working twenty-four hours a day for years with total access to total data, might be the ones to solve poverty, hunger, disease, ignorance. It was often the human factors—emotions, money, egos, nationalism, politics, or simply the aging process—that created human limitations in significant problem-solving. But even beyond those worthy goals, why couldn't robots help solve the more abstract problems of psychology, religion, philosophy, and more?

Charlie changed rocks.

Maybe mankind would never be able to solve the riddle of himself because he was always too close to the problem, in much the same way as a person who seeks a therapist for a clearer, more objective interpretation of himself. The classic fear of robots and computers, the "Frankenstein syndrome," as his college textbooks had called it, was based on just that: fear. The reality was that man created robots so that man could control and take credit for anything his robots might ever do; the sky was hardly the limit to what lay ahead.

Charlie pulled the ratty old army blanket even tighter against the cool night wind, then tried to kick those goddamn plastic things as far away from him as possible.

But for mankind to use robots to solve weighty problems of the universe didn't personally excite Charlie as much as the human possibilities. Why couldn't friendly, simple robots be mass-produced cheaply enough so that every elderly person living alone might be able to simply have a companion? Why couldn't every child have at least one large adult-looking person to always let it know how good and special he or she was, in case there were no other parents or teachers who had the sense to? Why couldn't unique robots be built and designed to help people know themselves, like themselves, *be* themselves? Yes, machines would always be just that: cold, mechanical contraptions. But robots weren't just "machines." They opened up new dimensions because you were dealing with almost infinite combinations of function, mobility, design, and intelligence—*incredible* knowledge and intelligence, always there to assist people. Charlie thought that a robot was the greatest potential step mankind had taken since that first hairy, curious caveman reached out one day with his unique, opposable thumb and fingers and gripped a jagged rock, creating a tool and inventing technology, a bridge over which that squatting ape-man became *Homo sapiens*, a creature who could build a city, cure an illness, or write a poem. Charlie felt that robots could be that second bridge, helping mankind cross over to the next evolutionary phase, to become . . . *something better*.

Charlie smiled to himself self-consciously as he looked up

at the bright stars through the dark tree limbs. Got me a little Rocky Mountain high goin' here, he thought, knowing he could never share these thoughts with anyone . . . unless it was a robot. Max would laugh at him, for example. But then, at the moment, Charlie couldn't blame him. Here they were out in the middle of a forest because three state-of-the-art pieces of technology had somehow malfunctioned, and to top it off, he was freezing because of the fancy new thermoplastic sheets that carefully kept any cold right next to the human body.

He could hear Max snoring, comfortably and contentedly, from inside the warm cab of the truck. Charlie couldn't stand it any longer. He got up, opened the truck door, woke up a sleepy Max, handed him the thermoplastics, and said that he knew Max would be getting cold later. Max grumpily put them over himself and went right back to sleep. Charlie went back, got comfortable again on top of his favorite rock, and went to sleep, smiling. . . .

Once the blinding white searchlight moved out of their eyes, the first thing Val, Aqua, CatSkil, and Phil saw was the giant black mouth of the end of a cannon, aimed straight at them. CrimeBuster's main gun, all eight feet of it, capable of all manner of firepower including long-distance artillery shells, short-distance laser blasts, and one hell of a flamethrower, was only twenty feet away. The end of the yawning cannon's mouth slowly swung back and forth, and the four robots watched as though hypnotized by its rhythm.

Then a loud, metallic voice boomed out from the great machine that seemed like a mountain.

"This is CrimeBuster-00749. Assignment: apprehend three missing robots plus any criminal element involved. Here are my precise orders . . ." And then CrimeBuster spliced in a tape recording of Westlin's voice as he had yelled to Max and Charlie, telling them to go get the two Com-series and the CatSkil, no matter what. Then CrimeBuster went back to his own voice, which sounded a little like a cross between Broderick Crawford and Jack Webb. "Warning: You are now under laser-beam cover, with focused heat capacity of ten thousand degrees centigrade per square centimeter. My standard armament includes seventeen conventional offensive weapons, fourteen defensive weapons, and one really incredible

133

stink bomb. You are now detained because your shapes and mobility have triggered my Suspicious Persons program. Identify yourselves."

It was suddenly quiet again on the sleepy dark street. The four bushes slowly turned and looked at each other. Then CrimeBuster watched as one of the taller bushes, the one with the suspicious green cloud of smoke around it, turned and led a hasty retreat. All four bushes suddenly moved off, heading for a nearby shadowy alley.

CrimeBuster's computer did some split-second calculations in selecting just the right weapon to fire. When CrimeBuster had been in the prototype stage many years before, he had tried to stop a hijacked armored car using only a single .22 caliber bullet. Shortly after that episode, a drunk was breaking into a soft-drink machine at an oil refinery, and CrimeBuster had opened up with his massive flamethrower after releasing a barrage of artillery (giving the drunk a quick opportunity to dive for cover), which resulted in raging fires and explosions that lit up an entire city for three days and nights. The choice of firepower was quite important for moral, legal, and crime-stopping reasons, so CrimeBuster's computer was programmed to quickly come up with the appropriate weapons to fire in any potential situation, from a tea party to a command raid. But four fleeing bushes did cause it some extra time and computations. However, within seconds, CrimeBuster's third gun port slammed open, and a single barrel shot out.

It was a classic thirty-five-millimeter machine gun, and it now blasted away at the street at the feet of the fleeing undergrowth, tearing up chunks of asphalt and stopping the suspects instantly. In fact, the four suspects quickly side-stepped back to where they had been standing, and CrimeBuster continued the discussion as though the entire vulgar but necessary incident with the machine gun had never happened.

"Identify yourselves within five seconds," CrimeBuster stated, "or you will be detained and/or destroyed."

Two of the taller perpetrators seemed to exchange looks, then one stepped forward.

"I am BushBot-60034," said a male voice.

Then the other one stepped forward.

"I am BushBot-60035," said a soft, feminine voice. "We are part of the Mobile Decoration Corps. We are assigned to G Sector."

"Move aside," added the male voice, "and cease all interference with our programmed duties."

CrimeBuster's computer whirred into action so loudly it could be heard by the suspects; there was suddenly a great deal of data to correlate. After a moment, CrimeBuster swung its main gun over at the third tall bush. "Are you also a BushBot for G Sector?"

This new bush didn't answer right away. First it seemed to lean back a little, get comfortable, cause a green cloud of cigar smoke to emerge, and then finally answered. Sort of.

"You look like you just took first prize in an ugly contest."

CrimeBuster's computer then recorded a bizarre noise that sounded like a drummer's rim shot, but it was not logical that such a sound would come from inside a bush. Confused, realizing that this case was getting increasingly complex, CrimeBuster then trained its gun on the smallest bush. "And the small suspect?" CrimeBuster asked. "It does not resemble a BushBot."

"That's because it is a shrub," Val quickly said. "Now move aside and let us—"

But Val instantly found himself staring down the dark throat of a cannon.

"Remain stationary for photo IDs and computer check," CrimeBuster commanded. A second later another gun port burst open, only this time a small camera with a flash attachment shot out, clicked into position, and then FLASH FLASH FLASH FLASH, four pictures were taken, and the camera disappeared inside CrimeBuster's vast bulk. Meanwhile, CrimeBuster's huge data bank was thoroughly scanned for any information concerning BushBots or related background. The moment this was completed, CrimeBuster's reaction was to level his flamethrower at the four bushes, which was when Aqua realized that things were going from robotbad to worse.

"Mobile Decoration Corps fails to confirm identification. Highest probability is that you are criminals. I have data that says local police will resume morning patrol of this area at six A.M. They will retrieve you at that time. You will not move until then. This message will not be repeated. While waiting, you may enjoy a brief, musical interlude." Suddenly, a catchy Muzak version of "Lara's Theme" from *Doctor Zhivago* blared out of CrimeBuster's speaker.

They all just stood there for thirty seconds.

The next Muzakian delight was a medley of old Broadway show tunes. It was during ''Camelot'' that Val spoke quietly to Aqua out of the side of his speaker. ''Aqua, we need a program that will remove us from immediate danger,'' he said.

''Agreed,'' Aqua said.

''I have a suggested plan, but let me compute a few more moments to examine it for flaws.''

Val computed. And the band played on.

It was during the rousing finale of ''Seven Brides for Seven Robots'' that Val explained his plan to Aqua.

''Have you noticed that since leaving the warehouse shelf, our Pleasure Centers have responded not to the Robot Litany, but only when we touch each other?''

''Yes, Val, but now is not the time for interunit contact.''

''I know, but since for some reason we do not respond in the correct way, a fact we'll report to the repair shop at our first opportunity, perhaps we should recite the Robot Litany in hopes of neutralizing this obviously malfunctioning Crime-Buster.''

Aqua thought it over.

A flamethrower was looking her right in the eye in case it did not work.

''Yes, let's try it,'' she finally said.

Val stepped forward. The music not only stopped but three additional guns clicked into place.

''Excuse me,'' Val began, politely as always, ''but we are not criminals. That would be illogical, since we are bound by our Robot Litany: 'We Exist to Serve with Logic and Efficiency.' ''

Val and Aqua's Pleasure Centers showed absolutely no response, not a flicker, not a trace of color. (CatSkil's Pleasure Center only lit up when he could cause a healthy guffaw, and Phil was too young to even have a Pleasure Center.)

But in the middle of CrimeBuster's back, near his nerve-gas canisters, bright colored lights flickered, and a momentary hum was heard, which caused a circuit override in his other systems. When the pulsating sensation was over and CrimeBuster was again free to concentrate on his weapons, suspects, and programmed task, he managed to say, ''The bush-perpetrators will remain silent and—''

"We Exist to Serve with Logic and Efficiency," Val and Aqua quickly said together.

In spite of himself, CrimeBuster made another brief, humming sound, and his Pleasure Center glowed a bright orange . . . and it took longer this time for CrimeBuster to regain control of his mechanical faculties.

"You . . . will . . . cease . . . all . . . ."

But that was all CrimeBuster could get out before Val and Aqua quickly said the Litany again.

This time CrimeBuster reacted even more intensely. He was not designed to handle an overload in this area; he began to glow bright red, from somewhere deep inside.

"Weexisttoservewithlogicandefficiency," Val and Aqua said in a rapid-fire way and began inching backward as Crime-Buster's red glow was followed by smoke pouring out.

More Litany. More smoke.

CatSkil nudged Phil to follow Val and Aqua, and the four robots, still holding their bush disguises in front of them, turned and quickly hurried down the street, continuing to spout the Litany for CrimeBuster, who was definitely approaching melt-down.

CrimeBuster's lights flashed on and off; guns shot forward, bursting through gun ports, then slid back; the camera flew into position, FLASH FLASH, but then slid back inside where it continued taking pictures; the searchlight went whirling around; and strange pulsating noises grew louder and louder from inside CrimeBuster, along with the sound of tubes shattering.

At the far edge of the street, Val and Aqua made one last yell, "WEEXISTTOSERVEWITH—"

But that was all it took. CrimeBuster imploded.

Val, Aqua, CatSkil, and Phil raced down the street, past some dark houses and toward the thick woods.

They skidded to a stop at the edge of a small lake and looked quickly around.

"The CrimeBuster's inoperative condition is only temporary," Val said.

"Yes," Aqua agreed. "His circuit-jamming will soon subside. Query: Where is a good place to hide to avoid such a destructive, malfunctioning machine?"

They moved past some bushes, then they saw it.

A large house across the lake, about a hundred yards away,

was lit up like a Christmas tree. Music poured out of the windows. Dozens of people were milling around, some inside, some out on the deck which was over the lake, some out in the parking area in front, where many cars were parked.

"A human social occasion," Aqua said, recognizing the symptoms.

"It is not a good place to avoid the CrimeBuster."

"But Val, we seem to lack any alternative options."

They looked around quickly.

Then, from behind them in the town, they heard the loud roar of CrimeBuster's engines as he again regained control. That was followed by the loud whoosh of his flamethrower, then the rat-a-tat-tat of his machine gun, which was angrily stitching a series of holes in the side of a beautiful little '57 T-bird that was parked in front of O'Brien's Billiard Parlor.

CrimeBuster was on the march again.

Val looked at Aqua, then at Phil, then at CatSkil.

"You are more familiar with human social occasions than the rest of us," Val said as they quickly began moving around the lake, heading straight for the crowded, noisy house. "Perhaps you can share your programming on the subject and add to our data."

With the distant roar of CrimeBuster in their mechanical ears, Aqua quickly tried to describe to the other three how robot-servants usually functioned on social occasions.

But CatSkil wasn't listening. He just smiled to himself.

Nobody had to tell him how to crash a party.

CHAPTER 8

party (pär´ tē) *n.* 1. a group of persons gathering together for recreation. 2. a social coming together for the purpose of amusement.

• • • "Ladies and gentlemen, it's getting late and I just want to thank you again for coming to my housewarming party," said the tall, smiling woman in the tight, bright red pants and the silver sequined top as she stood in one corner and loudly addressed the bored, half-drunk people in front of her. "For all of you to come and celebrate with me in this way means a great deal to me . . . ."

"And I say this from the bottom of my heart," whispered the half-drunk interior decorator to his giggling assistant.

"And I say this from the bottom of my heart," the tall woman said loudly, with a sweeping, theatrical gesture. Only about three or four of the thirty people there bothered to applaud; they had been the only ones listening except for some robot-servants, which had paused attentively.

"As you know, I, Claudette DuBarry, am not an interior decorator," she said, sweeping across the room toward a distinguished-looking middle-aged man in a three-piece suit and his young, attractive female assistant. "But I have worked closely with this brilliant man and his talented assistant in creating this, my summer home."

Claudette hooked her arms in those of the interior decorator and the assistant and beamed at the assembled group, which did not applaud on cue, couldn't care less about the house, didn't know Claudette, and had only shown up because in the small town there weren't many parties thrown, especially not parties with free food and plenty of booze.

The interior decorator exchanged looks with his assistant. In despair, both had been drinking heavily all evening. Now all they needed was this additional humiliation, to be pointed to as the people who decorated this incredible house. The lack of applause was obvious to both decorators. Claudette, however, was experiencing her finest hour and did not notice that no one else there really cared whether she made a speech or jumped in the lake.

"I wanted a home environment that reflected a variety of socioeconomic, political, and artistic statements," she said, not noticing that four dark shapes just outside one of the windows, discarded their bushes, then quietly entered through the back door. "My home now cleverly combines the functionalism of Quonset, the warmth of adobe, and the traditional values of Colonial. . . ."

At that point, unfortunately, Claudette chose to explain even further about her house, not noticing that the people at the party were exchanging the kind of looks that normally occur when a bag lady wearing a top hat, seventeen sweaters, twelve skirts, and one squishy pair of sneakers goes by on a busy street, informing no one in particular that God lives in her totally immersible Sears coffee maker.

Claudette's house combined high-tech, rustic ski lodge pine, French antiques, Navajo rugs, African sculpture, and Mexican tourist pictures of bullfights on black velvet, and only once in the many months she had spent carefully selecting everything in the house did she momentarily pause and ask herself if perhaps the whole look of the house might be a little too busy.

Claudette's excited, loud voice and her sweeping gestures did happen to keep anyone from noticing that Aqua had put on a French maid's apron, picked up a tray of party snacks, and motioned for Val, Phil, and CatSkil to do the same. She shook her head at CatSkil, who also wanted to wear a French maid's apron. The four robots then quickly moved away from the back door and tried to imitate the other robot-servants, which were walking around offering drinks and cleaning ashtrays while Claudette droned away.

"That 1964 television was actually owned by a genuine

Nielsen family," she said, pointing with pride at a small brass plaque on the TV set. Claudette was totally into Middle America chic, as well as being totally into everything else. "That striking abstract painting, entitled "Destiny!," is an avant-garde work done by an albino genius who dips earthworms in Day-Glo paint and lets them wiggle off the canvas. Isn't it stunning!"

One woman who had known Claudette longer and better than she had originally planned to turned to her boyfriend and quietly said in a dry tone of voice, "You know, I was in the third grade with Claudette—even then, she was completely full of shit."

Aqua bravely walked right past Claudette just as she was finishing her speech, but the tall, strident woman was too caught up in her speech to notice any new or unusual robots at this point. "Go ahead," Claudette said, "call me bold, daring, provocative! But I believe a home environment is a personal statement . . . and *this* is what I have to say! Thank you!" She bowed to extremely scattered applause—*really* scattered.

Val, meanwhile, was walking around with a white napkin over one arm, holding a tray of drinks. CatSkil was proving to be a very popular bartender because of how strong he was making the drinks. Phil's rear wagon had a tray across it (since they had taken out all the stolen hardware-store parts and hidden them outside before entering the house) and was scooting around, supposedly dispensing potato chips, cheese dip, and M&M's; in reality, he was just staring at everything, wide-eyed. When you're born in a forest and only thirty-six hours old, it doesn't take a lot to impress you. And Aqua was taking the most risks, openly approaching people the way a robot-servant is supposed to do, asking them if they wanted something to eat, such as stale cheese with a tired piece of bacon wrapped around it.

Claudette's speech finished, the party chatter and music returned to its previous volume. Claudette mingled, smiling at everyone, basking in her imagined glory, until a dark cloud appeared on her little horizon. Claudette noticed that one of the robot-servants, one she didn't remember seeing before, had a bent collar, oil stains on her pink and gold dress, and a rip in her neo-dermis, under which some wiring was exposed. Furious at how the careful look of her party was being ruined by such a sloppy robot, Claudette came striding across the room toward Aqua. . . .

CrimeBuster created a huge cloud of dust as he skidded to a stop at the edge of the lake. His six eyes picked up the light and the noise across the lake, and his entire top half swiveled to take in the scene. He saw a party. His CrimeBuster computer quickly went on yellow alert; parties were often sources of sex, drugs, and rock 'n' roll. If all of CrimeBuster's circuits had been functioning, he would have decided it was illogical for his suspects to be hiding at a party. However, internally, CrimeBuster wasn't in terrific shape.

During his nineteenth nervous breakdown a few moments ago, CrimeBuster had burnt out tubes, shorted out wiring, and worn out circuits. His Litany-jammed mechanisms were partly melted and fused together in some areas of operation. In others, he was locked into "On" position. And one of the areas in which he now was permanently set on "Go" was "Perpetrators, Search and Destroy." His computerized blood lust had sent him screaming down the streets after the escaping BushBots, radar bowls turning, lights on and functioning. He had immediately tracked them to the edge of the lake. And now, with the tracks leading around the lake to the house, he suddenly knew he would catch his suspects. His computer made a mental note to never again allow suspects to recite the Litany so fast that it would immobilize his unit. Next time, he would shoot first and recite the Litany later.

CrimeBuster rumbled straight down into the lake, aiming straight for the house, not bothering to take the time to go around on dry land. The lake was deep at this point, almost fourteen feet. CrimeBuster's underwater lights, spear guns, and shark repellent all automatically came on as he disappeared under the lake like a monstrous submarine. . . .

Claudette towered over Aqua, glaring at her soiled dress and fingering a large open rip. Claudette's face was red. She couldn't believe it. This was her big party, her big moment, all the other robot-servants swirling around were in perfect working condition and looked precisely the way they were supposed to, yet here was this dirty pink machine with mud on her shoes and leaves tangled in her torn dress, not to mention an open rip in the neo-dermis on the side of her head.

"You look terrible! What did you do? Fall off a cliff before arriving at my party?"

"Yes, ma'am."

"Sarcasm from a robot?" Claudette yelled, startling a few nearby guests. "What is that, some new programming option for party servants?"

"No, ma'am," Aqua started to say, but Claudette's shrill voice cut her off instantly.

"Are you one of the extra models I phoned the Rent-A-Bot people for over two hours ago? And you're just *now* arriving?"

"Yes, ma'am," Aqua said, forcing a smile. The nearby guests were just drunk enough to feel humiliation for a robot. "But if I may explain—"

"Explain?" Claudette shrieked. "Do I listen to explanations from the garbage disposal when it malfunctions?"

And with that, she stalked away, making an aristocratic gesture of dismissal. Aqua could only nod in a subservient way and then go back to circulating among the guests with her tray of snacks. But then Aqua noticed that Val was motioning to her. She casually moved over toward Val by the bar, where CatSkil was pouring drinks and where Phil now waited.

"Question," Val said quietly when Aqua was near enough for the four robots to quickly put their heads together.

"Proceed."

"You have programming for human social occasions. We lack this data. Assistance requested."

"The appropriate behavior mode for robot-servants at a party is to . . ." Aqua paused, and her computer rapidly beeped and whirred, double-checking her information before she finally said, ". . . mingle."

"Audio problem. Repeat, please."

"Mingle: to join, unite, or take part with others for social purposes."

They nodded, and then all four headed in different directions, like a football team breaking from a huddle.

CrimeBuster's underwater journey across the lake was delayed by the presence of a number of suspicious clues. As he neared the far shore CrimeBuster had paused to study a number of objects his underwater lights had spotted and his net had scooped up. Crime, as CrimeBuster knew and often said, could be anywhere, so he had paid close attention to the stuff he found on the bottom of the lake.

His mechanical fingers were now puzzling over the contents of his dragnet. His computer began filing away the following data: "Beer cans, dented and rusty—three; car tires, deflated—two; fishing hooks—nine; fishing lures, worm design—five; inflatable rubber toy turtle, green, ripped—one; Vegematic, with optional slicer-and-dicer attachment, broken—one; condoms, used—four; penny, Indian head—one." CrimeBuster's computer first tried to examine the possibilities of all these objects being involved in the same crime, but a drunken, fishing-trip seduction involving a Vegematic and a rubber turtle was just too remote a possibility for even CrimeBuster's eternal vigilance on the subject of wrongdoing. After several minutes, CrimeBuster decided to carefully store all the potential clues in plastic evidence bags, then his tank tread bit into the mud. He churned his way to the far bank, then suddenly roared up out of the lake and glared, dripping wet, at the brightly lit, noisy party. . . .

Phil rolled to the middle of the large room and stopped. His head pivoted wildly, trying to watch all the passing colorful creatures at once. He couldn't believe his optic sensors.

Rabbits were interesting, squirrels were intriguing, and that one noisy camel had really made his day, but what in the world were these things? Phil's eyes were wide open, his ears twitched, and he was getting plenty of input—almost sensory overload—but he had no idea how to store, organize, file, or interpret the information.

From twenty feet away, Val noticed Phil's agitated state, realized the problem, then hurried over, almost colliding with another robot-servant. Val bent down beside Phil, speaking quietly.

"Phil, I know this is the first time you have ever seen human beings. . . ."

Val then turned and looked at the passing parade that swirled and staggered around them. One man in the corner was nodding sympathetically to some boring woman whose main attraction was that she was drunk and had mentioned that she was new in town. Another woman in a purple dress with matching hair was loudly lecturing several other people on how her Indian guru was so effective and genuine because he was Cherokee instead of being from the Subcontinent, where "all the good ones have been gone for years." A middle-aged army colonel was explaining to a vegetarian why eating bloodred meat was the real key to survival in what he referred to as "the coming post-Atomic War era." A former punk rocker who hadn't updated his zoot suit or yellow hair in the last fifteen years was snorting a green powder he referred to as "soycaine, man, it's great." A recently divorced man wearing a clothing style too young for him was confiding to a friend that he'd really been looking forward to "scoring a lot now" but realized as he surveyed this and other parties that he found the whole process very depressing. A woman who had known the hostess for years as an old and trusted friend was quietly pocketing an expensive ashtray. A man and a woman who had been aware of each other all evening from across the room were still lonely but had made no move to go over and meet each other. One man bragged about his new car. Another about his job. An unhappy drunk played a joyous tune on the piano. And a woman got up on the coffee table to dance but slipped and fell into a large bowl of bean dip.

Val put his arm around Phil and finally spoke quietly, saying "There just isn't time to explain. . . ."

Phil nodded but kept staring. Val went back to serving drinks.

Just outside, CrimeBuster's searchlight spotted the discarded but familiar bush disguises almost immediately. They had been neatly stacked between an electric-blue Rolls-Royce and a tobacco-brown electric Pintette. All six of CrimeBuster's eyes now stared at the party. He could see many people, sometimes just moving shapes, through the windows and patio doors. He could hear loud music, forced laughter, and endless chatter.

CrimeBuster, still unobserved by anyone, rumbled over to another side of the house for a better view.

Just then, a large green truck with "Rent-A-Bot" on the side raced up through the night and came to a stop. Two men got out, mumbling about how they were behind schedule, hurried to the back, and opened the rear doors. Two maid-robots and one butler-robot climbed out.

"Hurry, we're running late," the driver said to his partner, then turned to the three ServBots. "You three, report inside at once!" Seconds later, the two men had jumped in their truck and raced off into the night, leaving the three robots in a cloud of dust. The three robots saw the house, turned, and started walking toward it.

"Halt! Suspicious persons will halt and identify themselves! Do not move!"

CrimeBuster wasn't taking any chances with anybody. There was too much funny stuff going on concerning this strange assignment. First, those BushBots sneaking out of town, then a bizarre party that was an obvious hotbed of criminal activity, now these alleged ServBots, not to mention all that crap at the bottom of the lake that probably spelled trouble.

The three ServBots, not nearly as sophisticated as the Com-series but certainly smart enough to know when a powerful searchlight was blinding them, realized they were being given contradictory orders.

"Excuse me," the butler-robot said, stepping forward. His right arm was permanently holding an empty tray at shoulder level. "Our primary assignment is to quote report inside end quote." He nodded politely, then all three turned and continued toward the party, totally ignoring CrimeBuster and his laser rifles, which were trained on their every move.

CrimeBuster was getting sick and tired of being ignored; to show disrespect for an officer of the law was to show disrespect for the law itself. CrimeBuster's grenade launcher burst out of a gun port, then flipped a hand grenade with a ten-second delay at the feet of the servants.

The butler-robot saw it, smiled, slowly bent over, picked it up, put it on his tray, looked at CrimeBuster, and said thank you. The two maid-robots smiled and nodded their appreciation, and all three proceeded toward the house. . . .

Inside, a drunk suddenly turned the stereo up full blast. He was tired of the guy playing the piano, because that was making the crazy broad on the coffee table continue to dance with her dress up over her head, not a pretty sight by any means. So the loud explosion of the hand grenade was drowned out by the vibrations of the stereo. Then someone else pulled the plug on the stereo and helped the woman back up on the coffee table.

Outside, CrimeBuster made a last quick surveillance of the area, establishing a perimeter before going in for the suspects.

146

Pleasant to the core, Val was trying to be a good serving butler and doing his best to be efficient, even though he had not forgotten that his primary goal was to avoid the malfunctioning CrimeBuster. So he served drinks and took orders with courtesy and promptness, his only delay in returning with drinks caused by the fact that CatSkil, the bartender was trying to hustle a blond maid-robot.

A woman with long, tie-dyed hair snapped her fingers in Val's face. "I'll have a vodka," she said. Val handed her a drink. She sipped it, then made a horrible face, looking at Val in disbelief.

"This tastes like a banana daiquiri!"

He nodded pleasantly and responded by reciting from memory what he knew to be the appropriate remark. "Yes," Val said, "I know what you mean. Mountains always make me feel closer to God for some reason."

Her shocked expression lasted ten seconds, then she whirled around and yelled at Claudette. "This stupid robot spouts nonsense. He can't even bring the right drink!"

Claudette charged over, starting off at angry but making it to furious by the time she spoke, since she had noticed Val's dirty, torn clothes. "You idiot! I refuse to have my party spoiled by you malfunctioning morons! You arrive late, you look terrible, and now you can't even bring a person the right drink! Now I want you to concentrate and do a quiet, perfect job for the rest of the evening! Are there any questions about that? Any questions at all?"

Suddenly, there was a question.

"*How long can a person live without brains?*" CatSkil asked, rumbling over to the rescue and positioning himself between Val and Claudette. Everyone looked a little stunned by this, especially Claudette.

"What . . .?" she finally said.

A number of people now gathered around. The piano player finally shut up. The woman got down off the coffee table. It grew quiet.

"*How long can a person live without brains?*" CatSkil asked again, puffing on his cigar, looking generally pleased with himself, as always.

"I don't know," Claudette said, still stunned by the very idea of being interrupted by a weird cigar-smoking robot she

147

didn't even recognize. "How long can a person live without brains?"

"*I don't know,*" CatSkil said. "*How old are you?*"

There was a long quiet moment as Claudette's jaw dropped open, than the room erupted in laughter. Claudette's face turned as red as her plastic pants, and she turned and stalked off, planning to call the Rent-A-Bot company immediately and then her attorney to begin proceedings.

"*This place reminds me of a fancy hotel I once stayed in,*" CatSkil continued, now holding center stage as more people gathered around. "*Room service had an unlisted number.*"

The bap-bap of the rim shot was almost drowned out by the roar of laughter. They were just drunk enough to think CatSkil was hilarious. However, the loud, electronic rim shot carried outside, where a large, black, menacing figure heard it.

CrimeBuster screeched to a stop.

His computer instantly cross-indexed that strangely familiar sound. Within seconds, CrimeBuster knew he had last heard it from one of the bush-perpetrators that were obviously inside the house. CrimeBuster knew he did not know what the suspects looked like, since they had cleverly worn green, leafy disguises, but now he had proof, on tape, that logically and legally allowed him to invoke the "no-knock" clause of law enforcement. CrimeBuster rumbled past a window, getting ready for a wide turn to build up momentum for his charge through the wall of the house.

Inside, all the people were listening to CatSkil and laughing, not noticing the large black figure roll by the window. But Val saw it.

He caught Aqua's attention and motioned to the window. She saw it, tapped Phil on the shoulder, pointed toward the door, and they began slipping away. Val worked his way through the laughing crowd of people next to CatSkil, trying to motion to him to head for the door.

CatSkil shrugged Val off and went on telling the people at the party about a man who was killed by a weasel. They screamed with laughter.

A stuffy, middle-aged man nearby leaned over and whispered to his unsmiling wife out of the side of his mouth a single word. "Jewish . . ."

"*I stayed at a hotel once where the bellhops were tip happy,*" CatSkil said, again ignoring Val, who had glanced

148

out a window and seen the reflections of a flashing red police light. *"I ordered a deck of cards, and the kid made fifty-two trips."*

That was followed by a rim shot, cigar smoke, a big laugh from the crowd, and the entire nearby wall of the house caving in; CatSkil would later claim that it was he, not CrimeBuster, that brought the house down.

The wall exploded inward, and amid flying wood, plaster, and bad artwork, CrimeBuster moved ten feet inside the house, siren wailing at full blast, red lights flashing, turret spinning, and all guns popping into view!

There was total panic. People screamed and ran, falling over themselves and broken furniture.

In the instant confusion, Val and Aqua exchanged worried looks from across the room. CatSkil smiled to himself, enjoying anything that ended up going so totally and wonderfully wrong.

"This is CrimeBuster-00749. Warning: there are suspicious persons on the premises. No one move until identification of everyone is complete—"

But the local minister and his wife continued tiptoeing off the patio. Instead, they almost went to heaven; CrimeBuster fired one of his many side guns, a loud M 16 automatic rifle, which pulverized a large aquarium, sending bits of glass, water, and rather surprised goldfish into the air and causing more screams.

This time, everyone did freeze. Including Val, Aqua, CatSkil, and Phil. They hadn't made it out the door in time.

"Repeating previous message," CrimeBuster said through his bullhorn. "No one move. Everyone is under suspicion."

Claudette was finally coming out of shock. First her party was being ruined by broken machines, now her beloved home itself was being wrecked. She hadn't spent her entire adult life marrying and divorcing three wealthy men to have everything end up in a shambles.

"What do you mean, *everyone* is under suspicion," she said, striding forward, hands on her hips. "I am Claudette DuBarry, I live here, I even designed this house!"

CrimeBuster's six eyes instantly scanned her.

"You especially are under suspicion," CrimeBuster replied through his bullhorn, giving his powerful voice an irrelevant S.W.A.T.-team-commander-talking-to-the-barricaded-suspect quality.

It was at this point that several men at the party regained their composure and stepped forward to stand beside Claudette. After all, she had provided free food and drinks. "What the hell, who does this robot think he is?" one man said. "Unplug the bastard," said another.

"I'm not going to have my dream home invaded and destroyed by a malfunctioning piece of machinery! Get out!" Claudette yelled. "You're not working correctly! Report yourself to the nearest repair shop!"

Several men picked up some broken pieces of furniture and started to try to surround the huge, black robot.

"Halt!" CrimeBuster warned, wondering if he should inform the group in general how quickly his laser guns could melt a human body, reducing it to an ugly burnt spot on the thick shag rug in a millisecond. "My armament is activated! I have proof that the perpetrators are here!"

"Let's see your proof," Claudette demanded.

A number of computer noises, several mechanical clicks, and a small whistle was heard from inside CrimeBuster. Then a small slot appeared and a vertical strip of four photos slid into view, not unlike those from the old fifty-cent photo booths. Claudette and several of the men bravely stepped forward and looked at the photos CrimeBuster had taken only a few minutes before of Val, Aqua, CatSkil, and Phil.

Val and Aqua exchanged looks, then again froze, acting like the other indifferent robot-servants, as Claudette studied the photographs.

"What is it?" someone in the crowd asked.

"This idiot," Claudette began, "has just given very clear pictures of four bushes."

"Bushes?"

"Bushes. I told you it was malfunctioning! Now who is going to help me throw this piece of junk out?"

A dozen men picked up makeshift weapons in the rubble and slowly began advancing toward CrimeBuster, who routinely clicked a large gun out of every side, each aimed at a potential attacker. The men paused, staring into eternity.

Val quietly stepped forward and stood to Claudette's right. "Excuse me, but if I might make a suggestion. Reciting the Robot Litany may be the solution."

"Yes," Aqua added and moved to Claudette's left. "It has a calming effect on our robot computers."

"Okay, okay, good idea," Claudette said, then turned to the people at the party and raised her hands in the air like a song leader. Val and Aqua, meanwhile, retreated toward the door, with CatSkil and Phil following. "Let's calm it down with that stupid Litany."

CrimeBuster, meanwhile, having overheard Val's and Aqua's voices, was making an instant cross-reference, and within the better part of a second CrimeBuster knew that he had last heard those voices from behind bushes. . . .

"Warning! Perpetrators are now heading for the door!" he said, swinging his guns in their direction. "Suspects must remain in place and—"

"WE EXIST TO SERVE WITH LOGIC AND EFFICIENCY!" yelled Claudette and everyone else in the room.

"Negative!" CrimeBuster said, already beginning to heat up inside. "Cease repetition of the—"

"WE EXIST TO SERVE WITH LOGIC AND EFFICIENCY!" Claudette was waving her arms back and forth, leading the group in saying it over and over.

"LITANY BEING USED TO SABOTAGE CIRCUITS!" CrimeBuster blared out over the Litany and the sound of his own warning bells, burning wires, and exploding tubes. It took much less time than before for CrimeBuster to reach the crisis point, since so many of his safety mechanisms had burned out the first time. "THEREFORE, EVERYONE IS UNDER A . . . UNDER A . . ."

But he never got the rest out. The Litany was causing him to freak out.

Glowing red, domed top spinning in a mad circle, CrimeBuster lurched forward and fired his main laser blast, which sizzled right through the house and into the lake, causing a loud hissing sound and an instant fish fry. People screamed and dove to one side, and CrimeBuster pivoted wildly, knocking out another wall, which fell backwards. His machine guns went off in every direction, causing everyone to hit the dirt fast. CrimeBuster then fired off a flare, which hit a large, tacky chandelier that came crashing down, just missing several people.

"He's wrecking my home!" Claudette screamed. "Stop him!"

It was too late. There was total pandemonium. Everyone was scrambling to get out. Every window frame and doorway was clogged with people trying to escape. Some dove off into the lake. The only ones not running away were Claudette's SweepBot, which calmly rolled out of a linen closet and began trying to sweep up, and Claudette's robot-servants, which automatically continued serving drinks and offering little pieces of ham that had been stabbed by colorful toothpicks.

CrimeBuster fired his main cannon into another wall, which came crashing down, then plowed backward over some rubble, his sudden weight on one end of the house causing the deck to fall into the lake with a loud splash and the chimney to fall off. Then he wandered off into the night, totally out of control.

Screams from fleeing people and the crash of a house falling in on itself, roof and all, filled the night air in every direction. Even Claudette had gone wailing off into the night, after first falling over a small lawn statue of a black stable boy, which former owners had self-consciously painted white and Claudette had purchased and repainted black.

From some bushes one hundred feet safely away, Val, Aqua, CatSkil, and Phil stood and watched the chaos. People were running, crawling, and swimming away in every direction, the house looked like a Wirephoto of a bombed-out building, and CrimeBuster was rolling in circles and firing his flamethrower straight up into the night air, causing more screaming.

"Data request," Val said quietly.

"Proceed," Aqua replied.

"Do you have data on why humans enjoy such social occasions?"

Aqua thought a moment.

"Negative."

They turned and moved off into the night, first collecting the borrowed robot parts from the hardware store. They were anxious to attach them to Phil to improve his unit.

The last sight anyone at the party had of CrimeBuster was of him rolling back into the lake and slowly sinking from view. Three witnesses (two women hiding under a car and a man who had climbed a nearby tree) later claimed that CrimeBuster's last words were quite clear. "You have the right to remain silent. You have the right to have an attorney present . . .'' But that was all they could understand before he bubbled below the surface and the cold water closed over the bullhorn, making the rest of it sound like a cross between blub-blub-blub and the mating sound of a humpback whale.

Chapter 9

haven (hā¹vən) *n*. 1. a sheltered anchorage; port; harbor. 2. any sheltered, safe place. 3. refuge.

• • • Max was freezing.

He pulled the thermoplastic sheets tighter around his body as he lay curled up in the cab of the truck. It was still dark. Max touched a button on his wrist watch. "The time is . . . 4:13 A.M." said the feminine voice of his watch. Max could hear Charlie snoring just outside on the ground. Funny, he thought, shivering, he didn't remember it being this cold when they had gone to sleep.

He lay there, the gear shift knob prodding his butt, realizing he couldn't go back to sleep. It was just too cold. Besides, his poison oak was really beginning to itch. In an hour or two it would be light enough for them to travel. Max hoped that they could find the missing bots first thing in the morning rather than late in the afternoon. He couldn't wait to take a day off, go home, get in bed, and have his wife spoil him a little. Her red hair had some gray in it now, but that special look in her eyes was still there when she looked directly at Max. She would bring him coffee and the newspaper, plump his pillows up, make his favorite meal for him, generally fuss over him before joining him in their large, warm bed.

Max decided he could use some fussing over.

The mud on CrimeBuster's lower half had completely dried

154

and his tank treads now worked fine as he rumbled through the dark forest, trying to pick up the trail of his suspects. He had been in the lake for almost twenty minutes, and the water had extinguished some burning wiring and cooled down overheated circuits, actually allowing CrimeBuster's computer to again function rationally. He had then charged up out of the lake like Godzilla, scaring the wits out of Claudette and her guests, who had just then come wandering back to the demolished house. But CrimeBuster hadn't paused as the people had again screamed and headed for parts unknown. He had hunted down enough suspects to understand the criminal mind; the suspects wouldn't be in the immediate vicinity. CrimeBuster consulted his internal clock, which gave him the correct time for the seventeen major cities of the world that are interconnected through Interpol, and discovered it was 5 A.M. Dawn would be at 5:58 A.M., and the light would be of immense help in tracking the perpetrators.

For a brief moment, CrimeBuster reflected on how working alone like this involved a certain loss in effectiveness. A backup partner that he could interface with concerning strategy, analysis of clues, criminal motivation, priorities, and more would have been very helpful. But CrimeBuster knew that crime busting was a lonely life. However, he reminded himself as he crashed through a thicket, somebody had to do it. . . .

At 5:58, when a distant rooster crowed as the orange morning sun peeked over a nearby hill, the little corner of the farm had already come to life. Birds in the nearby trees were making a racket, some cows in a nearby pasture were having breakfast, there was a lot of activity behind one of the haystacks, and a tractor was already cultivating some acreage.

The tractor driver, a late model FarmBot, wore bib overalls and a green John Deere cap. He had a blank, neutral expression painted on his face and a long, fake straw coming out of his mouth area. He was programmed only for plowing and milling and maybe a little hog sloppin', so even though he and his tractor rumbled by the haystacks, he had no reason to stop or comment on what he saw.

CatSkil peeked around the haystack once the tractor had gone by and nodded to Val and Aqua, who had paused in their work in case their noisy tools caused the tractor driver to stop and investigate. But once the coast was clear they went back to work, continuing to weld, solder, wire, and screw new parts from the hardware store onto Phil's unit. Phil, however, took CatSkil's nod to mean it was safe to again turn on his little Traffic Enforcement Designator helmet, and the little siren filled the air and the red light flashed as it spun in circles.

Val and Aqua, having had a rough night and getting dangerously low on energy, just stopped and glared at Phil.

Phil shut the light and siren off. They went back to work.

But then Val paused, setting his tools aside. "This Optical Logic Scanner won't work after all, not unless Phil has a much more sophisticated computer." He pointed to a new improvement they had just labored for an hour to add to Phil. "He can store more data now, but he still can't handle pattern recognition and evaluation."

He looked at Aqua for a response, but she kept her eyes on her project and worked harder than ever.

"Aqua, these minor improvements are not worth our time-energy expenditure. What he needs is a complete overhaul, and we lack sufficient equipment."

Val waited for Aqua to look up, nod, and quit work. Only she didn't do any of the three.

"Besides," Val added, seeing the orange sunlight pour over the yellowish field of waving wheat, "the CrimeBuster is after us and will be here soon."

That certainly will get Aqua to stop wasting time and energy, he decided. But she kept working, tightening screws on Phil, replacing old tubes with new ones, adding new wiring, and double-checking his new systems.

Val looked up at CatSkil. CatSkil shrugged.

"Aqua? Wouldn't it be logical to discuss the wisdom of additional work before continuing?" Val asked.

Apparently not. Aqua kept working, faster than ever, adjusting, experimenting, improving Phil any way she could.

"Aqua?"

Finally she responded, though she kept right on connecting a new input system to one of his audio receptors. "This is the first robot I have ever created and programmed. He will be the most efficient I can make him."

There was a long pause. Val didn't speak for a while.

Birds sang. Cows ate grass. The tractor chugged around in neat squares. And Aqua just kept right on working.

Aqua's actions didn't . . . make sense.

Then Val remembered she had fallen off a cliff. A stray phrase flashed through Val's mind, but he couldn't quite place it: *in sickness and in health* . . .

"Aqua, you are expending your own energy packs too rapidly. And we have no spare energy packs."

The voice of reason was like a distant cry in the wilderness; Aqua continued replacing one of Phil's blinking tubes with one of her own.

"You're being . . ." Val began, realizing it was time to just come right out and say it, just come right out with the blunt, ugly truth, just say it and let it hang right out there in front of God and everybody, ". . . illogical."

No reaction from Aqua. No denial, no explanation, no response whatsoever, unless you counted the way she kept right on doing what she was doing.

Val picked up a screwdriver, bent over, and joined her.

They both paused, looked at each other a long moment, then began working together.

"Look, little boy, that just doesn't make any sense," Charlie said, looking down at the four-year-old boy who stood surrounded by grown-ups in the alley behind the hardware store. It was 6:30 A.M.

"His name is Brian," Brian's mother said.

"And if he says he saw something, then he saw something," Brian's father said.

Max and Charlie exchanged looks, and Charlie knew he'd have to be a little more tactful.

"Look, Brian, what do you mean you saw 'the Easter Bunny except with no ears and with bright lights?' "

Brian looked around at all the faces watching him, then shyly buried his face in his mother's side.

Max rolled his eyes. This was all he needed. First, he'd awakened practically freezing to death in the cab of the truck, no coffee, nothing to eat, finally the sun comes up, he and Charlie get lost three times, spot the town, start asking questions, hear that the hardware store was robbed, a crowd gathers, then this little kid speaks up. Maybe he saw something to do with their problem, maybe he didn't, only now the kid clams up. Max started to scratch his poison oak rash, then realized there were ladies present.

He went over and examined the strange way the fence was cut open in the rear of Klein's Hardware while Charlie made one last try with their only eyewitness.

"Brian, could you tell me what you saw, please?"

The little boy looked up at his parents, who nodded, then he held his hand about three feet off the ground. "He was just *this* high . . . and magic."

"Magic," Charlie repeated, without inflection. He too was tired, grumpy, and itchy. "Magic . . ." he repeated, nodding. They needed to hear about magic right now in a big way.

Charlie forced a smile at the people in the town.

"Is there anyplace to get some breakfast here this time of morning?" Charlie asked.

"Well," drawled one old-timer who took forever to get the pipe out of his mouth and then point, "you might try that crazy city woman's party by the lake, the one that got crashed by that robot. I hear she had free food and—"

"Hold it," Max interrupted, striding back over. "What robot?"

Then they heard fourteen different versions of what had occurred at Claudette DuBarry's party the night before.

Three minutes later, Max and Charlie drove up to the edge of the lake and looked across at what used to be Claudette DuBarry's house.

It was a smoldering pile of rubble, totally flattened. The morning sun made it clear just how completely the house was wrecked, leaving Claudette in a mild state of shock. She was sitting out in front of her demolished house as Max and Charlie drove around the lake. Claudette had a dazed look on her face. Her hair was messed up, her silver blouse was torn, and her tight red pants were ripped. Most of her guests, now gone, had gotten a little ripped, too.

Max and Charlie stopped their truck but didn't get out. The scene before them was pretty bizarre.

The robot-servants were still wandering around, automatically offering drinks and dusty snacks to some drunks who were staggering and tripping over the rubble. The interior decorator and his assistant were opening yet another bottle of champagne and chuckling together. And the SweepBot was mechanically shoving its small broom back and forth against the small mountain of rubble, which was like trying to sweep back the sea.

"Have you seen any valet or comedian robots?" Max asked the tall woman who was sitting in front. He was impatient and got right to the point. But the woman just ignored them, then angrily waved away an offer of some snacks from a passing robot-servant. She got up and staggered back through her rubble, looking for her Day-Glo worm painting, hoping that "Destiny!" hadn't met its destiny.

Max and Charlie exchanged looks. This wouldn't be the town they'd pick to come for a relaxing weekend someday.

Then the interior decorator and his assistant, arm in arm, came stumbling forward, giggling so much they could hardly talk. It had all been too perfect: first Claudette had paid them a great deal, then all that crap she had insisted upon was forever destroyed.

"You want to know what happened?" asked the interior decorator, almost yelling.

Max shook his head and began to turn the truck around.

"Her house got hit by a train!" the assistant yelled. "You want to know why?"

Max and Charlie didn't. They were driving away as fast as they could, so the two drunks yelled after them as loud as they could.

" 'Cause she didn't hear the weasel!!"

They both fell to the ground, screaming with laughter, tears streaming down their faces. The truck skidded to a stop. Max and Charlie looked at each other with the same thought: the CatSkil. They knew they were back on the track and began looking around for tracks to follow. . . .

Bossie, an unimaginative cow with an unimaginative name, slowly wandered through a corner of her pasture, munching grass still wet with dew, while her large cowbell occasionally made a clanking noise. Otherwise, the small pasture was quiet, except for some snorting and pawing sounds from the other end of the field. Bossie glanced over in that direction, her droopy big brown eyes half open, then she looked back toward her breakfast, which she found more interesting.

Several days ago, Bossie had sort of gotten the general idea about what was expected of her from the nice farm couple that owned her, Ellis and Edna Ruth. Edna Ruth had herded her off to this small, separate pasture, and Ellis had backed his pickup in and carefully unloaded a powerfully built bull named Lord Parmenter IV. Then Ellis and Edna Ruth had left the two of them alone and gone back to their farmhouse, joking about how Bossie was getting a visit "from the Lord on this Sunday morning." Lord Parmenter IV had majestically strutted and pranced around, apparently very impressed with himself and quite aware of Bossie. That had been three days ago.

Lord Parmenter IV was a muscular, two-ton animal that had won twenty-two blue ribbons and sired over 300 offspring, counting both natural and artificial ways of getting the job done. He was an impressive beast and he knew it, and he wasn't shy about coming over to visit Bossie.

The only problem was, he just didn't do a thing for her. Oh, he was all right, fairly handsome, mildly attractive, but he seemed more interested in himself than in Bossie. Besides, Bossie wasn't a young cow, easily impressed. She found herself basically indifferent to Lord Parmenter IV; when the Lord had come galloping over she acted as if he was in the right church but the wrong pew. Confused, he kept trotting in circles, not knowing that Bossie might eventually give in but that she secretly hoped, in her heart of hearts, for some good-looking devil who could really make her blood boil.

Bossie's breakfast and Lord Parmenter's prancing around were both interrupted by the loud, rumbling sound just over the hill. Both animals paused and peered over the old-fashioned, four-foot-high stone fence that surrounded the little pasture.

They saw an incredible sight. Something very big, very strong, and very mean was coming straight for them!

Both the cow and the bull unconsciously took a few steps back, not sure what was coming or how close it would get to their field before veering off. The thing was, though, it didn't seem to be changing direction. It was headed straight for the solid stone fence, a fence built to last a hundred years!

As it came closer, they could see that the large, black, domed creature had a number of small hornlike projections sticking out from it. It suddenly picked up speed as it neared the fence.

Metal armor against solid stone makes a terrible racket, and by the time both Bossie and Lord Parmenter IV had stopped running and turned and looked back, the frightening creature had plowed right through the fence and was headed straight across the field, apparently planning to go out the same way!

Bossie's eyes fluttered. Her heart skipped a beat. This was more like it.

And since this tall, dark, and handsome stranger was ignoring her totally, that really did it.

Love at first sight. And Bossie decided not to be bashful about showing it.

"Mooooo .   . . ." she offered.

CrimeBuster skidded to a stop, pausing so abruptly in the field that he slid an exta two feet on something he didn't even like to add to his data bank. He couldn't quite identify the sound. His computer whirred and beeped, but since he couldn't recognize it, obviously it had nothing to do with crime stopping, so he revved up his engine and started up again, tracking the sound of a tractor just over the next hill. Perhaps the person or persons, robot or robots, in charge could be interrogated concerning the missing suspects. But then CrimeBuster's fourth eye picked up some movement on the starboard side.

CrimeBuster's world consisted only of cops, criminals, and citizens. But now he was faced with a cow. Just an ordinary cow, his computer reassured him, in spite of the strange way she batted her long eyelashes at him and the way she drooled and the way her brown eyes kept stealing glimpses of his cannon.

CrimeBuster rumbled on. Then two tons of angry bull slammed into his side.

The collision knocked some wiring loose, jarred several circuits, dented some metal, broke three headlights, and didn't do the bull any good either.

But Lord Parmenter IV wasn't just good-looking; he was brave and scrappy, too. He backed up, even though he now had stars in his eyes, and pawed the earth with his right front hoof, getting ready to charge again.

CrimeBuster whirled, and his flamethrower clicked into place. Lord Parmenter IV bellowed and charged, his horns and head dipping low, too low for the bull to be instantly turned into the world's biggest well-done hamburger.

CLANG. CrimeBuster had several more tubes smashed and lost two more side lights, and the dazed, staggering bull backed up for yet another charge.

Just as CrimeBuster's machine guns clicked into place, Bossie trotted over and licked Lord Parmenter IV's face. She had had no idea he cared for her this much.

CrimeBuster did not fire, not wanting to endanger the innocent hostage this criminal was now hiding behind, then realized he couldn't really spare the ammunition if he wanted to continue on his primary assignment. The large, black robot turned, with one eye on the bull, and raced across the field, blasting a hole in the stone wall on the far side. It exploded into gravel and CrimeBuster rumbled over it, heading for the sound of the tractor, still hot on the trail.

In his wake, Bossie and the still dizzy Lord Parmenter IV nuzzled each other happily. Bossie knew she now cared for the brave bull and would settle down to a contented existence and raise his calves, although deep down she also knew she would never forget the bold, handsome stranger that was leaving her life forever.

It was two hours later when Max and Charlie saw the billowing black clouds of smoke in the distance.

"What the hell can that be?" Max asked.

"Looks like it's coming from that farm over there," Charlie said, heading the truck in that direction.

Max and Charlie drove past a pasture with a stone fence around it that had been blasted through, near a cow and a bull that didn't even glance their way; they seemed to have eyes only for each other.

"Look at those tracks, Max, and how that stone fence has been destroyed."

"Think it's that CrimeBuster that's wandering around?" Max asked, looking around nervously.

"Could be. We'd better report it."

They went bouncing up a hill in their truck, then paused and looked down on the strange scene in front of them. A series of three haystacks were burning, and black clouds of smoke boiled up into the blue morning sky.

"What the hell is going on?" Max asked of no one in particular. They drove closer, stopped, and got out.

"Look, Max. There's a lot of excess robot parts scattered around."

"Yeah, and look at that," Max said, pointing to the charred, blackened body of a robot near one of the haystacks. "Looks like that CrimeBuster blasted one of the ones we're looking for."

"Which one is it? Can you tell?"

They moved closer, covering their mouths and noses with handkerchiefs. The smell of burning wire, rubber, and plastic was horrible. Before them lay a twisted, blackened metal shell. The arms and legs were curling masses of burning tubes and circuit panels.

"Looks like the CatSkil model," Max gasped out from behind his handkerchief, "but it's hard to tell. See an invoice number or anything?" Charlie's eyes were watering from the smoke as he turned the metal corpse over with his boot, causing ashes to rise. Then he looked around at all the scattered robot parts nearby, untouched by the fire. He picked one up.

"Max, look at this. This part is tagged 'Klein's Hardware.' Can you make any sense of all this?"

"I haven't made any sense of anything since 1969," Max muttered, then noticed an overturned tractor in the field next to the haystacks. "That CrimeBuster really went on a rampage of some kind. Any chance he blasted those two Com-series as well as the CatSkil there?"

"I don't see any remains of a Com-series. Besides, that would be too consistent. That CrimeBuster apparently is wildly malfunctioning—Hold it, Max. Look closer."

Charlie was bending over the burning robot corpse. There was part of a straw hat and some bib overalls that still hadn't caught fire. "This isn't the CatSkil after all."

"Damn."

"Looks like a FarmBot. It must have been riding that tractor and minding its own business."

"Maybe the CrimeBuster was trying to get it to talk about what it had seen," Max suggested.

"Maybe. But FarmBots aren't programmed to say anything except about the weather."

Charlie and Max moved away from the smoke as the fires began to burn themselves out. Charlie imagined with a shudder what the poor FarmBot must have gone through. Here was this violent, crazed CrimeBuster asking it questions, and all the FarmBot could do was say, "Hot enough for ya?" and "Yeah, we could use a little rain." Then WHOOSH! Wrong answers.

163

Max grabbed the CB radio and reported in, realizing that on the other end they were laughing at him. Charlie took a closer look at the soft robot earth of the half-plowed field, then saw a series of small robot tracks, followed by the huge tank treads of a CrimeBuster, hot on the trail. . . .

"They went this way," Charlie said when Max walked over to him. "What did the factory say?"

"They've been getting reports on that CrimeBuster all day. Three squads are out looking for it. But has anyone seen *our* three missing models? Not a chance."

Behind them, the haystacks and the burning FarmBot crackled, and sparks rose into the morning air. Max had a sore throat. He'd have killed for one of those bags of beer he didn't like.

"None of this makes any sense. . . ." Charlie said, thinking out loud. "You know, it's almost as if . . . as if those three robots are consciously avoiding us."

Max laughed so hard at the idea and teased Charlie so much that he was sorry he'd ever thought of it. They got in their truck and drove off, following the tracks.

The forest offered a canopy of thick branches to shield the four robots from the hot noon sunlight. They were slowly going up a steep hill. Val stayed forty feet ahead of the others, in spite of Aqua's efforts to walk beside him. She discovered that he was setting his own pace, as though he wanted to be by himself. Behind her, Phil stared at a huge tree stump covered in emerald-green moss. CatSkil brought up the rear, glancing at a cluster of large mushrooms; they reminded him of the empty nightclub tables he used to face while doing his act.

"Val," Aqua finally said. "You have not communicated for 3.479 miles."

She paused and waited for a response. Val did not answer.

"I also have a grade-seven computing ability," she said, which was about as high an IQ as a robot could have and still be mobile. "It is illogical to function with another unit on a regular basis and not use that unit's full capacities."

There was still no response from Val. They walked in silence, except for the crunching of dry leaves and the quiet sounds of machinery in motion. The birds continued to sing; the forest had accepted them.

164

Aqua puzzled over Val's strange behavior. The only association her data bank could suggest after a quick scan was that perhaps Val needed something Aqua had once heard humans discussing in a hot tub. The humans had mentioned that sometimes "people need more space." That, however, seemed illogical in relation to robots. After all, Val certainly had enough room to move his unit and appendages.

Aqua decided to quickly replay her own memory tapes of the last two hours to try to understand Val's strange behavior. She began her memory scan at a point after Val had joined her behind the haystack in trying to improve Phil. . . .

They had worked hard, then finally decided that everything possible had been attempted. They had stepped back to observe the new, improved Phil. He looked noticeably better. In fact, while Val, Aqua, and CatSkil were becoming more dirty and dented, Phil kept looking better and better, now sporting new, shiny gadgetry.

"Seventeen new parts," Val stated.

"Eleven recycled components," Aqua said, not mentioning how many small parts from their own units Val and Aqua had just given up to improve Phil.

"Plus general cleaning, tightening, and reconditioning of existing mechanisms," Val added. He and Aqua leaned closer to Phil. Even CatSkil watched with interest.

"Phil, are you interfacing well with your new equipment?" Aqua asked.

"Have you noticed a higher level of efficiency?" Val asked.

Phil looked up at the three larger robots, then suddenly made an electronic raspberry. Val and Aqua exchanged puzzled looks; the strange sound had a negative connotation. Phil pointed to Val's eyes, then his own. He pointed to Aqua's legs, then his own tank treads. Phil then folded his arms, his brain lights lit up a bright red, and he turned away.

Val and Aqua understood. "Now he wants super infrared night vision," Val said. His voice sounded tired.

"And large, bipedal locomotion," Aqua added, wishing she had been programmed for sighing.

Phil took off his red bow tie and tossed it on the ground, then rumbled forward, crushing it with his tank treads. He looked up to make sure he wouldn't get in trouble, then began a high-pitched series of beeps and electronic squawks. He rolled away toward a haystack and then stopped, immobile except for some black smoke that was coming out of his ear area.

"After getting these other improvements, Phil also now seems to want the new directional finder," Val said.

"With the advanced radar-sonar component," Aqua added, knowing that there was no way to acquire all the things Phil now wanted.

Val and Aqua set their tools down and leaned back against a haystack, their energy levels lower than ever. They were even too tired to chase Phil when he started going around in tight little circles and turning on the police light and siren on his Traffic Enforcement Designator. In the distance, Phil spotted several dairy cows that were grazing and took off, chasing them. Val and Aqua exchanged looks, each secretly tempted to just let him go, but they diligently got to their feet to go after him. CatSkil, however, held up his cigar hand and gestered toward himself, and he was the one who went after Phil.

They lost another thirty minutes at that point, since Phil sailed along, using his new equipment for better speed and coordination, merrily chasing the cows. He grabbed a cow by the tail and was happily pulled around the field by the cow, who was in total panic. Seeing CatSkil chasing after Phil didn't help calm the cow down any either. Finally, after having invented a new sport that could only be called cow waterskiing, Phil was retrieved, and the four robots set out in the direction of the hilly forests, leaving the spare parts scattered behind one of the haystacks. The FarmBot had continued cultivating in the nearby field.

Aqua now glanced over at the moss-covered stump as they slowly moved up the steep forest hillside and realized that in scanning her recent memories she could discover no reason for Val's silent behavior. She decided to increase her speed, until she was only fifteen feet behind Val.

"Val? I know you are examining variables, computations, combinations, and permutations," she said, excluding only condominiums. "But it is inefficient to be totally silent for long intervals."

Val made no sign that he had heard. They just kept walking single file up the hill, slowly, steadily. Behind them, CatSkil began humming the theme from *The Bridge on the River Kwai*.

"We have been functioning in synchronization until now," she said. "Communication is necessary for continued success."

Still no response.

Aqua turned around and went back to join Phil, who was idly pulling the heads off beautiful little yellow wild flowers as he moved up the hill.

But it was then that Val turned around.

"Aqua, wait."

Aqua waited.

"Aqua, as always," Val began, with some difficulty, "you are logical and accurate. And I have been extremely inefficient in not exchanging data with you. I just did not want to complicate your computer with problems that—"

"I function better with maximum input," Aqua said.

"Agreed," Val said quietly, then he smiled hesitantly.

Aqua made a small smile back, then they walked toward each other.

"Here is my thought," Val said, offering his arm to her like a southern gentleman. She curled her arm in his and they continued their walk, not unlike a mechanical Rhett and Scarlett strolling under magnolias. "I am not concerned with Phil's desire for miscellaneous equipment used by Traffic Enforcement and Gladiator models."

"I am equally unconcerned," she said. "Part of his insistence was due to our decision not to program Phil for subservience. And I do not regret it."

"I do not either. But as we saw, he still lacks important internal improvements."

"Yes. And it is now also obvious that even the resources of a human community are very limited in the parts we can acquire to improve Phil."

Val nodded. If a human hardware store with an entire section marked "Robotics" didn't have enough in supply to significantly improve Phil, Val didn't know where else to turn. "Compared to the repair shop or the main factory, there were relatively few parts available."

They were quiet as they walked, arm in arm, over the crest of a hill. Ahead, the trees were thinning out.

"Ideally, we should have access to an almost limitless number of spare parts . . ." Val said.

"Yes, and optional accessories . . ."

"Raw materials . . ."

"Tools . . ."

"Machinery . . ."

Their words trailed off. It was too much to hope for, to have acres of an almost infinite number of spare parts with which to improve Phil.

Then they got to the top of the hill and stopped and stared. Phil and CatSkil joined them. No one said a word.

Spread out below them was a small valley and a dirt road. Overhead, the clouds half-covered the sun and created a special, almost celestial, lighting on the clearing below.

The four robots saw acres and acres of an almost infinite number of spare parts with which to improve Phil.

To Val and Aqua, it was as though they had just stumbled through the misty chapters of a mythology book and were now actually standing in awe of a place that to a robot was a magical blend of Camelot . . . Valhalla . . . Atlantis . . . Oz. . . .

It was a junkyard.

Happily, the four robots hurried down the hill toward a place they hoped would be more than just a highly functional resting stop. A place that would turn out to be a haven.

A home.

CHAPTER 10

junk (jungk) *n.* 1. old metal, parts, glass, rags, paper, etc. 2. machine parts. 3. useless or worthless stuff; trash; rubbish.

• • • It was as if God was a robot and had smiled down upon them and sent them mountains of mechanical parts directly from that Great Machine Shop in the Sky.

Val, Aqua, Phil, and CatSkil approached the vast, sprawling, cluttered, heaven-sent junkyard with awe and reverence. They could only stare in wonder at the endless piles of shapeless, twisted, ancient metal and spare parts. They beheld crushed cars, rusty refrigerators, tarnished toasters, corroded computers, and many pieces of metal that would forever remain unrecognizable but might be, for the right purpose, still functional. So it was with slow, careful movements that the four lost robots stumbled out of the vast, tree-filled desert of Nature and into the oasis of lifeless machinery.

But then they exchanged excited, happy looks, and there followed an immediate laying on of hands. It was as though they had to touch every metal part in sight to make sure it was real; their experience became not just a series of visual delights but an experience in tactile excitement, too. Val and Aqua felt the greasy inside of an old-fashioned internal combustion car engine, marveling at its former utility. CatSkil felt the smooth, although now chipped, enamel of a broken washing machine. Phil scooted over to an old TV set and thrust his white mitten in among the tubes, feeling each cold, clear half-cylinder. Val grabbed an old circuit panel, then held it up to the sunlight, not knowing what it had been but quickly figuring out what it might be in a new, reincarnated life. Aqua lifted up some tangled wiring from inside an old casing, examined it, filed away what she learned in her computer, marked the location, and put it back exactly where she had found it. Their search continued at an almost frantic rate as more and more pieces of metal were grabbed, seized, snatched, clutched, caressed and fondled. CatSkil began to hum a strange tune that was somewhere between being a Gregorian chant and inspirational music that leaned heavily on the string section. A place that would have been a mere junkyard to a human being was to a robot a combination Garden of Eden, religious shrine, art gallery, Disneyland, and other analogies humans are simply not programmed to understand.

"My Pleasure Center is malfunctioning again," Aqua said quietly to Val as they explored the junkyard.

"Mine is, too," Val said. "Query: Could this be the closest we can come to the human concept of 'beauty'?"

"The probabilities seem high. Even Phil is quiet, apparently undergoing a minor sensory overload."

"I suggest the following program," Val said, speaking louder so that Phil and CatSkil could also hear him. "There is much to learn here, as well as many replacement parts for our units. However, we will logically save energy for needed repair work if we rest our units now."

"Should we cut our power usage back to ten percent for the next hour?" Aqua asked.

Val nodded. "In fact, my own energy pack is beginning to run low anyway." Val then tried to sound quite casual as he asked, "Can you feel decreasing power in your unit, Aqua?"

"Yes," she admitted. "But I didn't want to bother you with that particular variable."

"I function better with maximum input," Val said.

Aqua looked at her wrist and slid back a small panel, purposely angling the digital numbers in a pseudocasual way so that only she could see her readings. Val did the same to his wrist, also subtly hiding his data, which read "VALCOM–17485—ENERGY PACK: 22% POWER REMAINING."

"My unit has . . . fifty-two percent power left," Val said pleasantly, lying through his mechanical teeth.

Aqua saw that her wrist control read "AQUACOM–89045—ENERGY PACK: 17% POWER REMAINING." and she looked up, smiled sincerely, and said, "My unit has . . . forty-seven percent power left."

They each quickly slid their panels back over their digital numbers, then Val turned to CatSkil.

"CatSkil, are you experiencing any malfunctions due to power loss?"

"*A woman went to her psychiatrist and said, 'Doctor, it's about my husband. He thinks he's a refrigerator,'*" CatSkil happily began, with a quick flick of his cigar ashes. " *'That's not so bad,' the doctor says, 'it's a rather harmless complex.' 'Well, maybe,' the woman says, 'but he sleeps with his mouth open, and the light keeps me awake.'*" That was immediately followed by a rim shot, cigar smoke, and a nod from Val.

"Then we are agreed," Val said, looking at Aqua. "Let us each set our power usage down to ten percent for the next hour to conserve energy, since we are not close to an energy station." Val, Aqua, and CatSkil all adjusted their own levels, but when they tried to set Phil at a lower lever he ran, faking an end run but then going up the middle even with no blocking. CatSkil grabbed his left ear, Val got him by the wagon, and Aqua found the tuning knob on his Philco radio and cut Phil's energy down to ten percent.

Phil was stopped in his tracks. Val and Aqua sat down, side by side, on the ratty old front seat of a car that was sitting on the ground. CatSkil was close by, his power now greatly reduced.

"This afternoon, after giving our energy packs a brief rest, we can experiment and see what spare parts we can utilize," Aqua said.

"That would be both logical and effective," Val said. "Aqua, it still bothers me that our goal is not clearly defined."

"But Val, all of our energies have been devoted to trying to improve Phil and make him the best robot possible. Therefore, that would seem to be our goal."

Val mulled that over and couldn't find any flaw in the reasoning. He looked at Aqua and smiled.

"Logically," he whispered, trying not to disturb CatSkil or Phil, "you could conserve energy by resting part of your unit against mine."

Aqua smiled and put her head on Val's shoulder as he put his arm around her. Within minutes, the four robots were taking an electronic nap.

CrimeBuster finally realized he had been wandering in circles through the woods. He stopped, his periscope went up, slowly turning in a circle, and his radar bowls rose and began to turn. He tried to locate either fresh robot prints so he could keep tracking his suspects or any mechanical or life forms that might be of assistance in his efforts. Then he realized how unlikely that was. After all, the people at the party had recited the Robot Litany in an effort to confuse him and aid the criminals, then that FarmBot on the tractor had attempted to obstruct justice by only discussing the weather. What was this society coming to? CrimeBuster privately blamed the liberal JudgeBots.

CrimeBuster then realized he wasn't getting much from either his radar or from his periscope. Those particular parts worked fine, but somewhere in his system, CrimeBuster realized, he was suffering damage. It wasn't surprising. First his circuits had overloaded while he was forced to react to the Litany, then the lake water had sloshed in while he was in a vulnerable state with his gun ports left open, then he had been rammed by that stupid bull. CrimeBuster's energy pack was also low. He decided to conserve his efforts and lowered his periscope and radar equipment. It was time for old-fashioned, cops-and-robbers persistence.

CrimeBuster went crashing through the forest in an entirely new direction. He purposely chose the roughest paths, in an effort to outwit the fleeing criminals. He drove over rocks, across fallen logs, through the thickest undergrowth and up the steepest hills.

After an hour, he found himself with less energy and more injuries than ever before. He came to the top of a hill overlooking a vast clearing. Down below was a huge junkyard. CrimeBuster double-checked his ammo, clicked his guns into position, and rumbled on down to investigate.

Max kept eating while Charlie looked at the road map. They were on a dirt road, about ten miles from the farm, where they had just told Ellis and Edna Ruth what had happened. While Ellis went to make sure Bossie and Lord

172

Parmenter IV wouldn't wander away and then to clean up the burnt-out haystacks and destroyed FarmBot, Edna Ruth had made them both some sandwiches and given them a quart of fresh milk.

"Nice people, you know?" Max said, his mouth full of ham sandwich. "Not to blame us for the robot trouble."

"Who?" Charlie asked absentmindedly, his mind on the map.

"That farm couple. Nice folks. A lot of people would have gotten angry at us, you know, because we're from the factory. See? That's the difference between a FarmBot and a farmer."

"Max, I never said I liked robots better than people. I just don't think I'm smart enough to know how to improve people in this world. Just robots. Look at this, Max. That might be a place to go ask about missing robots." Charlie pointed at a place on the local map. Max looked at it and nodded.

"If we're going, let's get there," Max said, glancing up at the sun in the sky. Damned if he'd spend another night out here, cold and hungry. Before he did that he'd go back and tell Westlin to take this job and shove it up his integrated circuit. Charlie put the map away, started up the truck, and then went barreling down the dirt road, leaving a cloud of dust behind them. He reached for a sandwich and ate as he drove.

"Funny that there would be one out here in the mountains like that." Charlie said. "But it's on the map. . . ."

"What's that?"

"A junkyard."

confrontation (kon′ frən tā′ shən) *n*. 1. to face or boldly oppose. 2. a face-to-face, antagonistic meeting.

Two hours later, while Val, Aqua, CatSkil, and Phil, recently refreshed, busily looked through the junkyard, they had no idea they were being observed.

All four robots were on full power and again looking at a variety of parts, but this time with a strict eye for utility. Val screwed a tube, which he had taken from the back of an old TV set, into his leg panel. Nearby, Aqua examined the wiring in the back of an old fan to see if it might be compatible with her abdomen.

"Aqua, I think I've found a workable substitute for my broken digital neo-integrator."

"That sounds efficient, Val. And I may be able to splice this wiring into my SME-65 or my KU-69."

Phil watched Val and Aqua make their repairs and substitutions with a quizzical expression, then rolled over to a rusty car and took out a loose headlight. Phil put it over one eye, then looked up at CatSkil, who was smoking his cigar and looking more bored than usual. CatSkil looked down at Phil and his new oversized eye replacement and shook his head. Phil then scurried over to another pile of junk and found an old rubber boot, placed it beside his tank tread, then looked up at CatSkil in a questioning way. CatSkil again shook his head, then flicked away some cigar ashes. Phil tossed the boot aside and ran up to a rusty old inner spring mattress, picked out a large bedspring, and hooked it on top of his head. It wiggled back and forth and looked absolutely ridiculous. Phil looked up at CatSkil. CatSkil solemnly nodded his head.

Delighted with being able to create his own improvements, Phil then rushed over to an old, bent drainpipe. He quickly attached it to where his ass would have been if robots had asses and then raced off again after new improvements, now dragging a long metal tail after him.

CatSkil watched Val and Aqua's serious industry in picking out spare parts, then looked at Phil's version, decided he'd go with the kid; reached over, and put a large oil can on top of his head, like a triangular hat. What the hell.

Val and Aqua looked over and saw what both Phil and CatSkil were up to, but it didn't make sense. They were adding absolutely useless items to their units. Val and Aqua exchanged looks. Then Val reached for an old radiator, held it up to his chest, and began to wire it in place, while Aqua grabbed an old yellow plastic wastebasket, which she put on her head at a sporty angle like an Easter bonnet with all the frills upon it.

Then things really got out of hand. Not aware they were being observed, not even stopping to think what they were doing, Val, Aqua, CatSkil, and Phil began sifting through the absurd, discarded items and attaching them to their units.

174

There was a frenzy of activity as parts were wired, hooked, screwed, glued, and worn on different places on their bodies. Doorknobs. Housedresses. Typewriters. Bicycle horns. Steering wheels. Outboard motors. Accordions. Tubes. Wires. Anything. If it didn't move it was grabbed up and wired on.

Five minutes later, the frenzy of activity had stopped. The four robots had finally stopped acting like sharks who had just smelled blood. Now they stood in place, each looking more ridiculous than the other. Val had, among other things, a radiator on his chest, copper tubing over his right arm, a wind chime hanging from his left elbow, a trombone attached to his side, one foot in a bucket, and the other leg wrapped in a football knee pad. Aqua looked even sillier, wearing deer antlers on her head and a swim mask over her face, as well as several dozen other new parts that made the antlers and swim mask look low-key and sensible. CatSkil had a metal grid over his face, a "Yield" sign across his stomach, and he leaned casually against a surfboard. Phil wasn't even recognizable. He was best described as a heap of junk that could move. Phil was buried under all his new parts but still beeped with joy. At this point, the four robots exchanged looks, wondering what in the world had just happened. . . .

The four robots weren't the only ones who were curious about the scene that had just occurred.

"Interesting trespassers," said a young man from the top of a thirty-foot mountain of junk, who had been watching everything.

"Technologically fascinating," responded the young woman, who was sitting beside him. They spoke quietly, unnoticed by the robots below.

They were the owners of the junkyard and were what the local townspeople described as "sweet, but a couple of characters." Their names were Calvin and Susan Gort. They were thirty years old, and apart from each other, they loved anything having to do with technology. Susan wore her hair uncombed and a shapeless hat that kept the sun out of her eyes, plus thick glasses with broken frames held together with electrician's tape. She wore turquoise-colored work overalls with about a million little tools stuck in every pocket and dangling from every loop. Calvin, also in work overalls and wearing thick glasses, was one of those guys who could never get a date to the prom but knew not only how to fix your carburetor but even how to open easily a broken gym locker. Calvin wore a key chain on his belt with never less than a zillion keys on it, as well as a leather tool pouch now filled with nineteen tools, twelve of which Calvin had invented himself. Calvin also wore white socks, his cuffs rolled up, seven pens in his work-shirt pocket and was rapidly approaching advanced nerdism, if you only looked on the surface. Calvin and Susan's clothes didn't match, their hairstyles weren't in fashion, and they didn't do anything that was chic. The thing was, they didn't know or care about anything other than being happily married to the other one and having plenty of mechanical projects going all at the same time. They had purchased the rural junkyard six months before. They weren't used to many people or customers dropping by, let alone four strange robots.

"Two Com-series," Calvin noted.

"One is the new model with the Neo-pulse Frequency Modulation System," Susan added, who never knew what was up-to-date in *Cosmopolitan* but never missed an issue of *Popular Mechanics*.

"That CatSkil model is complete with cigar option."

"Perhaps we can study its NR-22 Closed-Loop Random-Output System."

"But what in the world is that small model?" Calvin asked. Phil was definitely a mystery to both of them.

"And what in the world are they doing?" Susan wondered out loud as they started to climb back down Junk Mountain.

"Obviously," Calvin explained, "they are customers, sent here by their human owner to acquire parts. Don't be so surprised at the idea of customers, Susan."

"But we've only had three in six months."

"I told you we'd make a profit this month."

"Calvin, of course we'll make a profit. We don't have any overhead."

He stopped climbing halfway down the pile of junk and just looked at Susan's smiling, pretty face. They each loved living away from the big-city confusion, but they also loved advanced technology; it had been a source of frustration until Calvin had seen the ad for the small-town junkyard set amid the mountains and forests six months ago. They had scraped together all their savings and bought it. But junkyards, it turned out, were not exactly a growth industry.

"Susan, you said you've loved living out here where the air is clean and the view is fantastic. Besides, we got all the projects going that we want to." Projects were what Calvin and Susan called their inventions or mechanical experiments. At the moment, they had twenty-seven half-started projects, including a soft alarm clock the size and shape of a double bed, a wind-powered pencil sharpener, a digital mousetrap, and a microwave toilet.

"I know, Calvin, it's just that maybe a junkyard surrounded by a thick forest isn't terribly profitable."

"Yes, but it does combine beauty and utility," Calvin said, smiling at her. "Like you."

Susan smiled sweetly, melting inside. She took his hand, and together they descended the junk pile, then walked around the junk until they reached the four robots. Their eyes never left Phil.

Phil looked up at them warily. His only experience with human beings thus far had been that collection of winners at the party. But he did not back away, only watched carefully as Susan took a tool from her belt and tightened up several loose screws on Phil's arm.

"Whatever this model is, it could use a little maintenance," Susan said, holding out her hand without looking up. Calvin automatically put the correct wrench in her hand from his tool pouch, and she went on tightening a few bolts on Phil. "It seems to combine the highly sophisticated 7000-series Differentiation System . . ."

". . . with amateurish level-three mobility," Calvin finished.

"Excuse me," Val said, walking up to them with all his ridiculous junk still on, "but Phil has a level-*four* mobility."

"And we connected a JBA-35 modifier to the Differentiation System," Aqua added, also joining the group, sounding quite intelligent for someone who was wearing a swim mask and deer antlers.

Calvin and Susan took it all in stride. Calvin bent over and peered closely at Phil, who peered closely at Calvin.

"How did you hook it in? With Number twenty-seven Inverse Wiring?" he asked.

"Yes, plus an experimental use of Electrostatic MagnoTape," Val bragged.

"What an exciting experiment," Susan said, genuinely

enthusiastic. Phil looked from one to the other as they spoke. "And obviously successful!"

"Thank you," Aqua said, smiling with pleasure. She too was very proud of Phil; it was the first time anyone had ever complimented him.

It was then that Val realized he had more stupid junk hanging from him than a Christmas tree. "I would like to explain our present excessive arrangement of spare parts," he began. But then he paused. Aqua looked at him through her swim mask, also waiting. "But I have insufficient data for an accurate explanation." Val suddenly longed for the days when he was an efficient robot that responded to normal programs and understood the logic of his own actions. But he was spared further confusion by the sudden presence of a raccoon.

It peeked out from behind some junk and watched the bizarre intruders in the junkyard. Susan noticed him and bent down, motioning him to come forward.

"It's all right, Rover. These sentient creatures are obviously not mischievous trespassers."

Thus encouraged, Rover the raccoon wandered over to Susan, who picked him up and stroked his back and rubbed him behind his ears, the way he liked. Calvin routinely leaned over and petted him, while Val, Aqua, and CatSkil had no particular reaction to the animal.

Phil went ape-shit.

He beeped, screeched, spun in a circle, reached out, glowed red, spun back the other way, glowed blue, and electronically indicated he wanted that raccoon more than anything he'd ever wanted in his whole life—all in the space of two seconds.

So Susan smiled and handed him over.

Finally, Phil got to have a pet, one he could hold in his arms and stroke with his dirty white mitten. The raccoon didn't mind it either; at long last love.

"Apparently," Calvin said, pointing to the bizarre appearances of what would have otherwise been two regular Comseries and one routine CatSkil, "you have been sent by your owners on an errand for spare parts. But why these?"

Susan made the mistake of turning to CatSkil. "Surely they are not to improve your looks," she said, smiling at CatSkil, who leaned back and got ready. Val and Aqua motioned for

178

her to stop, but she went right ahead. "Logically, they don't even fit; they are extraneous—"

Too late. Now CatSkil had her. He flicked his ashes in Susan's tool pouch, half-closed his eyes and said, *"Did you hear the one about the furrier who crossed a mink with a gorilla?"*

Susan blinked. Val and Aqua closed their eyes.

"He got a beautiful coat, only the sleeves were too long." Bap-bap, cigar smoke, and a satisfied look on CatSkil's face.

There was a long silence. Calvin and Susan could only stare. Phil, however, went into hysterics.

"What are you, an audience or an oil painting?" CatSkil demanded of Calvin and Susan, who remained speechless. They had heard about CatSkil models and knew how they worked internally, but they'd never actually been around one. They grew more interested in Phil's reaction. He was laughing so hard that Rover bailed out, thinking there was an earthquake. CatSkil turned away from Phil and motioned with his cigar toward Calvin and Susan. *"What's the matter? Can't you people hear over in this section?"*

"CatSkil, perhaps if we return to the business at hand," Val said, wishing CatSkil had an "off" switch.

"Laugh it up, folks, I love to see people who really enjoy life," CatSkil continued, getting out his best sarcasm the way some people, for special occasions, get out their finest linen.

"CatSkil, perhaps if we discuss other priorities," Aqua said, also trying to keep him from totally alienating two human beings who were not only courteous but might be of some practical help as well. CatSkil was just getting himself cocked and ready to fire again when the raccoon scampered away, and Phil quickly turned to chase it.

Val and Aqua just looked at each other, trying to figure out whose turn it was.

"That is a fascinating machine," Susan said, watching Phil rumble after unrequited love.

"Yes," Calvin agreed. "Before filling your order, I have a number of questions concerning his design—"

"Hello?" Max yelled from behind a large junk pile.

"Anybody here?" Charlie hollered.

Aqua and Val froze.

CatSkil yawned; first ya gotta care.

Val and Aqua's first thought was for Phil, but fortunately

the raccoon had led him on a merry chase down a winding pathway between large, twenty-foot high piles of junk, and he was safely out of sight. Val and Aqua stepped back until they stood beside CatSkil, their backs up against a tall stack of twisted iron parts. Still wearing a wide assortment of nonsense parts that they now hoped would help hide them, Val, Aqua, and CatSkil did not move an inch as Max and Charlie emerged from behind the junk pile.

Calvin and Susan turned to look at them, smiling.

"See?" Calvin whispered to Susan. "More customers!"

"Remind me to dig around later and see if we can find an old rusty numbered-card system," Susan whispered back, "so we'll know which part of the mob gets served first."

"Hello!" Calvin said loudly as a tired, dirty, disgruntled Max and Charlie walked up. Charlie almost tripped over an old lawn mower. "I'm Calvin Gort and this is my wife, Susan. We're in charge here."

"May we be of assistance?" Susan asked. It had been so long between customers that she'd almost forgotten just what she was supposed to say.

Max sighed. He knew weirdos when he saw them. But maybe they could get all this over with quickly. "We're from the General Motors plant just over the mountain. A couple or three units got left turned on or something and wandered off."

"Anybody tried to sell you some stolen robots?" Charlie asked in a not totally friendly tone. His poison oak had reached places on his body Charlie hadn't been aware even existed.

Calvin openly bristled at the tone, the question, and the implication. He never understood how anyone could accuse a poor person of being dishonest; it was too easy to make money if you didn't care how you did it. "First of all, I assure you that we do not deal in stolen parts or stolen property. We never have, we never will, and if you expect cooperation from us I'd suggest you not start off by insulting—"

"Look, pal, don't make a speech," Max growled. "We've been up all night. Just tell us if you know anything about any loose robots."

Calvin started to answer but then noticed that Max was now leaning back against what he thought was a pile of junk. Behind him two large eyes glared at Max, since Max was leaning against the pile of junk's black velvet Las Vegas-lounge jacket, wrinkling it. "You said some robots are loose," Calvin asked, "wandering around on their own, lacking supervision?"

"Something like that," Charlie said, idly noticing some deer antlers on top of some pink-colored junk that was off to one side, in the shadows. "There's two Com-series and a CatSkil model. Oh, and there's some crazy CrimeBuster loose, too."

It was at that moment that CatSkil decided that he had had just about enough; he started to readjust his arm slightly, preparing to flick cigar ashes down Max's neck. Susan saw it coming and instinctively tried to distract Max.

"Well, uh," Susan began eloquently, "why don't you just have the CrimeBuster find the other three?"

It did the trick. Max was so irritated that he moved away from the pile of junk, and the cigar ashes floated gently to earth, noticed only by Susan, Aqua, and Val, who quickly exchanged looks.

"Very funny," Charlie said, not smiling.

"Come on, dammit!" Max half-yelled at Calvin and Susan. "One thing I don't need is to waste time searching through all this worthless crap."

Calvin and Susan were taken aback by this.

"Excuse me," Calvin said carefully, emphasizing every word, not having quite believed his ears. "I want to understand something. Did you just make a disparaging reference to our vast assortment of mechanical parts? Did you just call them 'worthless crap?' "

Susan couldn't believe it either. She was genuinely shocked. "You find this abundance of technological advances to be . . . without value?" she asked.

Charlie rolled his eyes at the mountains around them and finally answered in a tired voice. "We don't have time to look through all this worthless junk!"

"Now have you seen any robots or not?" Max asked.

Calvin and Susan hesitated a moment, well aware that only a few feet behind the two hostile men from the factory were three robots who were purposely not moving or speaking. They weren't all that well-disguised either. It was just that Max and Charlie were tired and impatient and hadn't happened to really look in their direction . . . yet. If Val and Aqua had been able to breathe, they would have held their breath. CatSkil, on the other hand, picked this precise moment in the history of the world to try to blow smoke rings. He'd never learned how but always wanted to, so since he had a few minutes to kill, he gave it a try. The first few didn't work very well, but then he got the hang of it, and several almost perfect round circles of green smoke floated out of the junk pile, aimed at the back of Charlie's head. If either Max or Charlie happened to turn their heads just slightly . . .

Calvin and Susan began walking over to one side as they finally answered, trying to keep Max and Charlie looking at them and not in any other direction. "Let's see . . ." Calvin said, "we had some folks in today, but they were just playing and having fun with some spare parts. We haven't seen anyone that acted like robots. . . ."

"No," Susan agreed after serious deliberation. "We haven't seen anyone that acted like robots today . . . just some folks who were . . ." And then Calvin joined in and they finished the thought together. ". . . just playing and having a good time."

"Why the hell didn't you just say so?" Max asked.

"Come on, Max," Charlie said, gesturing for them to leave. "We got a lot of ground to cover." And with that, Max and Charlie moved off, walking back the way they came.

Calvin and Susan, arm in arm, walked part of the way with Max and Charlie, as though they were seeing off dinner guests. They smiled and waved, making sure the two men from the factory were, in fact, leaving.

"Come back any time," Calvin sang after them.

"Now that you know the way," Susan yelled happily, "don't be a stranger!"

"That's all we needed," Max grumbled as he and Charlie jumped into the pickup truck and roared off. "Mr. and Mrs. Gyro Gearloose . . ."

Val and Aqua stepped away from the stack of junk and quickly began taking off all their excess parts; their mood had sobered very quickly. Even CatSkil threw his own nutty attachments to one side, though he continued to practice blowing smoke rings.

Then Val looked around in every direction. "Query: When we constructed Phil, did we use any parts from a MagicBot?"

Aqua thought a moment. "Negative. Why do you ask?"

182

"He keeps disappearing," Val said, and then Val, Aqua, and CatSkil hurried off to find Phil.

Phil, at the moment, was chasing Rover the raccoon through twisted piles of metal, past rows of rusty truck parts, and around hollow shells of discarded computers, going deeper and deeper into the junkyard. There was a loud clanging noise that he kept getting closer and closer to, but Phil was pre-occupied with catching the raccoon. Phil was giving the raccoon a hell of a chase, but Rover knew the lay of the land better. The animal finally darted down a dark tunnel of stuff which was too small for Phil to follow and disappeared.

Phil screeched to a stop. He'd been chasing animals his entire life, and he knew when he was beaten.

He turned and looked around. No Val. No Aqua. No CatSkil. No familiar landmarks. Alone.

Above his head, bent, jagged pieces of steel and iron were overlapped, forming a roof for the corridor of junk he had wandered into; the sunlight and sky were hidden now, and the junkyard appeared to be a sinister jungle of metal to the little robot. Except for the distant clanging sound, everything was quiet. Then the wind came up and made an eerie whistle through the pieces of metal.

Phil rolled on but with hesitation, looking down the rows of rusty cars and wrecked machinery. It looked worse and worse. Phil began to make quiet little beeping noises, plaintive-sounding electronic whimpers. And the clanging noise grew louder.

"PHIL! REPORT AT ONCE!" Val sang out, but heard no response.

"PHIL! ANSWER AT ONCE!" Aqua's voice was raised to its highest decibel level, but it didn't do any good. Phil was not responding.

"Perhaps we should split up and search for him in different directions," Val suggested, and Aqua nodded. Then they turned to CatSkil. "CatSkil, would you help us look for Phil in that part of the junkyard over there?"

"Did you hear the one about the Jew, the chicken plucker, and the azalea bush all trying to get into heaven?" CatSkil began, with a flourish of his cigar. *"Well, it seems that St. Peter stops them and—"*

183

Val held up his hands in a halting gesture. "Excuse the interruption, CatSkil, but now is not the best time for a humorous story."

"Perhaps," Aqua quickly added, "you could hurry, just this once, to the conclusion of your amusing anecdote."

CatSkil nodded, shrugged, and spoke more rapidly. *"So St. Peter asks the Jew if—"* Suddenly, CatSkil's voice turned into rapid, high-pitched, electronic gibberish, similar to the sound of a tape recorder being "fast-forwarded." The whirring sound lasted a few seconds, then quickly slowed down and became audible again as CatSkil finished the joke. *"And so the guy says, 'I don't know, but the priest ate two of 'em!'"* That was followed, as the night follows the day, as the golden leaves of autumn follow the greenery of summer, by a rim shot, a puff of cigar smoke, and an almost but not quite perfect smoke ring.

Then all three robots headed in different directions, calling for Phil.

Phil, at the moment, was in total mechanical panic.

The portion of the junkyard he was traveling through was jagged and unfriendly, dark and foreboding, and he scurried along, lost and alone, like a metal Ichabod Crane trying to survive a Halloween race through the ghostly shadows of Sleepy Hollow. Ripped fenders created the image of grasping claws, metal springs cast shadows that looked like coiled snakes, and twisted wire cable gave the appearance of spiderlike creatures, poised and ready to pounce. From somewhere far away, Phil could hear the echoing sounds of Aqua yelling "Phil! Answer within ten microseconds!" and Val calling out "Phil! Hel-lo. . . ." But Phil couldn't tell where the voices were coming from or how close they might be. He just kept moving, even though the loudest sound of all was a loud clanking noise just ahead of him.

Just around a high column of wrecked cars waited a huge circular magnet. Held by a cranelike apparatus and thick metal chains, it was suspended thirty feet in the air over a big old Pontiac that carried a faded bumper sticker that read "Nuke the Black, Gay, Unemployed, and Handicapped Whales." Suddenly it dropped, CLANK! It hit the roof of the old car so hard the window glass shattered and the roof half-caved in, but it sucked the heavy car up into the air as if

184

it was nothing. The crane swung the magnet holding the car over to a rectangular steel pit. At one end of the pit was a heavy metal slab, which stood at a ninety-degree angle. WHAM! The magnet let go, and the car dropped into the pit. A long moment later, the impossibly heavy metal slab began to tilt forward slowly . . . then faster . . . falling . . . and the earth shook! As the metal slab was slowly raised back into its upright position, waiting for a new victim, a side scoop slowly pushed the Pontiac pancake off to one side. The crane had already swung back, and the magnet, like a hungry predatory bird, was seeking new prey. Immediately, as though forced to feed the ravenous metal slab, the magnet began sailing off after a new victim.

Phil.

The little robot had come screeching to a stop after rounding the corner, only to stare in horrified fascination as the large car was pulverized from a three-dimensional object into one with only length and width. Phil's green eyes blinked as the magnet went back up into the air slowly and the crane swung it over . . . closer . . . closer. . . . Phil had to keep tilting his head back to watch it.

And then he understood. He was next.

Beeping loudly for Val and Aqua, Phil whirled around and did a wheelie, laying rubber behind him, but the magnet had the ability to fly and went right after him, no longer circling in the sky like a lazy hawk but suddenly a fierce, single-minded killer that swooped down.

The crane operator, over in a small box, was a simple robot, not unlike the basic old model that was used as a forklift operator back at the factory. The CraneBot had no facial expression, no sophisticated reasoning ability, and no reason at all to hesitate in going after Phil. His mechanical hands routinely worked the levers; his assigned function was to scoop up and smash any loose metal in the vicinity, period.

Phil beeped as he dodged and raced along as fast as he could. The magnet was twenty feet in the air and dropping quickly . . . eighteen feet . . . sixteen feet . . . no matter which way Phil turned, it followed . . . fourteen feet . . . twelve. . . . Phil changed direction . . . so did the magnet. . . .

Val and Aqua walked into the vast open area and suddenly

stared, openmouthed, at the horrible scene in front of them. They were a hundred feet away, helpless to do anything.

Phil's lights flashed on and off, his beeping became shrill. His tank treads were whirling so fast they sounded like a passing freight train.

The CraneBot, safely in his box on the opposite side of the vast open area, routinely worked his levers, and the magnet was ten feet over Phil's head . . . eight feet . . .

"Can Phil outrun the mechanism?" Val asked.

"The machine is too . . . efficient," Aqua replied quietly.

Helpless, they watched as Phil faked left, then went right, but the magnet had been at this a long time, one of the veterans of the game, and was now only six feet above Phil . . . then four feet . . . then . . .

Phil's metal body jumped up, CLANK, against the huge circular object. Three feet was close enough for small metal objects, since magnetism did the rest.

Giving one last, long, horrible beep, Phil was plucked up in the air and swung over toward the rectangular crush zone.

Aqua closed her eyes.

Val put his arm around her.

Phil was dropped into the crush zone.

He hit so hard he bounced, losing any number of tubes and circuits upon impact.

Val watched the huge rectangular metal slab that was now upright at one end of the pit. . . . It began to move slightly, quivering, released from its upright position but not yet descending.

The CraneBot reached for a small lever, and just as he started to throw the lever forward, his metal hand stopped. The CraneBot's eye lights went out. His tubes flickered and died.

The metal slab remained upright.

And from a simple box just inside the chest area of the CraneBot, where a simple lever marked "On-Off" was kept, CatSkil withdrew his hand, casually shoved the CraneBot over, and then blew an absolutely perfect smoke ring.

It took twenty minutes for Val and Aqua to retrieve Phil from the crush zone, check him out to make sure he wasn't seriously damaged by the fall, and begin heading out of the mazelike junkyard. Still shaken up by the whole experience,

Phil held Val's hand tightly as they walked along. Aqua walked beside them, and she and Val discussed how desperately important it was for them to improve Phil to prevent him from ever getting into such trouble again. After they talked about it for a few minutes, Aqua turned and looked back at CatSkil, who was about thirty feet behind, just rolling along as usual, bothering no one unless given half a chance.

Aqua turned and walked back beside CatSkil, letting Val and Phil go on ahead. On one side of the path was a tall stack of washing machines and on the other were giant, worn-out generators of some kind. Aqua looked at CatSkil closely. "CatSkil, you performed very efficiently in rescuing Phil's unit."

"*There was this jockey, see, who always ate beans before a race, and—*"

"CatSkil, wait, please!" Aqua's sudden request made CatSkil stop in mid-joke, something that happened about as often as the planets lining up. "I want to tell you something."

CatSkil turned and looked at Aqua, giving her his full attention.

"CatSkil, I want to say something," she said softly. "If the reason you left the warehouse was to assist Val and me as your way of being our friend, then I want you to know that you have performed very, very effectively."

CatSkil, unable to look Aqua in the eye, busied himself with flicking his cigar ashes for a moment, then they just walked along side by side, enjoying the quiet stroll together.

Still holding Phil's hand, Val glanced back at Aqua and CatSkil. He couldn't hear what they were saying, but he saw CatSkil smile instead of sneer, and he knew something unusual, something positive, had just happened. Val smiled himself, happy they were all safe and that their units were relatively sound, noting that this basic tribal grouping would be known among humans as a "family;" for the first time, Val realized how effective it could be.

Val glanced back again. There was something about the way Aqua and CatSkil looked at each other briefly that caused a memory circuit ghost. Val suddenly remembered a scene from an old western movie called *Shane* that he had watched on the wall-size vidscreen owned by Horace Smith, or Smitty as he had insisted Val call him. Val had watched the film with Smitty while making him sandwiches, and he noted that at first glance the film seemed to contain a classic romantic triangle that humans, for whatever reasons, often enjoyed. Van Heflin was a rancher, Jean Arthur was his wife, and Alan Ladd was the mysterious gunfighter who stayed with them and proved to be their friend. However, Val recalled, there was never a hint of direct romantic interest expressed between the loyal rancher's wife and the quiet gunfighter; it would have been out of character, inappropriate. And yet there was a special, unspoken, what-might-have-been bond between them. (Val wouldn't have known about any of those human subtleties except that Smitty's wife, Pat, had mentioned it, in spite of the fact that Smitty didn't care and was impatient for the gunfight.) As Val glanced back at Aqua and CatSkil, he wondered why that tiny memory had kicked into his primary computer scan. . . .

Aqua and CatSkil were walking briskly past a dozen rusty, dented, empty file cabinets, which reminded Aqua of something. "CatSkil! I just this millisecond discovered a huge blank spot in my data bank concerning CatSkil. Val and I spend many hours trying to get whatever Phil wants or needs, but no one has ever asked you what *you* want. What is it you desire, CatSkil?"

"This woman opens a refrigerator, see, and there's this large white rabbit stretched out on his back, smiling at her. She says, 'What are you doing in there?' And the rabbit says, 'Well, this is a Westinghouse, isn't it?' The woman nods, and then the rabbit says, 'Well, I'm westing.' "

Halfway through the rim shot and the cigar smoke, Aqua held up her hands urgently. "No, CatSkil, please. This one time I would like you to attempt to respond more clearly. Please . . . tell me. What is it you really want?"

CatSkil stopped rolling, so Aqua stopped walking.

CatSkil did not shoot his cuffs, wave his cigar, or speak out of the side of his mouth. He made an effort to speak quietly and normally. But could not. He tried harder than he ever had to make words come out of his mouth; there was something he was trying to say and couldn't. Aqua held his hand, gripping it tightly, and leaned closer. "You can do it, CatSkil. . . . Tell me what you really want. . . ."

CatSkil closed his eyes and with an incredible effort finally whispered, "To . . . stop . . . telling . . . jokes . . ."

It was very quiet then, as CatSkil tried to recover from the extreme energy loss that the struggle had taken, but the way Aqua squeezed his arm as they walked on made it all worth it.

Val paused, realizing that the sun was getting low in the sky. They still weren't out of the junkyard yet. Val wasn't even sure exactly which way would get them out; the narrow paths between the junk kept curving. Val and Phil paused and waited for Aqua and CatSkil to catch up with them. Val was just about to begin to interface with Aqua concerning the best direction to go when a large, dome-shaped shadow loomed over the four robots.

Phil noticed it first and began to shake and beep.

Then CatSkil saw it, stopping in mid-puff.

Then Val and Aqua turned as the sun and part of the sky were blacked out by the huge shape, which had rumbled up over a small hill of junk and now looked down upon them. CrimeBuster's flamethrower was cocked and ready, along with nine other weapons, and his first order made it clear that he wouldn't be tricked again.

"Do not move or recite the Robot Litany, or you will be instantly incinerated," CrimeBuster blared out over his bullhorn.

Val's first computer analysis of the situation was that now it wouldn't matter which way was the quickest way out of the junkyard.

It was all over.

CHAPTER 11

end (end) *n*. 1. a limit; point of stopping.
2. the last part of anything; final point;
finish. 3. a ceasing to exist; death or
destruction.

• • • CrimeBuster had entered the junkyard very cautiously.
It had occurred to him that perhaps he had been making the
classic mistake of underestimating his criminal opponents. So
CrimeBuster resolved that this time he would pick the time
and place of his capture very carefully, and this time he knew
how to prevent any problems. Logically, he had them outarmed.
Therefore, the only way they could cause him problems was
if he allowed them to speak or move.

CrimeBuster had been tracking the four robots since they
had left the crush zone, waiting for them to regroup at a point
where he could capture them all together with no extraneous
variables, such as the interference from the people at the
party.

And now, finally, he had them in his sights. All eighteen
sights.

The tallest suspect stepped forward, and even though he
was staring into the end of the flamethrower, he began to
speak.

"An explanation of our activities would seem to be in
order," Val began, but he got no further.

"INCORRECT," roared CrimeBuster. "DO NOT SPEAK
ANOTHER WORD, OR YOU WILL BE BAKED AT A
TEMPERATURE OF 2000 DEGREES."

Val believed him.

"Due to the extent of the property damage you have already caused and the mathematical probabilities of further escape attempts between here and the factory," CrimeBuster said, "the logical, practical decision is to destroy you now." And with that, every single weapon CrimeBuster possessed shot out and clicked into position. "The first one to move will be the first one destroyed."

But at that moment Val, Aqua, and CatSkil all moved simultaneously, getting in front of Phil, trying to shield him.

"You have forced me to overreact," said CrimeBuster. "This is your last data input: 'A CrimeBuster Always Gets His Man.' "

Val and Aqua gave each other a long look and held each other's hands.

CrimeBuster's flamethrower, artillery cannon, laser gun, and one hell of a bazooka were carefully aimed, one each, at each of the four robots, and CrimeBuster was just about to let loose when Calvin and Susan came sailing out of the sky, screwdriver and wire clippers in hand, and landed on top of CrimeBuster.

The huge black machine whirled around in a circle, trying to dislodge them, but they held on tight. They had heard the commotion, investigated, then climbed to the top of an even higher pile of junk and, with little time to think or plan, they had leaped onto the huge CrimeBuster, which now began blaring out warnings to them.

"HALT! ATTACKERS WILL BE DESTROYED IF YOU DO NOT SURRENDER NOW!"

And then to emphasize his point, CrimeBuster began firing his M 16's in every direction. Val, Aqua, Phil, and CatSkil hit the dirt just as a spray of bullets ripped up the junk behind them.

"Calvin!" Susan yelled. "Can you reach it?"

CrimeBuster furiously spun in a tight circle.

"No!" Calvin yelled. "I think it's over here—"

Without stopping, CrimeBuster spun Calvin off into a pile of old wiring. Susan held on with one hand, her legs flying out in the air behind her, as CrimeBuster became a bucking bronco. Val and Aqua, meanwhile, rushed over, helped Calvin to his feet, and were just about to inquire politely as to his immediate plans when he ran back and leaped onto the rocking, spinning machine. Susan, on the other side, was clutching a gun-port opening.

"Can you reach it?" he yelled over the horrible grinding noise of CrimeBuster's engines and artillery shells, now being fired.

"Almost!" Susan yelled back.

Val and Aqua, hiding behind a wrecked car, could just barely see through the cloud of dust that Susan was stretching toward a control panel but couldn't quite reach whatever she was trying to disconnect.

"The R-17 wire!" Calvin yelled. "Cut it!"

"I'm trying—"

CrimeBuster heard and understood. Every gun he possessed went off at once; explosions started going off all over the junkyard. Dirt and tiny metal pieces rained down on Phil's head. Everywhere, junk was being burnt, blasted, and destroyed! Grenades were launched! mortar and bazookas were fired, flares went off—but Calvin kept trying to inch his way around the lethal fireworks that came flying out of every porthole. CrimeBuster pulsated, inside and out, with red lights. Alarms went off. He increased his speed, backing up, careening off one stack of crushed cars, knocking them over, then charging forward into some heavy scrap iron.

Guns fired!

CrimeBuster roared!

Junk exploded!

Calvin yelled!

Phil beeped!

CatSkil joked!

And Susan quietly managed to clip a tiny red wire inside CrimeBuster's main control panel, and suddenly everything was still and quiet.

CrimeBuster became totally inactive instantly. One second he was a raging mechanical monster, the next he was a lifeless, motionless hunk of metal. Calvin and Susan had put his lights out.

They climbed down off the black metal statue amid the cloud of dust that was still swirling and hugged and kissed each other. Calvin's glasses had flown off, Susan's hair was messed up, the tools in their tool pouches had flown out in every direction, and Calvin was missing his left boot. But

192

except for a few scratches and being tired and dirty, they were fine.

Phil found Calvin's glasses and brought them over to him. CatSkil got his boot, flicked his cigar ashes into it, then returned it to Calvin. Val and Aqua hurried over and began to dust off the two humans.

"Thank you both for preventing our units from being destroyed," Val said.

"Well, the CrimeBuster was obviously malfunctioning," Susan replied, smiling, then looked over at CatSkil.

"*He was so stupid,*" CatSkil intoned, gesturing with his cigar toward the lifeless CrimeBuster, "*that if a doctor told him he had sugar in his urine, the next morning he'd pee on his cornflakes.*"

They all did their best to go right on with the conversation. "From a purely technological point of view," Calvin said, "making it inoperable is a very simple procedure."

Calvin and Susan picked up their scattered tools, put their shirttails back in, and glanced around to see how much damage had been done to the immediate battlefield. Val, Aqua, CatSkil, and Phil regrouped and assessed their own damage, which was minimal. Then Val looked at Phil and smiled, and Phil looked up with wide, happy green eyes and beeped at Val.

"Aqua, once again the Phil unit was almost destroyed, first by the automobile crusher and now by this malfunctioning CrimeBuster. We need to plan for his future so he'll be efficient and take better care of his unit."

"I agree," she replied. "Otherwise, eventually he'll be deactivated, discarded, or destroyed as worthless."

They had begun to walk on through the junk, and Calvin and Susan joined them. CatSkil was most of the way through a joke about his mother-in-law, who talked so much that when they took her to the beach she got her tongue sunburned, when suddenly the four robots stopped and stared at a shocking sight.

Halfway up a pile of metal scraps, wedged in between a pile of rusty axles and some corroded sheet metal and leaning out at a grotesque angle, was a dead robot. It startled them to be suddenly face to face with the rusted hulk of a long-inactive robot. The head of the robot had a vacant brain area, a mouth open as if in a scream, and eye holes that were empty and rusted, with long brown streaks of corrosion running down the face like tears from eyes that stared into a forgotten eternity.

Val and Aqua flinched from the sight, and CatSkil quickly tried to shield Phil's eyes. Calvin and Susan exchanged looks, understanding. They all inched around the metal corpse, and Phil made strange little beeping sounds. They moved past it, but the vivid image of the dented, twisted body of what was once a beautifully efficient machine would always stay in their memory banks.

It was several minutes before anyone spoke. They had arrived at the edge of the junkyard.

With dignity, Val turned to Calvin and Susan. "Our primary objective is to improve the Phil unit and maximize his potential. Can you help us?"

"We gave Phil a directional finder, a unit safety monitor, and much more," Aqua quickly added. "But it is not enough."

"No, not nearly enough," Val said. "He needs entirely new equipment. But we not only have limited resources but limited time as well. Our energy packs are running dangerously low."

"We get energy packs through here occasionally, but we have none at the moment," Calvin said.

"Perhaps there are other ways we can help," Susan said. "What would you like us to do?"

Val and Aqua couldn't answer fast enough.

"Phil needs a newer, more sophisticated computer—"

"Better microprocessing chips—"

"Better size—"

"Utility—"

"Programming—"

"Wait, please," Calvin said. "What you also need for Phil's survival is for him to have a *function*."

"We can do a lot to help you," Susan added, "major maintenance and some minor modification, but if you really want all this done . . ." She shrugged apologetically. "There's only one place for you to go. . . ."

Then she turned and looked toward the mountains. On the other side was the factory.

Val and Aqua looked at each other, then they looked down at Phil. . . .

Calvin and Susan stood at the edge of their junkyard and watched through their binoculars until Val, Aqua, Phil, and CatSkil were just four tiny specks halfway up a steep mountainside. The late afternoon sun occasionally glinted off the metal shapes against the distant rocky landscape. Then, after some backsliding on the rocky shale, the four tiny specks were out of sight of the junkyard.

Calvin and Susan put their binoculars down.

"I don't think there's any way they can make it," Calvin said sadly. "They just don't have enough energy left."

"I know," Susan said. "But I hope they do."

It was the second time Val had slipped on the particularly steep slope and tumbled fifty feet to the bottom. He banged his already-damaged foot on a rock when he finally came to a stop, ripped his pants leg, and had a little pseudohair torn off the side of his head. Once Val managed to make it back to the top of the slope, they decided to rest briefly. In the last two hours they had suffered unit damage, and it showed. Aqua's left arm was half ripped off, following an effort to save Phil, who had slid backward, and her dress was more torn than ever. She was aware that the dripping inside was going on faster than ever, due to ripped lubrication tubes. CatSkil was missing his left foot and part of his forehead, and his jacket was ripped open in back. Not all of Phil's brain lights would go on now, and his power drill was the only one of his tools that worked properly. His bow tie-directional finder was at the bottom of a ravine he'd fallen into, and they were too exhausted to go back after it. They had no idea what had happened to his dirty white mitten.

They leaned back on rocks and a fallen log, noting that the sun was getting low in the sky. And they still had a long way to go. Both Val and Aqua knew that because of their reduced strength and capacities for geographical reference, their climb was going badly enough by daylight, but at night . . .

They didn't speak, not wanting to use the extra energy. Birds chirped around them; the forest prepared for the coming night.

"The atmospheric temperature is dropping a little," Aqua said in a quiet voice. "Do you think that will slow up our progress, since we now have torn neo-skin with exposed parts?"

Before Val could shake his head, a voice was heard which echoed up and down the steep slope.

"There was this drunk who was cutting through a graveyard one night, see, and he stumbles into an empty, freshly dug grave and passes out. Hours later, he starts to moan, 'I'm cold, I'm cold. . . .' Another drunk staggering by looks down and says, 'If you wanted to stay warm, you shouldn't have kicked all your dirt off.' "

The rim shot was not as loud and the cigar smoke was also very reduced, expelled without much force. CatSkil, too, was beginning to wear down.

"We need to continually monitor our energy-pack levels," Val said, also speaking in a quiet, subdued voice. He opened his wrist panel and read: 09% POWER REMAINING. He looked up at Aqua and forced a shrug and said, "I have thirty-four percent power remaining."

She nodded, then checked her own wrist panel, which read: 08% POWER REMAINING. She closed her panel, looked at Val, and reported that she had thirty-three percent power remaining. He nodded and they started climbing again.

The pine trees were casting long black shadows when they finally reached the crest of the mountain and began the difficult descent.

As internal parts sparked and died from lack of energy and other parts were simply broken or torn on the jolting trip, Val and Aqua's delicate mechanisms lost the ability to tell time. They didn't know if minutes or hours were passing. Up and down they went, mostly down now, assisting Phil, helping each other, trying to use gravity to help their journey without letting gravity suddenly end it. Twice they discovered they had gone in circles, but they knew that if they kept heading down the slopes they would soon end up close to the little valley and the factory.

"Val, I have been thinking. . . . The important thing is that if, just in case, one of us doesn't make it all the way back . . ."

"Yes, Aqua, I understand . . . . just on that slight mathematical possibility . . ."

"Then at least one of us must get Phil safely to the repair shop and tell them he is worth the expense of reconditioning and explain exactly how he does function."

"I agree, Aqua . . . because if neither of us successfully makes the trip with Phil, when he is found no one will understand that all he needs is upgraded equipment. There will be no one there to explain his true . . .*worth.*"

Some time later they crossed a small stream, splashing straight through it, not worrying about water damage. They were each so weakened and damaged that rusting wouldn't make any significant difference.

"If we do make it to the repair shop, Val, you know what they will do to your unit and mine, don't you?"

Val didn't answer. They all four splashed ashore and began the tortuous business of helping each other up the steep, muddy ravine. Aqua continued speaking in a quiet voice. "You know they will completely circuit-wash us. You know they will erase our memory banks. You know they will correct all our malfunctions, including the Pleasure-Center response we each cause in the other. And you know once we are overhauled and totally efficient that we will not only lack the present interest we have in each other but we will be sent to separate owners. Do you know those things, Val?"

At the top of the ravine, after dragging Phil up through the mud, Val turned and spoke in a quieter voice than Aqua had ever heard him use.

"Why do you think we've never turned back?" he said, and Aqua realized he had known so much more than he had ever indicated from the very beginning.

They started down a dirt road, Val and Aqua walking very slowly in front, CatSkil and Phil very slowly bringing up the rear.

"You and I can avoid the factory repair shop and stay together," Aqua said.

"Yes," Val acknowledged. "Or we can improve Phil, for better efficiency. And his survival."

"Correct. Those are the choices."

Then they both turned and looked back at Phil.

Phil was off to one side of the road, staring at a big butterfly with wings the color of a deep blue lake. The butterfly was sunning himself on a flower, with Phil's face only six inches away; whenever it slowly moved its wings, Phil would slowly rotate his radar ears at the same time.

Val and Aqua looked at each other and smiled, leaving the road because going cross-country was the fastest way back to

197

the factory. Although speed wasn't terribly important, actually, since they each secretly knew they probably wouldn't make it anyway, not to mention what the coming darkness would do to their efforts.

Max and Charlie were watching the four metal specks through binoculars. The robots were only several miles away, but it was miles full of chasms, rocks, ravines, and cliffs. They were happy, however, just to have spotted them again.

"They can't be going that distance," Charlie said, more to himself than to Max.

"They'll never make it, no sweat."

"We'll never make it!"

"Look, they're going slow. They're running down."

"Good. So am I."

They got in the truck to go pick them up.

"I just realized we haven't been monitoring Phil's energy pack. . . ." Aqua said as they walked through a meadow that had a huge, uprooted dead tree in the center.

"Correct," Val said. "We assumed that due to his size he has been consuming energy at a lesser rate than we have."

Aqua peered into Phil's brain lights, looking for a tiny digital readout that she'd never looked at before. When she looked up, her expression was very strange.

"Assumption incorrect," she finally said. "Phil's energy pack has less than two percent power left."

Val's mouth dropped open. Aqua looked just as stunned.

Phil would soon, very soon, be lifeless, inoperative, nonfunctional.

Dead.

Assisting Phil as much as they could, and now noticing that his lights were dimming and his beeps were subdued, they continued on, moving through a dense thicket.

"Phil's movements are already slowing down," Aqua said.

"His lights are almost gone."

"He'll never make it."

"Unless we carry him."

"Will we have the extra energy?"

"Yes," Val said, "as long as we avoid the camel cave."

They had to go not only around huge boulders but even around small rocks; they couldn't spare the energy for climbing now.

198

Even CatSkil avoided logs and thick bushes. When one of the four robots seemed tired, the others would help as best they could, until they themselves had problems.

The sun was an inch off the jagged horizon and the sunlight was a softer yellow when they finally paused under a cluster of Douglas fir trees. They leaned back, resting, speaking slowly, not moving at all. Val and Aqua were off to one side together, and Phil and CatSkil were thirty feet away. The factory was still not in sight, and they had no idea how much further it was.

"The repair shop shouldn't be much further away," Val said, knowing he had no idea where it was.

"I doubt if we can make it in time to . . ."

"We have to."

"I know. But Phil's energy pack must be down to less than one percent. Query: Do you think we could carry him? Between the three of us perhaps we could do it."

Val, knowing it was impossible, said, "Yes, perhaps so." He then looked closely at Aqua. She was dented, dirty, torn, and had more loose wires than ever before. Not that he looked any better. Val had learned many, many things since first meeting Aqua, but acquiring programming for "charm" was not one of them, so he looked at her and said, "Your unit has undergone a great deal of damage. I have never seen you look as inefficient as you do now." He spoke pleasantly as always.

"I think the dirt getting into our wiring is accelerating our energy drain," she said.

"That sounds logical," he said. "Your logic is very consistent under any conditions, Aqua."

"Thank you."

Then Val used valuable energy to slowly walk over to Aqua. There was something about the way the soft evening light behind her made him forget her physical imperfections or even their problems at the moment.

He suddenly thought of the adventure they had shared, the struggles, the world of new data, how wonderful she was to interface with, so he smiled as he looked at her. He spoke very precisely. "Aqua, if I lack the energy to tell you later, I want you to know that I hope the very last thing about me they circuit-wash are my memory tapes of you."

She looked back at him, remembering how intelligent and

efficient a partner he had been. She had also never known a robot who would try to fight a camel. "Val . . ."

But then they were distracted by some unusual electronic noises, and they turned and looked over at the source of the sounds.

"CatSkil!" Val yelled, having a response as close to horror as his programing would allow. "What have you done!"

Aqua was equally startled, and they both rushed over, although their version of rushing at this point almost looked like slow motion. At first they couldn't believe their optic sensors, then they realized it must be true.

CatSkil was finishing an energy-pack transplant with Phil.

He had pulled out Phil's small, rectangular energy pack from Phil's right side and quickly switched it with his own. Phil's lights dimmed to darkness and he froze during the two seconds he had no energy pack. But the moment the new, fresher pack was clicked into place, Phil perked right up, his lights brighter than ever, his motions as he swung his head around and moved his arms faster than before.

CatSkil, however, now suddenly looked and sounded very sluggish, as though he was a drunk about to pass out. His cigar ash was a dim light, the light on his pinkie ring was flickering, he didn't have the strength to wave his arm around anymore, and his voice was slow and deep.

Val and Aqua now stood beside the two robots, one livelier than ever, the other almost gone.

"CatSkil!" Val stated. "It is illogical for you to perform this energy-pack transplant!"

"Phil's energy pack, which you now have in your chest, is almost dead," Aqua said. "And we have no replacement packs."

But even as they spoke they knew CatSkil had been aware of all that before he gave Phil his energy and took the bad pack for himself. Further discussion with CatSkil on the point was extraneous.

Aqua tried to look at the readout on Phil's new energy pack, although it wasn't easy. Not noticing the consequences of what had just occurred, Phil was busy enjoying his new energy. He spun in a circle, waved his tools, blinked his eyes happily, and beeped to everyone in general and no one in particular. Aqua, however, finally managed to see the all-important computerized numbers.

"Val, there is a surprising new development," Aqua said, "CatSkil's old energy pack, still has forty-two percent power remaining."

That didn't seem logical to Val either.

"How could CatSkil have used up so little power?" Aqua wondered out loud. Val decided to check. He walked over, opened CatSkil's circuit box in back, checked, closed it, and turned to Aqua. "Apparently, he has been selecting low-power jokes."

At that moment, CatSkil's arm that held the cigar suddenly dropped to his side. He didn't have the strength to hold it up anymore. The light in his pinkie ring was just barely visible as a dying flicker. Val and Aqua looked at CatSkil and quickly tried to compute what they should do or say next.

The wind came up, rustling the long green grass around them, and the yellowish light of the setting sun painted the scene in beautiful light. Finally, Val placed his hand on CatSkil's arm and asked his friend the only logical question.

"CatSkil . . . why did you give Phil your power? Why?"

CatSkil made a slow, squeaky motion, a parody of his former way of leaning back whenever he began a story. His voice was like a phonograph record slowly winding down, getting deeper and deeper. *"My mother-in-law needed a blood transplant once . . . ."* He paused, waiting to see if he had the energy to finish. *"But we had to give it up. . . ."* His eyes turned from Val, and he gave Aqua one last long look. Then his eyelids slowly closed forever, even though by sheer force of mechanical will, he finished the joke; he wouldn't let himself be done until the punch line was reached. *"We couldn't . . . find . . . a . . . gorilla. . . ."*

CatSkil even got out a single "bap" of his rim shot as he went offstage. The light in his pinkie ring was out. He was motionless, now merely a hunk of lifeless metal.

Once he heard the punch line, Phil began to shake with laughter, harder than ever. His lights flashed, his cube-shaped gray head rocked around, and he happily beeped up a storm. He looked up at Aqua, but the expression on her face was so sad and the sudden silence so complete that Phil looked over at Val, who placed his hand slowly on the shoulder of CatSkil's lifeless body.

Phil stopped laughing.

For some reason, his uncle CatSkil was totally motionless,

arms hanging at his sides, eyes closed. Even the light in his pinkie ring was out. Phil quickly looked from Val to Aqua and back again, then finally realized that CatSkil had blown cigar smoke in someone's face for the last time.

It was several minutes before Val and Aqua could leave CatSkil's lifeless metal shell, even though they logically knew they should. Finally, they each took one of Phil's hands and led him away, through the long shadows of the coming evening, leaving CatSkil under a quiet tree, as though he would be able to sit there and to enjoy the coming sunset over the mountains.

Every few yards, Phil's head would pivot completely around and he would watch, waiting for CatSkil to come surging along, waving his arm, joining them. Val and Aqua tried to reassure Phil, but they did not know what words to use. So as they continued their journey, almost forcing Phil not to go back to CatSkil, they journeyed in silence. Phil kept turning and looking back, even when CatSkil was hidden by the forest shadows.

Max and Charlie were outside the truck, peering down at some robot tracks in the soft earth.

"Be getting dark soon," Max said, glancing at the sky.

"Yeah, but we got 'em," Charlie said. "I just called the factory and confirmed that the type of energy packs they have will be wearing out any second now. Besides, see how deep in the earth these tracks are compared to the other tracks we've seen? That means they're going slow, very slow. Which means they're almost finished. Let's go and—What are you sitting down for?"

"I'm tired, okay, I'm twice your age and I'm tired."

"Come on, let's go! We can get them and be back by dark!"

Relax, will ya, hotshot? I'm just resting for a second."

"Aw, come on, Dad, let's get this over with!"

Max slowly got to his feet, smiling. Both men seemed a little embarrassed as they got in the truck.

"You haven't called me that in a long time . . . son."

Charlie sort of smiled and nodded. "Didn't mean to get so irritated, it sort of slipped out."

"Don't apologize, it sounded . . . nice." Then it was too

202

much for both of them, so Max gruffly slapped his son on the arm and growled, "Let's go get those 'bots.' "

"Right!" Charlie said, gunning the truck forward happily. And for just a moment, Max saw that same special look in Charlie's eyes that he had loved for so many years in his mother.

For Val, Aqua, and Phil, the concept of time blurred into a repetitive haze of trees, rocks, and motion. The landscape melted together like a watercolor. They didn't know which ridge was which, or whether five minutes or two hours had passed. Val and Aqua staggered on, with Phil scooting in circles around both of them. At one point Val and Aqua descended a hill, started to fall, then just let themselves tumble on down; logically, it conserved energy to reach the bottom of the hill that way. Overhead, the sun continued to sink in the sky, not caring that three machines were racing it over the mountains and losing.

Max and Charlie spotted CatSkil's lifeless body, went bouncing over a field, parked, and got out without saying too much. Oh, Max mumbled something about how now the funny man didn't seem so funny, and Charlie had to explain to Max how the screws held CatSkil's top half and bottom half together as they took him apart to make it easier to lug him over to the truck. They tossed him in the back of the pickup, where his arm flopped over the side, the cigar permanently clutched between dead gray fingers. When Max hurled the bottom half of CatSkil, his legs, vaudeville trunk, and tank treads, into the back with a loud clank, Charlie did say something about how it was a valuable machine. But otherwise, they didn't say anything as they got back in and drove on, sometimes following the tracks, other times circling around a ravine or rocky area and again picking up the trail. It was late and they were dirty and exhausted and they both knew it was now over, except for picking up the pieces.

Val and Aqua were crawling now, up to the top of a ridge. They had exposed tubes, broken wires, limbs that didn't work properly and half their lights were out. But they kept going. Phil moved in a frisky energetic way beside them, having no idea he was the reason for all this effort.

As they reached the top of the ridge, clutching handfuls of grass and dirt to propel themselves on, the golden rays of the setting sun reflected off their metal faces. The last streaks of yellow in the western sky were yielding to the dark blue of evening.

Then Val saw it.

He managed to lean up on his elbows, then finally he struggled to his feet, swaying a little. His telescopic vision was no longer functional, but he finally made his optic sensors focus well enough to be certain.

"Look . . . the factory . . ."

Val helped Aqua struggle to her feet, then she too peered off into the distance. And she could see it too. "The repair shop . . ." she said softly.

In fact, the giant factory complex was still many miles away, miles filled with trees, rocks, steep slopes, dangerous ravines and chasms, and soon, darkness. For practical purposes, they might as well have gotten excited about spotting the moon. But their thoughts were not entirely practical at the moment. . . .

Val staggered on toward the factory, but then paused again after ten or twelve feet, his back to Aqua.

"You did it, Aqua," he said without looking back. "You made it."

"You . . . did . . . it, Val. . . ." she whispered. "I knew you could. . . ." It was at that moment that Aqua heard strange sounds inside, and then she realized she had no feedback from major parts of her body. Using all her energy, she slowly opened her wrist panel and looked at the energy pack reading, just as it changed from "01% ENERGY REMAINING" to "00% ENERGY REMAINING."

With no energy left, she ever so slowly looked back up toward Val and reached out one hand toward him. His back was turned, and he did not see her last gesture, and there was no way anyone could have heard her last word, "Val . . ." because even though her lips formed the word, no sound came out.

Then all lights faded and all motion left her body, and gravity gently closed her eyes for her. At that moment she became a beautiful, pink and gold statue on top of a windy hill as the sun went down and purple twilight filled the forest.

She was a statue with one arm stretched out toward a robot who did not even know she was no longer there.

"Aqua, there's one last subject . . . I want to talk with you about," Val said slowly, his eyes never leaving the factory in the distance, "but . . . I'm . . . running . . . out . . . of . . ."

It was then that he began to turn toward her.

"Aqua?"

Ever so slowly, almost not able to move himself, Val turned and looked in alarm at Aqua's closed eyes and motionless body and her hand outstretched in his direction. He completed his turn and stretched out his hand toward her, but the distance between them was too great.

As he slowly tried to walk toward her, he realized that his main computer was suddenly getting no feedback or input from his feet . . . or legs . . . or waist. . . . He knew it was almost night, but was that why everything was suddenly so dim?

"Aqua . . . wait. . . . Aqua? I want . . . to . . . discuss . . . one last human . . . emotional . . . phenomenon . . . with . . . you. . . ."

He thought he kept moving, but he wasn't sure. Why had it gotten so dark suddenly? Aqua's image was just a faint outline in his mechanical retina, but he kept struggling toward it. Strange, not being able to feel your chest . . . or arm. . . .

"I . . . want . . . to . . . ask . . . what . . . you . . . know . . . about . . . l . . . l-l-l . . ."

Somehow his hand found her hand and that felt good to him, and it was nice to have something good at that moment, since his lights quietly went out and the world gently faded to black.

The two machines did not move or sway in the evening wind, but the tall, golden grasses around them did, and the trees murmured. The two machines remained frozen and lifeless, just standing, leaning toward each other, holding hands—even when a curious smaller machine, making puzzled beeping noises, rolled over to them and prodded each of them, waiting for a response.

Phil pushed at Val's leg gently and beeped, then he tugged at Aqua's dress and cocked his head to one side, not understanding. He repeated his actions and his questioning beeps many times, and he watched and waited many times,

205

but nothing happened except that the purple color grew deeper in the sky.

Finally, reluctantly, having electronically sensed that Val and Aqua somehow weren't really there anymore, Phil turned and slowly rolled away. He paused several times, and looked back, and he kept looking back until it was too dark to see them anymore.

It was almost too dark to go on any further when Max and Charlie drove up a steep ridge. Charlie had finally worked up the nerve to mention to Max that at one point he thought that he had seen four robots through his binoculars instead of three. But Max had quickly said to forget it: in the first place Charlie was probably seeing things, and in the second place they only wanted to bring back the three missing ones they were responsible for; no use confusing the head office with details. When Charlie insisted he had seen four, Max laid down the law: if it doesn't have an invoice number, it doesn't exist. Charlie gave up. He was tired and hungry, too.

They might have missed them if they hadn't been silhouetted against the purple western sky on the hilltop. There was nothing further to say, and Max and Charlie got out and grabbed Val, Max taking his head and shoulders, Charlie the feet. Even Charlie didn't object as they lofted the expensive, precision-made robot and sailed it through the chilly night air. It landed with a loud clank in the back of the truck, near CatSkil's two inoperative halves. Aqua was next. They lifted her stiffly, then clumsily shoved her over the side of the rear of the truck. She landed on her side bounced a little then lay still. Max hurried over to the passenger side of the truck, but Charlie paused as he walked around the truck, squinting through the violet semidarkness. For a moment he thought he had seen something up on a high ridge, like a small robot watching everything going on below. If there was a little robot or something there, it was very hard to make out, because of the bushes and trees. Then it seemed that the strange image turned and slowly rolled away, paused, looked back one more time, and then moved on out of sight. Inside the cab of the truck, Max hit the horn impatiently. Charlie knew he was tired and that the dusky half-light often played tricks with lights and reflections, so he decided to try to forget it and not say anything to anyone. Charlie got inside the truck and turned on the headlights, and then he and Max slowly, carefully made their way down the mountainside toward the factory, their mission accomplished. They had successfully found all three malfunctioning machines, but somehow neither Max nor Charlie felt a sense of victory.

Before long, the truck's headlights became a single tiny light that slowly bobbed along far below, out of the hilly forests and into the sleepy valley, leaving the tree-covered ridge dark and quiet and peaceful.

Epilogue

future (fyōō′ chər) *n.* 1. the time that is
to come; days, months, or years ahead.
2. what will happen; what is going to be.

• • • Charlie and Max were almost at the end of their ''sentence'' in the motor pool a month later, one rainy morning about 4 A.M., when Babe Aldrin found them. She had heard that Westlin had not only sent them to the service department but assigned them to the graveyard shift as well. Originally he had told them to work there for two weeks as punishment for screwing up, but Max and Charlie had quickly protested, so Westlin had calmly made it a month instead.

Babe came down the stairs, whistling. She had made a late flight herself and was still up, so she decided to try to take care of a little private business for herself and her friend, Patsy, who worked at the plant in charge of the Logic Testing Division. Patsy was brilliant and well-liked and smiled as broadly as Babe did whenever company executives were around. The scam that the two of them had had going for years, dealing in slightly defective robots on the side, was something they had in common, as well their mutual interest in what they called their ''three gentlemen friends''—Black Jack (in Las Vegas), Johnnie Walker Red (with a twist of lemon), and Robert Redford (even if he was pushing sixty and now playing a crusty but lovable doctor on a TV series).

''Max? Charlie?'' Babe yelled, her voice echoing loudly in the almost empty motor pool. Then she saw them. Max was working on the inside of a black CrimeBuster, Deluxe Model, repairing some wiring, while Charlie was pounding out a dent in the side.

"Looks like a bull rammed it," Charlie joked.

"Quiet, Babe will hear you," Max said, but Babe had spotted them and strolled right up, giving them a huge smile.

"Hi, Max! Hi, Charlie!" Babe said. "What are you doing in the motor pool?"

"Westlin," Max muttered and paused to go get a Coke from a nearby machine.

"Too bad," said Babe, as if she didn't know all about it.

"Yeah, well this isn't as bad as last week," Charlie said. "He had us doing boring insulation work over in the Extinction Department. You ever work all night trying to stuff an eighty-foot blue WhaleBot?"

Babe laughed politely, then hooked her arm in Charlie's as he strolled over to the Coke machine, joining Max. Beside it was a company bulletin board. Among the homemade ads for car pools and garage sales was a newspaper clipping. It featured a little news article with the headline, "Junkyard Owners Capture Dangerous CrimeBuster."

"Say," Babe said, quickly buying both Max and Charlie a soft drink, "I was telling some people about those robots that wandered off last month. We searched the woods in my helicopter for them all day, remember?"

"Yeah, I think I remember," Max said dryly. "Why? What about 'em?"

"Oh, nothing. I just heard you finally found 'em. But I was just wondering whatever happened to them."

"Nothing much," Charlie said. "Wasn't any big deal."

"They get 'em fixed or what?" Babe asked.

Max went back to continue his repair on the inert Crime-Buster. He looked out the huge factory window. The rain had finally stopped. In an hour or two the sun would be coming up and Max could go home.

"Well, it was a funny thing," Charlie said, taking the time to answer Babe rather than resume work right away. "This CrimeBuster here malfunctioned too, you know. But we've overhauled and tested him and he works fine now. But those other three . . . they never could figure out what went wrong."

Charlie went back over to the CrimeBuster work area, where Max was tinkering away. Babe stayed hooked onto Charlie's arm. Max knew Babe wanted something and that she didn't care what had really happened to the robots. "They put new energy packs in them," Charlie continued. "Then they circuit-washed them *three* times, switched tubes, chips, wires, everything, but they kept malfunctioning. We kept sending them out, the owners kept sending them back."

Charlie shrugged, so Babe looked sympathetic and mumbled, "Sad . . ." Then she lowered her voice and looked around furtively, and that's when Max knew it was coming. "The reason I ask," she almost whispered, "is that I've a friend, Pat Clipner, over in Logic Testing, who is looking for a good deal, see, and willing to pay *beaucoup* bucks for—"

"Forget it," Max cut in. "Too late. The hotshots in the front office never could figure out what was wrong. They just finally closed the books on them and took the loss."

Babe looked crestfallen. The robot black market would have to continue without her this week.

"So what finally happened to them?" she asked.

Max shrugged and said, "We junked 'em."

The rain had stopped by the time the sun came up over the junkyard. It was a particularly beautiful morning; the early morning sunlight reflected off wet, glistening piles of metal, creating sparkling reflections. Calvin and Susan were up early, starting their day as usual by sitting in torn, overstuffed chairs in front of their little trailer that served as both office and home and was located in the center of the junkyard. It was their custom to have coffee and read the morning paper together before starting work on their various inventions and projects.

Aqua, looking alive and well and reconditioned, emerged from the trailer with a tray and served Calvin and Susan their coffee.

"Thank you, Aqua," Susan said.

"You're welcome, Susan," she said, then offered Calvin his coffee and his usual sweet roll. When Calvin and Susan had reconstructed her, the top half of Aqua's body, with its pink and gold dress and fairy-tale collar, had been salvageable, but they had had to add a new bottom half, so Aqua now wore a pink and gold pants suit. But it was still Aqua, as pleasant as ever.

A small robot wearing a Traffic Enforcement Designator helmet came scooting up, holding the morning paper. At first,

Calvin and Susan had been impressed with Phil's ability to navigate his way through the junkyard maze every morning to the driveway entrance to the junkyard, get the paper, and bring it back to them. Then they realized that, considering the way Phil had found his way back over the mountains to the junkyard using only Val's input concerning direction and the North Star, well, getting the morning paper was a piece of cake.

Phil rumbled up to hand Calvin the newspaper, but at the last second, CatSkil rolled up and grabbed it for himself. CatSkil now looked exactly the same following his massive reconditioning (he had refused to allow any changes), and he was still CatSkil, inside and out. Just to annoy Calvin, CatSkil now sat beside him and began to browse through the paper.

"CatSkil, just once," Calvin said, "I wish you'd let me read the sports section first."

CatSkil blew the world's most perfect smoke ring into Calvin's face and kept right on reading.

From around the corner Val emerged carrying a small circuit connector. Val now wore a pair of red plaid pants, a bright blue sweater with a little alligator on it, and a golfer's cap, which, for reasons passing all understanding, he seemed to favor. Susan privately thought he looked like a junior executive on his day off, the kind who went to the club on Saturdays to hang around the bar and drink instead of playing eighteen holes.

"You were right, Susan," Val said in his usual nice tone, which hadn't changed at all. "Thanks to your using Number Fourteen Flexi-Cable when you were reassembling all of us I no longer have a walking impediment because of my foot laceration."

It was at this point that Phil turned on his little flashing red light and imitated a machine that could fire off an M 16: rat-a-tat-tat.

"However," Val said, a little sadly, "Phil still seems to want to be a CrimeBuster whenever he is enlarged and improved."

Val and Aqua walked over to an outdoor workbench where they had a special project of their own. They uncovered the plastic tarp that had kept everything dry during the rain, picked up their tools, and went right to work.

Calvin looked up at CatSkil and asked, trying to keep the

irritation out of his voice, "Are you through yet, CatSkil?" CatSkil's only response was to casually flick cigar ashes on Calvin's head.

"Calvin," Susan said, "I don't think you should complain about not getting the sports section first. Not when we've got all this nice company and service, and all we have to do is maintenance and find some new energy packs every once in a while." Then she looked over to where Val and Aqua were working. "You two need anything today?"

"We could use some magnetic wiring, please," Val said, being careful not to let any grease get on his blue sweater. "Number six would be fine.

"And some smaller grid components," Aqua added.

"Okay, I'll look around," Calvin said, sipping his coffee. He looked up at the sky and the mountains. The rain had made the smell of pine very strong in the air, and it was going to be a beautiful day, once the last of the gray clouds wandered away.

Rover the raccoon scampered into view and rushed into Phil's arms, who happily beeped and scooped him up. Then Phil and his raccoon went over to watch Val and Aqua, who were at an important stage in their project. Even Calvin and Susan watched.

Val tightened a screw, and Aqua then connected the wires to the energy pack, and at that moment, for the first time, the brand-new, tiny robot came to life. She was about half Phil's size, with a round, transparent brain area, two arms, and small metal wheels instead of tank treads. She had large, cute eyes. She looked at Val, then at Aqua as Aqua attached her red bow tie-directional finder to the top of her head like a little bow. Then she turned her head and looked at her big brother, Phil, who loudly beeped a hello.

In a quiet little electronic voice, she made her first beep right back at him. Then she looked up at Val and Aqua again. Smiling at her, they reached for their tools. They already knew several ways to improve her.

Calvin turned to Susan and said, "Do you think those two will ever be satisfied with what they build?"

But it was a different, louder voice that answered him.

"This agent brings a small dog into a nightclub. The dog is a brilliant piano player—plays Bach, Beethoven, then goes into some terrific jazz solos. He's sitting there playing when

212

*two bigger dogs come in, pull him off the stool, and haul him
outside. The club owner looks at the agent and says, 'What
happened?' The agent says, ''Ah . . . they want him to be a
doctor.' ''*

Bap-bap.

Cigar smoke.

Satisfied look.

And back to the sports section, not that he hadn't finished
with it, but because it was still bugging Calvin that he was
taking so long with it.

Calvin and Susan nodded, agreeing with CatSkil's keen
grasp of the obvious.

Val and Aqua worked together, a perfect team, pausing
only to smile illogically at each other every once in a while as
they worked on the tiny new robot. Phil and his raccoon both
crowded in closer, getting in the way. At the sight of the
raccoon, the tiny robot suddenly emitted a high-pitched series
of squeaks and beeps.

The electronic baby talk didn't make sense to anyone yet,
not even Phil, but there was time to figure it out, all the time
in the world.

The work progressed, the morning wore on, but no one,
human or robot, happened to look up and see a misty band of
rainbow colors which ended just above them and was now
fading away in the bright morning light.